Jason waited . . .

He turned slowly, sighting through his viewfinder for fresh inspiration. He found it on the straight rise of gray cliff that soared above him—company.

Curious, Jason focused his zoom lens on her face. She was astonishingly pretty. A new face. He wondered whether she had been up there during his conversation. She had regarded him a little too curiously, and in the game he was playing curiosity could kill a lot more than a cat.

Jason climbed the path. Then he started off after the woman, keeping well back. It would be interesting to learn exactly why she was on Galbraith. And he meant to let her know that he was interested.

ABOUT THE AUTHOR

Eve Gladstone believes that romance and adventure are a constant challenge. For *Enigma*, her fourth foray into Intrigue, Eve was inspired by the primitive beauty she observed on her visits to Monhegan Island, off the coast of Maine. Eve lives in a New York City suburb with her husband and a compatible assortment of dogs and cats.

Books by Eve Gladstone

HARLEQUIN INTRIGUE

23–A TASTE OF DECEPTION
49–CHECKPOINT
75–OPERATION S.N.A.R.E.

HARLEQUIN SUPERROMANCE

297–ALL'S FAIR
324–ONE HOT SUMMER

Don't miss any of our special offers. Write to us at the following address for information on our newest releases.

Harlequin Reader Service
901 Fuhrmann Blvd., P.O. Box 1397, Buffalo, NY 14240
Canadian address: P.O. Box 603,
Fort Erie, Ont. L2A 5X3

Enigma
Eve Gladstone

Harlequin Books

TORONTO • NEW YORK • LONDON.
AMSTERDAM • PARIS • SYDNEY • HAMBURG
STOCKHOLM • ATHENS • TOKYO • MILAN

For Jonathan Gleit,
with a world full of wishes.
Build a tall dream.

Harlequin Intrigue edition published April 1989

ISBN 0-373-22111-8

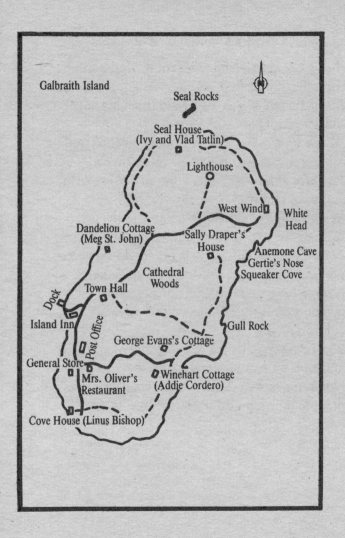

Galbraith Island

Seal Rocks

Seal House
(Ivy and Vlad Tatlin)

Lighthouse

West Wind

White
Head

Dandelion Cottage
(Meg St. John)

Sally Draper's
House

Anemone Cave
Gertie's Nose
Squeaker Cove

Cathedral
Woods

Dock

Town Hall

Island Inn

Post Office

Gull Rock

George Evans's Cottage

General Store

Mrs. Oliver's
Restaurant

Winehart Cottage
(Addie Cordero)

Cove House (Linus Bishop)

CAST OF CHARACTERS

Addie Cordero—She was sent to find a killer before he could find her.

Jason Farrell—Was his sensuality a mask for a sinister nature?

Steven West—His family home had sheltered a murderer, but was it a guest or an owner?

Veronica West—She was a gifted actress with many roles to play.

Kevin Morgan—This physician's plans for Addie's "vacation" were anything but restful.

Linus Bishop—His artist's perception revealed the island's many beauties . . . and its dangers.

George Evans—He was Addie's nearest neighbor, but the thought didn't give her comfort.

Tim Gruesin—His life was a game of strategy, and he didn't like to lose.

Noah Roberts—He and Gruesin had a game plan, and he wouldn't tolerate interference.

Prologue

The gulls followed the Port Clyde ferry out for a mile or two sounding their hollow cries into the chill morning air. When no more leftover bits of breakfast rolls and pastry were tossed into the boat's wake for them, they began to drop back, one by one, into the fog until there was only a solitary straggler left sitting on the bow. After another mile or so, the last gull launched itself off and flew back toward the mainland. And then there were none.

The ferry plowed on into a sea that became increasingly rough. Some passengers went below complaining of sea-sickness. Others took to the lounge for more coffee and pastries. For a while Addie Cordero sat alone daydreaming, enjoying the brisk air and even the choppy ride.

She thought of the bright summery coast she had left behind and of tiny Galbraith Island lying ten miles out from the mainland. The ferry was passing through fog as thick as freshly carded sheep's wool, the kind of fog that could obliterate the boundaries between time and distance while keeping apart two aspects of reality, both the one she was escaping from and the one she was heading *to*.

As the ocean breeze slid cool caresses along her cheek, Addie found her thoughts turning to Pam Hellman's warning.

"Don't count on a vacation," the assistant district attorney had said just before Addie left Boston for the trip to Maine. "Enigma is a lot smarter crook than you are detective."

"Obviously," Addie had said. "He's been able to murder four women—"

"That we know of," Pam threw in.

"Murder them and leave no clues to his—"

"Or her—"

"Identity. No clues except for a slip of paper found near the last victim's body. A scribbled note of ferry schedules to Galbraith Island, and a date of arrival . . ."

"And you," Pam added, "as a graphologist—"

"Psychologist using graphology as an analytical tool," Addie reminded her.

"Right. You said the handwriting didn't belong to the victim and could belong to the killer. And remember that if it *was* the killer's handwriting, then there's the possibility of Enigma being on Galbraith Island."

And then Pam had asked Addie to go to Galbraith and find Enigma using the one clue they had available. Addie had accepted the job with almost too much alacrity. There was a sense of adventure attached to the trip. She'd enjoy breaking away from the usual order in her life. And best of all, the trip coincided with the unpleasant ending of an affair. Addie was eager to do something new. Actually finding the mysterious criminal dubbed Enigma by the Boston district attorney's office almost seemed a side issue.

Learning to forget Rafe, who had gone to Europe without her, and putting her life back together, were Addie's priorities.

During the drive up from Massachusetts, she'd thought of little else, and so far the ocean winds hadn't blown the image of Rafe away. So far Enigma hadn't done much to distract her.

Allowing herself to fall in love with Rafe had been a decision of such spellbinding stupidity that even now it left her wincing. She hadn't paid the slightest attention to what her experience as a psychologist told her about him. Smug, opinionated, insensitive, even ruthless defined Rafe, and she'd known it from the beginning but had written off the clues because they didn't square with what she wanted so desperately to believe about him. She hadn't even paid attention to the obvious evidence of his selfish nature in his handwriting.

Then, after a year, he'd said goodbye...Addie, my career is calling me to more interesting ports. She'd said so long and cried a roomful of tears. And still she thought about him; the only solution was action, keeping her mind exercised.

So Addie was traveling out to Galbraith Island with the express purpose of putting her life back together and incidentally searching for a multiple killer. Drawing her sweater close around her against the morning chill, Addie knew there was something a little off kilter about her priorities just now, but assumed it would all be sorted out somehow. For the moment she wanted the wind to blow her cares far away, out to sea, out to the end of the world.

She noted suddenly that passengers had begun to collect once more on the deck, leaning against the railings and waiting like so many birds on a high wire. Then she heard a collective sigh. The fog had begun to burn off, and there was a hard edge to the horizon.

"There it is. See?" A woman in jeans and a heavy sweater spoke slowly, and yet with enthusiasm, to a small child whose nose barely reached the bottom railing. "Galbraith Island."

"Where, Mommy? I can't see it."

"There, darling, use your eyes."

Addie went over to the railing herself and gazed off into the distance. Galbraith appeared as a smudge on the horizon; a drawing badly erased by an impatient hand. Galbraith Island, small, primitive. A place where she knew no one, where there was no sheriff, and no electricity or telephone in the cottage she was renting. For the first time an edge of fear crept over her. Perhaps she had bitten off more than she could chew. If she did confront Enigma there it would be the first time she had ever met a murderer face-to-face without the safety of the court and gun-toting guards to protect her.

Though the note had indicated an earlier arrival, it was even possible that Enigma could be on the ferry boat right now, standing just as she was at the railing watching the island take shape. She glanced hastily around at her fellow passengers but they were as innocent appearing as she.

"Finding Enigma is top priority in the department," Pam had told Addie, "and so far this handwriting sample is the only concrete evidence we have to go on." Pamela Hellman was in her element as an assistant district attorney with a caseload of murders and assorted mayhem on her hands. "The victim, Eda Barnstable, was the widow of the estimable lawyer, Barney Full-of-baloney Barnstable, who died last year in a suspicious automobile accident. Barney was a power in this town. The law firm he represented wasn't happy about his death and still isn't happy about the fact we haven't closed the case on it."

"And you think Eda Barnstable's death is connected to her husband's?"

Pam shook her head. "All options are open. Not only because Eda was the widow of Barnstable, but because I have a gut feeling her death and three other unsolved murders we investigated are connected. I haven't been in the D.A.'s office for ten years without learning to pay attention to those tiny vibes I get along my spine at certain times," Pam added. "Sometimes cold evidence isn't the only reason for acting. Enigma is the name we've given the killer. This handwriting sample is our only clue, if it *is* a clue. According to the time schedule, he's on Galbraith now and we may not have a minute to lose. How about it, Addie? Are you game to make a stab at an ID?"

"I'm game," Addie had said, "although I can think of two people living in happy retirement in Phoenix, Arizona, who won't be happy about it. They want me to stick around for a long, long time. After all, I am Mr. and Mrs. Cordero's only child."

"I don't expect you to go alone, Addie. We'll send a backup along with you if you'd just say the word." Pam had looked worried, perhaps because of Addie's enthusiasm. "I'm asking you to take on something that could be dangerous and all of a sudden I'm getting nervous."

"Pam, forget about sending someone along with me. Meeting in the dead of night, behind a rock, under the full moon, that sort of thing? Not exactly my style." Then she added in a hopeful tone, "And Enigma might not even be on Galbraith. The setup is rather implausible."

"It's the implausibility I don't trust. Addie, a backup is a good idea. I know you like being in total control of your life, but sometimes you have to put your trust in someone else, too."

"It's not a case of wanting to be in control. As a matter of fact," Addie admitted, "I think bits of my life are flying off in all directions. But I just don't see the sense of a backup. All I have to do is find a person whose handwriting matches the sample we suspect belongs to the killer of Eda Barnstable."

"That's right. Find Enigma and back away," Pam warned. "No heroics. Remember, when the police discovered Mrs. Barnstable dead in her apartment, her hand was closed around a small piece of paper. You were called in to determine whether the script was in the widow's handwriting."

It wasn't, Addie remembered. The strokes were muddied and aggressive, the capitals large and excessive, indicating immaturity. It was also clear the writer was of a particularly vicious nature. He was smart, cold, calculating and did not like to be crossed. And if the handwriting *was* Enigma's, it was the first clue the killer had left behind.

"So if you find the handwriting that matches the one we have," Pam went on. "Just ID the owner and scoot out of there, that's all we ask. You're not a policewoman, you're a psychologist in the Boston court system. We're asking you to volunteer your expertise but that's all. We'll take over from there.''

It hadn't seemed like much when Pam had asked. But now, as the island ceased being a shadow in the distance and instead became a lump the size of a piece of coal, Addie wondered what had possessed her to refuse Pam Hellman's offer of backup. Galbraith Island was certainly a long way from anywhere.

Chapter One

"Excuse me, could you point me in the direction of Winehart House?"

The stranger Addie had accosted on the dock examined her with interest, measured her suitcase with his eye and said, "You must be the new tenant."

She regarded him with surprise. "Yes, how'd you know?"

"It's a small place. There isn't too much going on we don't know about. Especially when a house in a desolate spot stands unoccupied. Welcome to Galbraith Island."

"Thank you. Desolate spot? You make it sound ominous. A minute ago I was thinking how happy I was to be here."

"Civilization too much for you, eh?"

"Just about. Incidentally, I'm Addie Cordero."

"Linus Bishop." He held out his hand. He was a courtly old gentleman with long, white hair, a bright red bandanna around his neck and smudges of paint on his shirt. "Winehart," he said, shaking her hand vigorously, "you'll find it along the town road, up the hill, say half a mile as the crow doesn't fly, second, no third path to the right. There's a little beat-up sign you can't miss. Incidentally," he added with an apologetic smile, gently mimicking the tone she'd taken when she'd introduced herself, "sorry about calling Winehart House desolate. Galbraith is a small place, after all. And you'll find we're a friendly lot."

She hoisted her suitcase. "I understand. Thanks, Mr. Bishop."

"Tell you what. Stop at the general store. They have the one and only ve-hi-cle on the island. You can ask them to bring your suitcase up for you."

"Great, thanks a lot. I have to order some groceries, anyway."

"Good idea. Fitzgibbon will be hanging around once he discovers Winehart has a tenant."

"Fitzgibbon?" Addie asked tentatively.

"Maine coon cat. Salt-and-pepper longhair with yellow eyes the size of traffic lights. Likes lobster, but will settle for canned tuna or cat food."

"Thanks for telling me. I like cats." She took a deep breath of the fresh island air. It smelled good. "Sometimes, however, they don't like me."

"Allergy?"

"Well, not lately," she said. "But I haven't been around cats for a long time. Maybe I'm cured."

"Well," he said smiling, "Fitzgibbon will either cure you or kill you. Enjoy your stay."

"I intend to, Mr. Bishop."

"Please, call me Linus."

"I will," she responded, "if you call me Addie."

He nodded and seemed about to walk away when abruptly he stopped. "Know anyone on Galbraith?"

She shook her head. "Not a soul."

"Artist?" he asked.

"Wish I were." It seemed an odd question to Addie. Odd but harmless.

"Writer?"

She shook her head slowly once more, wondering what he was getting at. She'd have to reveal her talents for graphology eventually, but she and Pam had decided it would be best to treat it as an adjunct to her work and one she wouldn't mention except casually. "I've written a few papers for professional journals, if that's a help."

He smiled in a puzzled way and she decided to put him at ease at once. "I'm a psychologist."

"Psychologist," he said, his eyes lighting up with interest. "I think Galbraith at present is short of psychologists."

"But the truth is," Addie told him, "I'm on vacation."

He laughed. "Know what you mean. Tell you what, settle in and when you have a little time, come visit me. I live at Cove House. It's the third house past the general store but closer to the water. You'll probably find me in my studio behind it. Better pick up a map at the general store. It'll come in handy."

"I'd like to visit you, but won't I be—"

"Disturbing me?" he cut in. "Not at all. Even when I'm working I like company."

"Thanks, I'll take you up on that, Linus."

Addie breathed a deep, satisfied sigh as she went along the town road toward the general store. Things certainly worked quickly on Galbraith Island. If Linus Bishop was a sample of local friendliness, she'd have her handwriting samples in no time at all.

Linus Bishop. The name sounded familiar. Artist. Watercolor seascapes, she thought. Well, she'd soon find out.

She sighed again, taking in the fresh island air and its salty tang. The sky here was a deeper and more serene blue than it was back home, and the sun was a gold button heading for its zenith. The sounds of Galbraith were just what she'd expected, too, the slap of water against the dock and gulls beseeching a fishing boat coming into shore.

"Small, but fully packed with the glories of nature," was how Pam had described Galbraith. "If you want to be out of this world, Addie, that's the place. And," she'd added, "the natives are very friendly. There's not much doing on the island except for the painters who paint and the writers who write, the gardeners who garden and the fishermen who fish. The water's too cold for swimming. Everybody else hangs around and waits for the evening. There are parties and dinners and visits for cocktails. They'll welcome a newcomer. Not counting day-trippers we're talking maybe fifteen, twenty people. Start with them and go on from there.''

"Sounds so deliciously simple when you put it that way,'' Addie had commented dryly.

"It is a working trip,'' Pam said, adding with some enthusiasm, "but you'll love the place.'' Addie knew Pam had spent a couple of weeks on Galbraith the summer before her twin sons were born. "But,'' Pam added suddenly in a serious warning, "you could be very lonely if you're not careful. There's no electricity, no telephones, except for the one at the Island Inn, and no organized nightlife. If you don't find yourself invited to the parties, you could be awfully bored.''

"I'm not going for the nightlife,'' Addie reminded her boss. "This trip is strictly business. When I want a vacation, I'll vote for Club Med anytime.'' But she *had* been looking forward to getting away, of feasting her eyes on another kind of landscape, basking under another kind of sun.

The natives of Galbraith were indeed friendly, Addie found out again when the owner of the general store offered to let her hitch a ride up to Winehart in his Jeep along with the groceries she'd ordered and her luggage.

"No,'' Addie said, thinking what a nice day it had become. "I'd rather walk. Linus Bishop did suggest I buy a map of the island, though.''

"He would, since he designed it, but it's a good map, and we're proud to sell it. Every stone and pebble on Galbraith has a name and sometimes even two. The nice thing about Galbraith is that part of it looks as wild as the day it rose from the sea. You'll think you've discovered something, that's how untamed Galbraith seems, but you haven't. It's all been here forever. Also,'' he added, looking at her with interest, "we warn new visitors to the island about the strong undertow on the eastern coast. Don't even dream of swimming there. And the cliffs on that side are high and when damp, dangerous. Sometimes, mostly in winter of course, the waves smack against the cliffs and rise fifty, seventy-five, sometimes even a hundred feet. Awesome sight.''

Addie took the map in her hand. "And dangerous, too, I suppose."

"If you came up against one, you wouldn't be around to offer your opinion."

Friendly, beautiful Galbraith. "Tell me, when's the next boat out?"

The store owner laughed. "Where are you from?"

"Boston."

"Galbraith is a piece of cake."

"Glad to be here, I think." She opened the map. It was artistically drawn, and it said the money paid for it went to the Galbraith Preservation Society. What, she wondered, besides life, might need preserving here? She located Cove House on the map easily enough, as well as the Winehart cottage. All of the houses were drawn in with a delicate, finicky hand, each one named. Some names were overly cute, some deadly serious. Well, she seemed to have her work cut out for her, but who ever said looking for Enigma would be easy?

There were fifty families on the island, half of them fishermen living there year-round and pretty much eliminated as possible suspects. Of the remaining property owners, most were members of the island's art colony; some would be in residence over the summer months, some would rent out their cottages, and others would not arrive until later in the summer. There were, in addition, a small enclave of wealthy families who had built their summer houses on Galbraith.

Addie was to confine her search to the members of the art colony, vacationers and the few wealthy families who were currently in residence.

The signpost pointing to Winehart Cottage was indeed at the end of a twisting path that led off the town road. The sign had been knocked over, and Addie found it when she accidentally smacked her foot against it. The house itself was at the end of a winding path of flagstone with growths of wild thyme in between the stones. Trees on either side of the path leaned into each other, forming a leafy overhang through which the sun slanted. The house was small and sat on the hillside. It once might have had a view overlooking the sloping west end of the island. However, tangled undergrowth and a small forest combined to surround the place, keeping it cool, dark and more than a little mysterious.

Fitzgibbon was waiting for her. He sat on the porch railing watching her out of his traffic-light eyes, as though somehow he'd known she was coming.

A dead shrew lay on the welcome mat.

"Oh, Fitzgibbon, thanks a lot," Addie said, recoiling slightly. "But it's a present I could have done without."

The key, as she had been told, was on the lintel. Its whereabouts, she had no doubt, was known to everyone in town. She opened the door and was greeted by the usual smell of a damp house; a scent of mold and upholstery that needed airing. The interior had been newly painted so there was also the pungent aroma of oil and turpentine.

She stepped into a narrow hall that held a small table and a kerosene lamp. Fitzgibbon dutifully followed, twisting around her legs and rubbing up against her.

To the right was the living room with a brick fireplace at the far end and a plump country couch upholstered in flowered chintz. To the left was a bedroom, painted white and furnished with simple maple pieces. One pleasant surprise was a series of lithographs in both rooms, contemporary landscapes of the island in old frames. The artist was a past owner of Winehart. Addie pushed the curtains back and opened the windows to let in some air.

The hall also led back to the kitchen, which was furnished prettily in oak, had a gas stove, a wooden icebox and another fireplace. The kitchen opened onto a porch, which ran the whole width of the house. That, with a small bathroom, was all there was of the Winehart cottage.

Just enough, Addie thought, because she had every intention of keeping her housekeeping duties to a minimum and letting the Boston district attorney's office pick up her dining-out tab. Her groceries had already arrived along with some chunks of ice, so she began to unpack.

Within the hour, Winehart Cottage was completely aired out and bore the mark of human occupancy, including several vases she'd filled with wildflowers that she'd picked outside the kitchen porch.

Though tired from the nonstop drive up from Boston and the choppy ten-mile ferry ride out, Addie grabbed the map of Galbraith. She'd stepped off the boat from Port Clyde knowing no one and within two minutes she had made a friend in Linus Bishop. Perhaps a hike around the island would net a few more fish. It was too nice to stay indoors anyway.

"Hey, anybody here?"

Apparently her wish was already on the way to being fulfilled. Addie heard the front door open. She came into the hall and was startled to find a very large man standing by the door. In fact, he seemed to take up most of the hall's tiny space.

"Do you always come charging into people's houses without knocking?" she said with an uncomfortable little laugh.

The man ignored her question, raking her with his eyes. "I'm your neighbor from down the road. George Evans." He put out a huge hairy hand and shook hers vigorously, holding it a shade longer than she liked. "Saw the present Fitzgibbon left you," he remarked with a grin. "I disposed of the corpse over the side of the porch."

"Thanks," she replied, controlling her nervousness. "I was hoping Fitzgibbon would handle it for me. You his owner?"

"He's my owner," the man said flatly. "I didn't catch your name."

"Addie Cordero."

George Evans wore denims and a well-worn plaid shirt that was splattered with paint. He was a tall, powerfully built man with a head of unruly reddish hair. He towered over her in the most menacing way as if he was used to using his size to control a situation that might otherwise be uncomfortable.

"Pretty isolated back here, Addie. Not a house within a thousand feet except for mine," he said. "A lot of undergrowth. The Wineharts always liked their privacy."

"I'm not sure anything can really be isolated on an island that's scarcely a square mile in size," Addie said defensively, although she hardly knew what she was talking about. She thought, with the most extraordinary lack of logic, that she didn't want him in her house, didn't want the feeling that if he took a deep breath he might expand into every corner and squeeze her out.

"Don't let the size of Galbraith fool you. It's a pretty curious place, and sometimes a square mile has a funny way of seeming endless. How long are you here for?"

She brushed past him quickly, opened the door and went out onto the front porch, waiting there for him to join her. "The Wineharts said I could have it for as long as I want. They never did find another tenant."

He looked at her curiously. "Odd they rented to you. As a matter of fact, I'd heard they were coming up."

"Really? I guess they changed their minds." The truth was there'd been a hurried deal between the Wineharts and the Boston district attorney's office. Addie walked down the steps as George closed the screen door behind himself.

"Not everybody likes the isolation here."

"The Wineharts explained that to me, Mr. Evans."

"Mister! Man, nobody calls me mister on Galbraith. It's George to kids and grown-ups alike. What's Addie short for?" He followed her along the curved path that led to the town road, refusing to break off their conversation.

"Adele, but I never use it."

"Well, Adele," he said, ignoring her comment. "My studio is down the road two hundred yards. You'll see the sign. I'm one of the year-round residents of Galbraith."

"Year-round?" From the moment she'd met him thoughts of Enigma had been battering around in her brain. But, if he never left the island, he couldn't be her quarry. She relaxed a little. "Doesn't it get lonely in the winter?"

"It's not a prison, Adele. I leave Galbraith whenever the mood hits me. I hit all the well-known spots in Boston and New York."

"Boston." She said the word so softly it was clear he couldn't catch it. "I suppose you go there often to visit the galleries."

He gazed at her for a long moment. "Are you talking about Boston or New York? Like I said, I leave here whenever the mood hits me, go wherever I want, do whatever I want to do. You know, when I have a hankering for a good time."

"Ah," she said, offering him a smile that wavered in spite of all her efforts to appear nonchalant, "the big city's the place to have a good time, all right."

"Hey," he said in a jovial tone that didn't quite match his appearance. "It's not bad on Galbraith, either. Summer's a blast. Stop by my cottage, have a glass of wine. You'll get a chance to see my work." The last was said with the air of offering her a great gift. "Come any time, the studio is always open."

Like Linus Bishop's, she thought. What was it Pam had said about being lonely on Galbraith? So far they seemed to be coming at her from all directions. One Enigma, two Enigmas, three Enigmas, four. Her head whirled.

"Perhaps I will," she said politely, waiting to end the conversation. She'd have to, she supposed, although reason told her she should have someone in tow when she did—if she could find a person to trust.

"Oh, by the way," she remarked, "I hope you don't mind Fitzgibbon visiting me. Linus Bishop said to buy him some cat food, which I did."

"He's a sucker for pretty women," Evans said, grinning at her. "The cat, I mean, but I suppose Linus, too. Don't worry, if I want Fitzgibbon, I'll know where to find him. *Ciao*, for now."

Addie watched him walk away. She couldn't forget Pam's cool recital of the facts about Enigma. "This year four widows have been found murdered in apparently unrelated circumstances with too many coincidences. Although their killer or killers tried to make all their deaths look like suicide, forensic evidence proved otherwise."

"Three murders and with Eda Barnstable we have four."

"The similarities continue," Pam had told her. "The victims were all of a similar age. They lived alone and were without close relatives or friends. And, to top it off, there were large sums of money missing from each of their estates. Their bank accounts had been closed out suddenly and the victim was dead a short time later. In each case a bank officer had tried to warn the victim not to close the account, but the officers were told the victim had a personal financial adviser. And at the time of death there was no sign of a break-in, which meant the victim knew the murderer. Concerning the last victim, Eda Barnstable, we're just now trying to unravel her affairs. We'll feed you the information as we get it. The modus operandi remains the same, however; the killer killed but apparently didn't want it to look like it."

"An unwilling murderer of a delicate nature. Hates the sight of blood," Addie remarked. "Where have I heard that before?"

"But it's often true," Pam had said. "I'd guess violence is extremely distasteful to our killer."

Enigma. Vicious killer. Linus Bishop had asked her if she knew anyone on Galbraith. No, she had jauntily responded. Marvelous. Now he knew she was alone in the Winehart cottage. Why the devil had she fallen for the impassioned look on Pam's face and how in the world was she going to find a man who murdered Eda Barnstable, and

*possibly three others, all on the basis of a few words he'd
scribbled on a torn piece of paper?*

She had no answer to that one. Running out was one way
of looking at it. Either way, Rafe was in Europe without her
and she was on Galbraith because of her graphological talents and a sudden longing for solitude.

And, she realized, she might have just spoken to Enigma himself in the person of one George Evans who traveled to Boston on occasion when he felt the hankering for
a good time.

THEY WERE BELOW Gertie's Nose in a narrow rocky cove
called Squeaker, through which the waves burst, scurried
and splashed, then foamed down, only to burst up again.
The continual noise was enough to mask the sound of their
voices. The rock they stood upon was beneath an overhang. Permanently wet from the mist thrown up by the
waves, the surface was dangerous to anyone attempting to
move swiftly across it.

Steven West, however, didn't seem to be aware of the
immediate danger. He kept jamming his fists into his
pockets, then taking them out again as he traced and re-
traced his steps along the edge.

"You don't give a damn that they'll probably kill me
before this is all over." He'd said the words carefully, as if
trying not to betray his emotions, although an uncon-
scious tremor gave away his fear and uncertainty.

Jason Farrell watched the waves, admiring their force as
they surged into the cove. He was a tall, lean man with
sandy hair, inquisitive gray eyes and an air of quiet au-
thority. "No one likes to be double-crossed," he said, "but
the object is not to be caught."

"I'm telling you, I've a bad heart, Farrell. I don't know
if I can take this pressure. I have this itchy feeling they
know something, suspect something." The late afternoon
air had turned cool, but beads of sweat had formed on
Steve West's upper lip.

"Tim Gruesin and Noah Roberts are your business buddies. You've gone this far together. They're on Galbraith as your guests. They suspect nothing, Steve. It's business as usual, that's the idea."

"Yeah, right." Steve was still standing perilously close to the edge with the waves rushing below him. Jason eased himself nearer, suddenly ready for trouble. Steve whipped around. "I should've run for it when I had the chance."

"Don't even think it. Running out was never an option. With millions of dollars involved, you couldn't have reached your front door without our knowing it."

"I wouldn't bet on it, Farrell. In the end you people can be bought like everybody else."

Deep within the man's eyes, Jason caught a glimpse of something mean and dangerous. He'd have to put a stop to it at once; remind the Boston millionaire that he was no longer in control of his own life, that there were other forces involved, controlling him.

He reached out and grabbed Steve by his jacket collar and in a swift movement pulled the material tight into his fist.

"Hey, wait a minute, Farrell, what do you think you're doing?"

"Teaching you a little lesson."

In another second he had forced Steve up against the hard rock surface below the overhang. "Pal, I think you've forgotten where you are and who you're dealing with. This isn't the office of Boston Bank and you don't have a button to push here for help. You and I are all alone and it's a long swim back to the mainland."

Steve's eyes bulged and he opened and closed his mouth without uttering a sound. "No sirree," Jason said, pulling the collar a little tighter, "you're going to pay attention to what I have to say, and then you're going to tell me it'll be a perfect pleasure to go along. It would take very little effort for me to send you straight down into Squeaker and let the waves pick you up like a baby and rock you to sleep right out there in the Atlantic."

Steve's shoulders slumped. "All right, all right, I'll do what I have to. Just get your hands off me."

Jason released him and carefully dusted the shoulders of the banker's jacket and straightened the collar for him. "Fine, it's all set. You'll come out of this in one piece if you do what you're supposed to. And don't improvise."

With a quick, brittle laugh, Steve said, "Take it easy, Farrell. There's more than one way to skin a cat." He stopped, gave Jason a canny glance and said, "Give it any more thought? What we talked about in my office?"

A quarter-million-dollar bribe was what they'd talked about. Jason shook his head. The man didn't stay intimidated long. "The word was no then. It's still no."

"That may be the sorriest no you've ever uttered." Steve cast a glance at Jason that was pure hatred, then turned and went trudging along the overhang to the small dirt path that led to the crest of Gertie's Nose. From there it was only a short way to West Wind, his gray-shingled mansion that stood high on the massive cliff known as White Head, overlooking the sea.

Jason waited until West was gone and then made his own way along the rocks. They were slippery with lumpish green algae. Last-minute panic, that's what Steven West suffered from. It wasn't the first such instance Jason had had to deal with, nor would it be the last. As for the bribe, it had been offered almost as a reflex action and Jason had refused it the same way. A quarter of a million dollars. Routine. There ought to be a few laughs in the notion but he wasn't laughing.

Well, he thought, surveying the wild charm of the land and seascape, mustn't let the artistic moment pass. There were some things to be said for this sojourn on Galbraith Island, and the wealth of physical beauty topped the list.

He removed his camera from the case strung over his shoulder, positioning himself just beyond the spray caused by the waves thundering up through the narrow cove. He managed several black-and-white shots of the waves as they burst up into white, foamy jets, wanting to capture at least a portion of the astounding power and beauty.

He took several more shots, then turned around slowly, sighting through his viewfinder for fresh inspiration. He found it on the straight rise of a gray cliff that soared above him. Company.

She stood there at the crest of Gertie's Nose, her hand shading her eyes. The sun was directly behind her. She was a slender, shapely figure in jeans and a blouse of filmy stuff that outlined her figure quite clearly. He didn't recognize her. Her short dark hair blew around her face and she drew her fingers impatiently through it.

Curious, Jason focused his zoom lens on her face. She was astonishingly pretty, with large dark eyes, a small nose that had something clever and haughty in its tilt, and a wide, shapely mouth. A new face.

Suddenly she smiled and waved. Jason, taken aback, drew his eye away from the camera and looked up at her. For a moment they both remained very still, contemplating each other, then the woman waved goodbye and ran quickly, lithely away, skirting along the edge of the cliff. She jumped across the two foot gap that interrupted the path to White Head, and disappeared quickly from view.

As Jason snapped her joyful leap into the air silhouetted against the sun, he wondered whether she had been up there during his conversation with West. He knew, of course, that she couldn't have seen them below the overhang, nor could she have heard their conversation over the noisy play of the water coming into the cove. Still, she had regarded him a little too curiously and in the game he was playing, curiosity could kill a lot more than a cat.

Jason climbed onto the path that West had taken out of Squeaker Cove and shortly he, too, jumped the gap onto White Head. Then he started off after the woman, keeping well back but making no attempt to hide. It would be interesting to learn where she lived and exactly why she was on Galbraith. And he meant to let her know he was interested.

Chapter Two

It was nearly six when Addie wandered into town to pick up a few more things at the general store. She found Linus Bishop in the canned-food aisle, contemplating the range of pork and beans offered for sale.

"Thought you were going to come by this afternoon," he said.

"Hi." She found a can of asparagus spears and popped it into her basket. "Believe it or not, I took a walk up to White Head, wandered around a while and, by the time I got back to my cottage most of the afternoon had vanished. What are those smallish birds that look like sea gulls but aren't? They're all over the place."

"Terns, I imagine."

"One good tern deserving another," she said. "I'm sorry about missing this afternoon. Will tomorrow be okay?"

"My dear, never mind that for the time being," he said. "I'll stop by your cottage on the way to West Wind this evening about eight. Come along, why not?"

She drew her brows together. "West Wind?"

"West Wind belongs to Steven West and by extension to his second wife, Veronica. Saturday nights one or the other of us always throws a party. Kind of a round-robin all summer long. Their guests, our guests, we all mingle."

"But—" Addie began.

"No buts about it. We're informal on Galbraith, and I've had to put up with a lot of West's banker friends over the years. They're the types who don't buy paintings, they inherit them.''

Addie gazed at the artist. No, she couldn't even conjure up thoughts of Enigma with reference to Linus Bishop. Kindly, friendly, open and trustworthy best described him.

''I'll pick you up at eight,'' he was saying to her.

She gave a light shake of her head as if to clear it of cobwebs. Operating on instinct was no way to conduct an investigation.

''Oh, and both Wests are generous hosts, so save your appetite,'' he added.

Addie felt a little leap of satisfaction course through her. It was all happening so easily. This would be the perfect opportunity to meet most of her prime suspects. A couple of days and she might well be out of there. However, she thought it prudent to appear to waver on a bit about accepting the invitation, to keep up a shy, modest mien. ''Perhaps,'' she said with a smile of demurral, ''the Wests wouldn't be happy about your showing up with a perfect stranger.''

''Addie,'' Linus said, looking at her closely and with an air of having made a discovery he wanted desperately to show off, ''You *are* perfect. I can tell that at a glance. But believe me, there's plenty on Galbraith a whole lot stranger than you could ever be.''

''SO THAT'S WEST WIND,'' Addie said of the massive gray-shingled mansion standing at the crest of the cliff. She had seen the building from a distance on her walk earlier that day, and had admired its high, solitary beauty.

''Been in the West family from the day it was built a hundred years ago,'' Linus told her. ''Bankers from Boston, what the world calls old money, although the original owner, Cyrus West, made his money inventing a better mop pail. The current heir, Steven West, married the beautiful Veronica, late of the London stage. He's the fourth generation of his family to summer here. Large collections of turn-of-the-century seascapes, and no Linus Bishops. He flies up to Port Clyde from the city on weekends and takes his private launch out to the island. That handsome blue cruiser at the dock is his. Smile at him tonight and maybe he'll take you out for a spin.''

"I guess you're pretty friendly with them," Addie ventured.

"I wouldn't say that, either. He's a hard man to know, though he pretends at being hail-fellow-well-met. His wife's the life of the party."

The front door was open and Linus stood aside to usher Addie in. She heard the sound of laughter coming from a room just off the center hall where a group of people were already comfortably ensconced and enjoying themselves.

She hesitated for a moment on the threshold, full of sudden misgivings. Events were being propelled forward too quickly. And she had the odd feeling she was being set up by Linus, although she couldn't have explained why. She cast him a shy glance. He shook his head and said pleasantly, "They won't bite, you know."

"You're sure."

"Guaranteed."

Addie realized she had been holding herself tightly and knew she had to relax or she'd come away from the evening with nothing but a memory of failure.

Linus took her arm. He brought her into the large, comfortable room, tossing greetings around as though he were dispensing grass seed to the dozen or so assembled guests. The room had a peak ceiling and dark-panelled walls covered, as Linus had said, with fine old seascapes. A double set of couches covered in bright chintz and flanked by a number of deep velvet wing chairs faced an imposing stone fireplace in which huge logs burned cheerfully. A huge clerestory window at the far end of the room framed a dramatic view of the steely sea and the deepening early evening sky.

"Nice," she whispered to Linus. No, she thought looking at the assembled guests, an atmosphere so warm and

friendly could never harbor Enigma. But wasn't that feeling the criminal's stock-in-trade?

"Nice," Linus said, "it's that, all right, despite the absence of even one Bishop watercolor."

She giggled, feeling unexpectedly at ease, then she drew
herself up. She was there for one purpose only and that was
to find and identify Enigma.

"Come, Addie, I'll introduce you around."

Glancing quickly about, she was startled to discover
George Evans in one corner talking to the man who had
been taking photographs at Squeaker Cove that afternoon. The man, she remembered uncomfortably, who had
trailed her along the length of White Head. When she'd
abruptly turned and headed back through the woods that
covered the central part of the island, he'd turned back,
too. She didn't know at what point she'd lost him, but one
thing she was certain of, he'd kept his distance but it definitely had seemed as if he'd wanted her to know he was
there.

"Everybody, meet Addie Cordero," Linus announced as
though she were a prized and expected specimen.

"Come here, let me see her. Trust Linus to find a pretty
woman and bring her to us straight away." The accent was
British and the speaker was a slender woman sitting deco-
rously on a window seat with a fluffy, jet-black cat in her
lap.

"Of course, my darling," Linus said, taking Addie over
to her at once. "Addie, this is our hostess, Veronica West.
Where's Steven?"

"In the kitchen making a pest of himself with the servants. You know Steven," Veronica said, "he fancies himself a gourmet cook and doesn't quite believe the island
help can cut the mustard, so to speak." She put out a hand
with crimson-tipped fingernails. "How are you, Addie?
I'm so glad you could come." She was a beautiful woman
with high cheekbones and blond hair curled into intricate
ringlets. She shooed the cat away and got languorously to

her feet, dusting her hands across her bright red lounging pajamas.

"Better be on your best behavior, Veronica. Addie's a psychologist," Linus said.

Veronica arched an eyebrow. "Not an artist? Not a poet?" Her tone was playful. "Not a novelist or a playwright? Not even an actress? How absolutely wonderful."

"I'm afraid those are skills I've always admired," Addie said, "but haven't the least notion about."

"Imagine, a woman after my own heart." George Evans came up to her and put a heavy arm around her shoulder. "Somebody who admits she doesn't know the first thing about art."

"Well, I don't mean—" she began but he cut her off.

"Come on, Addie, let me introduce you around. She's my neighbor at Winehart Cottage," Evans explained to Veronica, "which makes me responsible for her."

Addie caught the careful look her hostess gave her and the almost imperceptible shake of her head. "George," Veronica said with a charming smile, "why don't you get me a nice, tall glass of vodka and orange juice?"

"Oui, Mem Sahib," he said, reluctantly removing his arm from Addie's shoulder and making an exaggerated bow.

While he was gone, Addie dutifully followed her hostess around the room.

"Sally Draper, poet," Veronica said of a gray-haired woman with an open smile and an ample bosom who swept up Addie's hand in a strong grip.

"Leave it to Veronica to introduce us by our titles," the woman said. "Sally Draper, poet. Sounds impressive even to me."

Her companion, a slender, dramatically beautiful woman with deep red hair was promptly introduced as Meg St. John. "I won't say playwright," Veronica remarked. "I'll say Meg writes plays."

"Comedies," Meg corrected her.

"Comedies, of course," Veronica said with a little bow, "and if I'm lucky I'll get to act in one any day now."

Meg St. John made a face, her long thin nose wrinkling in disdain. "I'm writing in a part just for you, Verry."

"That's what I'm afraid of."

Veronica took Addie's arm and brought her over to the couch where a young man with a headful of thick black hair and a flamboyant moustache sat hand in hand with an equally young, very pretty blonde, whose Wedgwood-blue eyes smiled at her. "Vladimir and Ivy Tatlin," Veronica said. The young man shot to his feet and with a grand gesture, took Addie's hand and kissed it.

"Very much pleased to meet you," he said in a thick accent.

"Vlad's a violinist. He emigrated from Russia and met Ivy along the way," Veronica explained. "In Italy, as I recall, where he was playing a concert. Ivy played the flute there in the Rome symphony orchestra. They met and the rest, as they say, is history. Do I have everything right, Ivy?"

Ivy shook her head and laughed. "You do every time, Veronica." Her accent was very American.

The two men sitting over a game of chess at a table in one corner were introduced as friends of Steven West's, bankers, the word said rather derisively.

Tim Gruesin, a balding, stocky man, cast an appreciative glance over Addie, then returned to the game, which he apparently was winning. His opponent, Noah Roberts, who was wearing an aggressive Hawaiian shirt, gave her a thin-lipped smile.

"Did I hear him say you were a psychologist?" he asked. His voice held the faintest unidentifiable accent, that of someone who had either come to America very young, or grown up in a home where a foreign language was spoken daily.

"I'm afraid so," Addie admitted with a tiny smile, "although it's not the sort of thing I usually announce about myself."

"Your turn," Gruesin growled to his partner.

"Excuse me." Noah Roberts gestured toward the board. "Duty calls."

Next Veronica brought Addie over to the photographer Addie had seen that afternoon. "Jason Farrell," Veronica said, her voice turning coquettish, "this is Addie Cordero. Talk to her, darling, I really must go see what Steve is up to." She left Addie alone with Jason after touching Addie's arm in a light gesture of apology.

Even from a distance Addie had thought that the photographer was a handsome man. She was curious about why he had followed her but she hadn't been particularly alarmed. After all, Enigma couldn't even know who she was or that she was on the island yet.

In the soft light of the West living room, the strong lines of Jason Farrell's angular face were deeply shadowed: his chin, which jutted slightly, held a deep cleft. She thought that his eyes were deep gray, but couldn't be quite certain of it in the dim light. There was something sensual about the man, a certain power that seemed constrained beneath the tweed jacket he wore like a uniform. She had sensed it that afternoon out at the cove as well.

Jason took Addie's hand in a strong grip. "I caught you on film." His voice was deep and warm and surprisingly full of good humor.

"Did you really? Then you *were* the man I saw out at Squeaker Cover this afternoon. I thought as much."

"And you were the lady on the rocks."

"You make me sound like some sort of exotic drink." She extracted her hand from his clasp and had an odd lingering notion that he had surrendered it reluctantly. "The trouble is, I'm superstitious," she said. "If you captured my soul in full color heaven knows what dire things might occur as a result."

"You're in luck. I use black-and-white film."

"Oh, that's all right, then. I figure the soul is definitely red, yellow and blue, and all the permutations thereof."

"A superstitious psychologist. Sounds ideal."

Addie laughed. "I suppose I am superstitious. I can't remember the last time I walked under a ladder." Then she added in a more serious tone, "But I also believe one operates just as often on instinct. Well, at least I do."

"And that's the kind of thing that can land you in all sorts of trouble," he said gazing closely at her.

Addie felt the color rise to her cheeks and knew he'd caught sight of it. She no more understood her sometimes foolish behavior than the simplest of her patients. One could be as scientific as one wished, except when it came to romance; then instinct turned into foolhardiness. After Rafe left for Europe, Addie had vowed she would never allow herself to fall in love again without clearly understanding exactly what she was doing.

"Of course I bolster what I know about myself and my patients with a few tricks some people wouldn't call scientific." Addie was aware of how defensive she sounded and thought that would fit the role she was here to play.

"You read bumps on people's heads," he said with a smile.

"No, but it's an idea."

"Ah, palms." He reached for her hand and turned the palm upward. "Mmm, I'd say a long life is indicated. Here, of course, this curve around the thumb, I believe it indicates a romantic nature."

She pulled her hand back. "Not palms, either."

"And not a romantic nature."

"I'd say you have a specific talent for pushing people back against a wall, Mr. Farrell."

Her remark seemed to take him by surprise. He frowned but after a moment grinned as though she had caught him out. "My students call me Professor Farrell," he remarked. "But my friends call me Jason. Won't you? And what's this other scientific specialty you're talking about?"

Addie felt an unexpected nervousness in the pit of her stomach. She had to be casual and she might have only one chance to advertise her expertise to the assembled guests unobtrusively. She suspected that Jason Farrell wasn't the kind of man to make a fuss about it and then she'd be back to square one. She gazed quickly around the room and saw a young woman in a dark cotton dress with a white apron over it heading toward them with a tray of canapés.

George Evans caught her eye at the same time and gave her a broad grin. She smiled back despite her distaste for the man and reached for a canapé. As she'd hoped Evans came quickly over to her.

"Handwriting," she said, turning back to Jason. "I, um, I sometimes use handwriting analysis to assist me in my psychological evaluations."

Evans, who had been listening carefully, was impressed. "Fantastic, the lady reads handwritings." He called out to Veronica West, who had just come back into the room.

"Really? How amazing," Veronica said, "Besides being a psychologist, just imagine. Here I am, my one and only talent totally abandoned, while everybody else here is so damn *clever*. Although," she added, coming over to them, "personally I think handwriting analysis sits somewhere between reading tea leaves and tarot cards. The hangman." She shivered. "You don't mind my being so frank, Addie, do you?"

"No," Addie said without the least bit of rancor, "not at all. You aren't the first person I've met who's expressed skepticism about handwriting analysis and I'm afraid you won't be the last."

"Really." The woman glanced at her guests as if to include them in her surprise. "I'm not at all sure what you mean."

"There's nothing magical about graphology," Addie said. "Your handwriting is as individual as your fingerprints."

"I was born with my fingerprints."

"There *is* conclusive research linking individual handwriting strokes and pen pressure to personality."

"I learned to write one way in school," her hostess said, "and I've pretty much stuck to it since then. I can't imagine how you'd discover a thing about me from that."

Lack of imagination, for one, Addie thought, for never altering her handwriting, no matter how her life might have changed. "Mrs. West—"

"Veronica."

"I'm afraid psychology and graphology are both imperfect sciences," Addie said with a little laugh she hoped didn't sound false. "You join two imperfect sciences together and you might have one effective tool."

Linus Bishop joined in, saying in a patient voice, "What Addie means, Veronica, is that graphology allows one insight into people's souls. As a result, she'll know how to deal with them, knows when to ease up if they're stubborn, or to press if they're undecided."

"If graphology is reading souls," Veronica said, "then, Linus darling, you and I are in total agreement. Graphology, as far as I'm concerned, is closer to witchcraft than science."

Addie laughed. "I wish it were as simple as that."

"And do you make a living from this talent?"

"As I said it's an added tool I've tried to use in my work, like a computer for keeping files."

A tall, distinguished man came up to them. Addie noted that the denim shirt and denim pants he wore looked expensive and were starched and pressed as though the wearing of such clothes was an effort to keep in step with the island's mores, whether he liked them or not. He put an arm around Veronica's waist and said, "Artists never make livings from their talent."

"She isn't an artist, darling, she's a psychologist. And she reads handwriting. This is Addie Cordero. My husband, Steven West."

Addie extended a hand and found it taken in a reassuring grip. "Welcome to West Wind." Steve's smile was friendly, if a little distracted.

"Thank you for having me."

"She came with Linus, darling," Veronica said.

"Linus always shows up with beautiful surprises." He released her hand.

Linus, hearing his name mentioned, drifted back to their group. "Speaking of me in vain?"

"Speaking of your lovely friend," Steve said. "Thanks for bringing her."

Linus beamed. "Oh, I aim to please."

"I imagine it happens to you all the time at parties," Veronica said to Addie.

Addie looked curiously at her. "I'm sorry, I don't know what you mean."

"Being asked to read handwritings."

"I usually don't bring the subject up, as a matter of fact." She turned and gave a meaningful glance toward Jason Farrell, who still stood nearby, as though she was trying to blame him for forcing the information out of her.

"The longer I live," Jason said, moving closer, "the more I'm convinced people know themselves very little, and that they're desperate to find out who they are and what they are by any means." His next remark took Addie aback. "It could be a pretty dangerous pastime, reading handwritings for fun or for profit."

"I don't know about that," Addie said. "A roomful of professionals, artists, writers and musicians, it would be a real pleasure, come to think of it."

"Addie, do read our handwritings, it would be so much fun," Veronica said.

"Even if you don't believe in it?" Addie asked.

"But everyone else does."

"I'd hate like hell to have everyone know my peccadilloes," Gruesin said without looking up from the chessboard. He laughed and turned to Veronica. "But I'll go along with it if we don't have to sign our names to our handwriting samples."

"Great idea." His remark was caught up by Meg St. John, the woman who had been introduced as a playwright. "I don't mind learning something new about myself, but I don't want to have to share it with the lot of you."

"I'm for that, too," George Evans said. "You tell me I'm a pushover for a compliment—" he began.

"She'll tell you what you are, George," Steven West said, "an arrogant bastard who can't paint worth a damn."

Evans, instead of being angry, let out a huge bellow, but Addie caught an odd glint in his eye as he moved past her toward the cocktail table where he began to stuff himself with food.

"Anonymity, what sense does that make?" Veronica asked.

"Meaning some of you are too shy to admit what an egocentric bunch you are," Linus said. "But how does that sit with you, Addie, analyzing our handwriting without knowing precisely who the writer is?"

"Somehow modesty doesn't seem to fit on Galbraith Island," Jason Farrell said lazily.

Anonymity was the last thing Addie needed. If Enigma *was* in the room, she wanted to know who he or she was as soon as possible.

"Modesty, no, anonymity, yes," Meg St. John insisted and Sally Draper, the poet, agreed.

Addie found it hard to repress a smile. She would have let them argue it out among themselves, let them think graphology was just a parlor game on the order of charades. Once again she had the feeling that everyone was being a bit too friendly, too convivial. It was simply not an atmosphere she imagined could support someone as venal as Enigma.

And Addie, after a moment's reflection, decided there would probably be full confessions before the party ended, it had been that kind of day. If so she might make the ID and then hail the next boat to the mainland. She might even take a vacation early. Fly to Europe. Casually bump into Rafe on the Champs Elysee. Walk right past him and not even smile a greeting. But, she reminded herself, she was trying not to think about Rafe.

"I'm game if you're game," she said, "provided you understand that what I am about to tell you will be a first reading handicapped by my not knowing the sexes, ages or conditions of health of the writers.''

"Addie, we do have to live with each other long after you're gone,'' Sally Draper commented in a soft apologetic tone.

Vladimir Tatlin pointed to himself. "I write with Russian accent. You'll know me without too much troubles.''

Everyone laughed and Addie said, "Ah, but I'll be the only one to read what you write and I promise, I won't give you away.''

"But remember, we don't want a sop to the truth, either,'' Linus said. "The whole idea of the game would be lost.''

"It's only a game,'' she pointed out. "I suggest,'' she said to the guests who had gathered around her, "that you each write a couple of lines of poetry on a piece of ruled paper and don't sign it. I'll read your poem aloud, and make my analysis of your handwriting. However, anonymity does mean some of the fun will be taken out of it.''

"Maybe that's true,'' Meg St. John declared, "but so will the queer looks we'd be giving one another after. Poetry sounds fine with me.''

"And no quotes from any of your plays, Meg,'' Evans told her. "I know every word you've ever written and a few you haven't managed yet.''

At that moment someone new came into the room, a slender man of medium height with long, wind-tossed hair, and wide-set deep brown eyes. In fact he was so good-looking that Addie drew in an unexpected breath when she saw him. He was dressed casually but in very elegant style, with a print scarf tucked into his shirt collar. "I took a long walk,'' he said apologetically, "and ended up at Seal Cove on the other side of the island.''

"Darling, come in, never mind,'' Veronica said, going up to him and taking him by the hand. "Dr. Kevin Morgan,'' she explained to Addie. "He's one of our guests and he has absolutely no sense of time or direction, isn't that right, darling? Addie's going to read your handwriting, Kevin, impossible as it is.''

"Is she?" Kevin gave Addie a dreamy smile.

"Kevin, of course, is a medical doctor, but he wants to be a poet, don't you darling?" she said.

Kevin smiled and shook his head, as though indulging Veronica in her fantasies. "Whatever you say, Mrs. West," he said with an emphasis on her married name.

"Here's your chance to shine." She explained the game to him, adding that Addie would read each poem aloud so each guest would be able to tell when his or her sample was being analyzed. "Your chance to be judged by your peers, Kevin. Just write one of your poems in your lovely, illegible script."

"But we shouldn't reveal which poem we write, any of us," Steven West reminded them. "Stick to the classics, Kev. There are a dozen of us here. You'll announce yourself if you use something you've written. I'll know," he added with a look of disgust, as though he had been privy once too often to the doctor's poetical musings.

"I write for myself, Steve, you know that."

"You said it, Kev, I didn't. Everybody here is agreed to straight anonymity, then, meaning none of us is exposed to dangerous guessing games."

"Dangerous?" Jason Farrell said. "My feeling is that graphologists keep the interesting part to themselves and hand the rest out as pap. Am I right?" His smile offered Addie a frank chance to defend herself.

"I wouldn't dream of feeding you pap," she said. "That's not playing fair." She wanted to turn from him but was held by the intensity of his gaze. A smile might have defused the moment, but it wouldn't come and then she saw his mocking look. Subtle, perhaps, but as certain as if he were telling her he could see right through her.

Her heart did an unexpected flip-flop. He might be Enigma after all, a charmer who could remove the floorboards out from under her without her ever knowing.

"I promised I'd analyze handwriting samples and I will," she said. "In fact, general anonymity gives me a chance to tell you a few things I might ordinarily keep to myself."

"Such as?" Jason asked, his gaze unwavering.

"Irritability, short fuses, someone on edge." She stopped short, aware of the imprudence of such remarks.

"So, if there's a madman among us, you'll know it," Jason commented, not bothering to keep the sarcasm out of his voice.

Addie tried to backtrack but didn't know if she could succeed. "I'll know if there's someone impulsive and quick-tempered, someone who carries a grudge or hurt, oh, that sort of thing. Someone who has the potential to act irrationally," she added with a laugh she knew must sound forced. "Don't we all?"

Jason's expression was immobile. "And just how often have you exposed people bent on mischief?"

Damn, she had asked for it, letting him bait her. She had to make it all sound like innocence and fun, nothing more. She chose her words as carefully as if she believed Enigma *was* actually among them. "As I said before, I use what I know as an aid to my work, that's all. People come to me with problems and I'm there to help. It's all quite cut-and-dried." She gave Jason an especially sunny smile. "And here I've a feeling I'm going to find a collection of elegant, cultured scripts and no hang-ups."

For a long moment, they all remained silent watching one another. Yet Addie ardently believed her words. Facing her was an intelligent and cultured group, she'd bet her life on it. There was no reason to believe Enigma was present, and that was all that mattered.

Veronica broke in with a brittle laugh. "Mischief?" she looked at Addie with a twinkle in her eye. "On Galbraith Island? My dear, nothing ever happens on Galbraith. That's the *point*, or so Steve says. Well, shall we begin?" she added, springing to life. "We'll need pencils and paper."

"Ruled paper," Addie reminded her.

"Why ruled?" Meg asked.

"So I can tell if you're an optimist or a pessimist. The rules and the sides of the paper act as guides to your behavior, as well."

"Ask enough questions," Dr. Morgan said, "and we can all become experts overnight."

The doctor was delicate in appearance and, Addie decided, rather poetic in a Byronic sense. She wondered about his own poetry and thought if she had the chance, she'd ask to see some of it.

"I'll haul in a couple of books of poetry," Steven West said. "I can't think of a thing at the moment except Dandelions by Henry Wadsworth Longfellow."

"Dandelions?" Sally Draper said with a laugh. "You mean daffodils and the poem is called 'I wandered lonely as a cloud.' The author, incidentally, is William Wordsworth. Really, Steve, your ignorance appalls me."

He laughed. "It appalled my teachers, too."

"Ugh," George Evans said. "'I wandered lonely as a cloud.' They beat that poem into my head when I was in grammar school."

"Everyone joining in?" Veronica asked brightly.

She was greeted with a chorus of agreement and when her husband returned with several volumes of poetry, everyone gathered around him. He held a book up. "Shakespeare, anyone?"

"Put all the books on the table," George Evans said in a cool, commanding voice. "Remember, the operative word here is anonymity."

Addie waited quietly as people sifted through the books or sat thinking. She saw Jason Farrell spend time over a slim, leather-bound volume. Then, without copying a word, he sat down and scribbled something quickly. Kevin Morgan made a great show of not consulting a book, but Meg St. John and the bankers fought over turf, which turned out, when Addie had a chance to check, to be a volume of English and American poetry. She felt every ounce of flesh tingle with apprehension. In a very short while she'd know for certain whether or not Enigma was among the guests at West Wind. The idea was both frightening and thrilling. She noted carefully that the book Jason had gone through and put down had been a collection of Shakespeare sonnets.

Ten minutes later, the guests had deposited their slips of paper into a wide-brimmed straw hat that Veronica had produced. "I'm going to mix them up like lottery tickets," she said, "then hand them to Addie. It's been a lot of fuss to keep your secrets safe and it won't be nearly so much fun, but here goes."

The hat was ceremoniously handed over to Addie who said, "I can take your handwriting samples out one by one and read them each off the top of my head, or I can spend a few moments studying them first."

"Oh, take your time, by all means," Steven West said in an interested tone. "If you're going to do a thing, do it right."

"I'd feel more comfortable that way," she said, offering an apologetic shrug. Then she put her hand into the hat. "You're right," she said gaily to Veronica. "I feel as if I'm about to draw a lottery number. And the winner is..."

Addie stopped and gazed transfixed at the slip of paper in her hand. So Enigma *was* there after all, sitting in that lovely firelit room. Enigma, the unknown quantity she had come to Galbraith to find.

Chapter Three

Suddenly nothing looked good from where Addie sat. The ripple of fear along her skin did not abate. Everything had been going along too smoothly. She should have expected a hitch.

Enigma was present in this most civilized setting and Addie had to find a contingency plan for breaking through the promise of anonymity. She continued to gaze at the slip of paper in her hand. She knew every stroke of that pen by heart. They matched the ones on the piece of paper found clutched in Eda Barnstable's hand. That knowledge did her no good at all.

"Somehow," Jason said, breaking into the silence, "I think the lady has hit a brick wall."

Addie caught his eye and said in a level voice, "Now why do you think that?"

"Furrowed brow. Intense concentration. I can smell the burning rubber across the room."

"Jason, darling, Addie's just being careful," Veronica said. "After all, she's going to tell us what we are and I've no doubt a few of us mayn't like it at all. Just imagine, some of us may leave West Wind with an entirely new set of insights about ourselves."

Steven West said, "Go ahead, Addie, take your time."

Addie drew herself up. She'd have to listen carefully to people's responses as she read each poem aloud; had to catch the lift on an eyebrow, or flutter of an eyelid, so she could match reaction to sample until Enigma stood alone. She sifted through the other poems and discovered snippets of interest among them: aggression, laziness, creativity, those who vacillated or took too much upon themselves. She'd have to be very careful and yet give them their money's worth.

What she could impart to each and every one of them could cause endless guessing games, endless quarrels all summer long. It was a social evening. It wasn't time to intrude, to cause rifts, to make them uncomfortable. After all, it was supposed to be just a parlor game, nothing more, except for the cold-blooded killer sitting in their midst.

"I'm not sure I want my handwriting read after all," Meg St. John said in an unexpectedly querulous tone. "I only went along with the idea because everyone else did. I've got my psyche to worry about. I like it just where it is, half hidden, known to me alone."

"You're an open book anyway, Meg," Linus said, grinning. "We know all about you just by watching you move."

"Give me a moment or two more," Addie implored them. "You're a complicated lot and I'd hate to shortchange you."

"If you find out we're all a bunch of scoundrels," Linus said, "you won't hold back, will you, Addie?"

"I'll call 'em as I see 'em." She glanced briefly over at Jason Farrell and found him watching her, his face completely expressionless. Was he the one she'd come looking for? Pity, if he were.

"What I want to know," Veronica said, "was did I make a mistake leaving the theater?" She had resumed her seat at the window, and the cat was once more in her lap.

"She's a graphologist, not a prognosticator, Verry. You'll see in my wife's handwriting," Steven said to Addie, "a woman of a very rare theatrical talent. It's the rest of the stuff I'll be curious to learn."

"No peeking, either. You won't know it *is* my handwriting," Veronica remarked. "Not from the poem I've chosen."

"I'll know."

"Shall we bet on it, Steve?"

He frowned at his wife. He was a little on edge, Addie thought with a frisson of fear. His handwriting, then?

"A banker who bets?" Steve said. "What would my depositors think?" His guests laughed, although his wife merely shook her head and trailed her red-tipped fingers down the soft, silken fur of her cat.

But to Addie, outward trappings meant nothing. A banker could no more hide what he truly was than a hobo.

Previously, when she'd been invited to read handwritings as a parlor game, she'd always entered into the spirit willingly. But this avid request for anonymity was new to her. She tried to remember who had sparked the idea but couldn't. Perhaps it had come about like spontaneous combustion.

But she had no wish to upset the equilibrium of their lives. She'd compromise, as she often did, and in the case of Enigma, she'd simply fudge the truth.

"Those poems we chose," Steven West remarked. "Do you take them into consideration?"

"No," Addie said. "You used them as your personal identification. I only look at structure and spacing; the forms of words, not their meanings."

West nodded, then joined his two house guests who were again bent over their chess game.

There was a little rustling in the room as her audience put aside drinks or plates of food, and assumed various poses of attention. The West house was one of the few on the island that had its own electric generator and Addie could feel its light vibration beneath the floor. The scent of candles drifted past, their fragile flames pushed by the night air that was flowing salted and damp through an open window. From outside she could hear the rustling of trees and the sibilant sound of the ebb tide caressing the rocks below.

She drew her hand through her hair, pushing at a mischievous strand that fell into her eye. There was laughter, voices just out of earshot, the fire crackling. A fire in July, but summer nights on Galbraith Island had a peculiar chill to them, as if the ordinary rules of the season didn't apply. Aware of the attention of her audience, she turned first to the poem by William Blake.

Enigma's contribution to the evening. Might as well get it over with, she thought. *Songs of Innocence*, indeed. She drew in a strong breath, then began to read the poem aloud in her soft, warm voice:

"Cruelty has a Human Heart
And Jealousy a Human Face.
Terror, the Human Form Divine
And Secrecy, the Human Dress.

"The Human Dress, is forged Iron
The Human Form, a fiery Forge.
The Human Face, a Furnace seal'd
The Human Heart, its hungry Gorge."

"William Blake, *Songs of Innocence*," Sally Draper said. "Called 'A Divine Image,' if I'm not mistaken."

"You're never mistaken, Sally," Meg St. John said, giving her a smile that held something a little spiteful in it.

"Meaning," Veronica said lazily, "if you know it's Blake, then you're the writer."

Linus Bishop said, "Wrong, Veronica, I know it's Blake, too."

"Let's have a show of hands."

"Veronica, give it up," her husband said irritably. "Go ahead, Addie. Ply your trade."

"I'm *plying* as hard as I can," Addie said, keeping her tone light, although as she glanced once more at the poem, that shiver flowed once more along her arms.

A determined, inflexible character. There were initial strokes that indicated resentment, and the muddiness of sexual appetite, combined with a backhand of self-interest. Underlying hostility, brutality threatening to explode. But, she saw it once again, intelligence in the pointed m's and n's. Alert, alert, alert, the handwriting seemed to say, like a fire alarm that can't be turned off because it's just out of reach. All the writer needed was a lighted match.

"Quiet," George Evans said suddenly, apropos of nothing, "the graphologist is thinking."

Addie looked up quickly. "Our quoter of Blake," she said at last, her eyes sweeping over her audience. How like a tableau it seemed: Linus Bishop cupped his right ear with his hand as though his hearing had suddenly failed him. Veronica almost too languidly petted her cat. George Evans poured himself a copious drink from a bottle on the buffet table against the wall. Jason Farrell leaned against the door at some distance, as though it were a game he'd rather not play. Meg St. John and Sally Draper sat on the couch, side by side, smoking cigarettes and sharing an ashtray. Tim Gruesin and Noah Roberts were still at the chess table and Noah held a chess piece in midair. Steve West lounged against the fireplace and the Tatlins and the doctor, Kevin Morgan, sat attentively on the second couch.

"I find this handwriting fascinating," she said at last. "The writer is determined, creative, extremely intelligent. This, mixed with a quick temper, could make him, or her, a fascinating if volatile companion."

"Volatile?" Tim Gruesin caught her eye and Addie thought the glance he gave her was the coldest she had ever received.

"Volatile, as in dynamite," she confirmed. "This writer wants his or her way, and watch out for the explosion if it doesn't happen."

"An explosion as in bang, you're dead?" The question was asked by Jason Farrell.

She regarded him coolly. "Explosion as in a slammed closet door, or a tire kicked. A temper tantrum with plenty of screaming. But," she added trying to make the analysis more moderate, "it's a temper quickly abated. Explosion today, but the reason is forgotten almost immediately and the sun comes out."

She gazed once more around the room, yet her analysis had yielded no quickened interest in an eye, or look of abject fear at being found out. But then, no one here knew who she truly was, or why she was there, or what she was looking for—or that she had found it.

She slipped the first piece of paper to the back and perused the next poem. Emily Dickinson, Addie recognized the passage from a college poetry class. She cleared her throat.

"The soul selects her own society,
Then shuts the door;
On her divine majority
Obtrude no more."

"Pretty," Veronica said, "but I'll have to think about what it means."

"Dammit, Veronica," her husband said. "Stop giving yourself away."

"I doubt she's given herself away," the doctor said. "You can copy a poem and not understand a word of it."

"Oh, thanks much," Veronica said, although she didn't seem perturbed at all over the barbs thrown by both her husband and their guest. "I get paid for reading poetry if you two jokers will kindly remember it."

Addie looked around the room, then said, "Penner of Emily Dickinson, I don't know who you are, but you're emotional, impulsive, yet decidedly a procrastinator. Emotional and impulsive," she reiterated, "you put off things and yet if someone chides you, your reaction is to be overly sensitive. You won't hide your hurt so much as admit it. However," she added with a smile, "you're usually fired by enthusiasm and your hurt tends to be short-lived." And you're a liar, she thought, omitting an obvious point in the way the a's were curled tight.

"Ah, now, here's one," she said, taking up a new slip of paper.

"Where the bee sucks, there suck I;
in a cowslip bell I lie;
There I couch, when owls do cry;
on the bat's back I do fly."

"Shakespeare," Meg St. John said. "*The Tempest.*"

"Congratulations, Meg, you are now about to have your handwriting analyzed." The speaker was George Evans.

Meg's answer was sharp, although her tone held a certain amount of familiarity in it. "I'm a playwright, you fool, as if you didn't know. I'd have to be pretty dim-witted not to know a few lines out of *The Tempest.*"

"Oooh, I love Shakespeare," Veronica mocked. "He's so full of quotations."

Addie waited for the laughter to die down, her eye on the poem. The handwriting had the characteristics of a British hand: it was attractive, the letters upright and careful, revealing the national characteristic of a certain amount of self-consciousness. The writing was mature; it had changed considerably from childish writing and showed intelligence and a feeling for handling details. She cast a quick glance at Veronica. Veronica was wrong about herself—if this were Veronica's handwriting the woman had changed considerably since she was a child. The self-consciousness of the writing made Addie uncertain of her guess, however. A self-conscious actress seemed a contradiction in terms.

She gazed across the room at Noah Roberts. She had detected a slight accent when he spoke. Might he not have been educated abroad? The small letters, the upright script; the poem might have been written by a man's hand. Roberts was a banker and had probably spent a good deal of time working with figures, which could account for the careful quality of the script.

Her audience was waiting. She smiled and plowed on, reading off the flattering characteristics and checking both Veronica and Noah Roberts for their reactions.

Veronica was a good enough actress to keep a straight face, and Noah, while paying attention, still threw an occasional glance at the chessboard. Addie learned nothing.

The next handwriting belonged to Vladimir Tatlin, of that she was certain. Vladimir Tatlin was right. She'd been able to match him to his handwriting easily. It was foreign in character, the careful handwriting of one who had learned to write and speak English as a second language. And he had, in fact, chosen a poem by Pushkin.

Ivy Tatlin's handwriting was equally easy to match. It was that curious half-formed cross between printing and script that told of her youth and education. She'd chosen a song by Bob Dylan and Addie found her writing indicated she was artistic, whimsical, intuitive and well adjusted. As for the others, they had made an eclectic selection: Chaucer and Alexander Pope, Kipling, T. S. Eliot, Lord Byron and Sylvia Plath. She read their poems aloud and tried to match reactions but had little success. They were a garrulous, charming lot, given to saying what they wanted with little fear. Addie told what she could, omitting descriptives such as greed or avarice, anxiety or tension, the usual problems found in every gathering. There were several beautiful handwritings, and others tight and controlled with tiny letters cautiously made; the handwriting of people who were assigned the meticulous care of funds or the calculations of the weight of bridges, but who hid their emotions.

Then there was the analysis she'd saved for last, the very poem to end the parlor game.

"Our revels now are ended. These our actors,
As I foretold you, were all spirits, and
Are melted into air, into thin air:
And, like the baseless fabric of this vision,
The cloud-capp'd towers, the gorgeous places,
The solemn temples, the great globe itself,
Yea, all which it inherit, shall dissolve,
And, like this insubstantial pageant faded,

Leave not a rack behind. We are such stuff
As dreams are made on; and our little life
Is rounded with a sleep.''

There was an appreciative silence for a moment and then a sudden small laugh. Veronica said, "Well, two minds beat as one. Two quotations from *The Tempest.*"

"Sensible," Sally Draper said. "We're all locked together on an island, for better or for worse."

"I wonder who our duo is?" Veronica mused.

"You're much too interested," her husband said. "You played Shakespeare often enough. I'd say you were one of them."

She laughed. "Darling, I haven't been an airy spirit for a long time. Go ahead, Addie, tell us what you've found."

"Artistic," Addie said of the dynamic, spontaneous hand. "But secretive. He'd—"

"He?" Jason Farrell raised his eyebrows. "I thought you couldn't tell the sex of the writer."

"That's true," Addie said flushing. "It's just that I— well, actually I don't really know why I said it."

"Perhaps because it's Prospero's speech," Veronica said. Her eyes, suddenly feral, lit up with a curious smile. The cat jumped down from her lap and sauntered over to Linus Bishop, whose lap he chose next.

"Believe me," Addie said, unable to resist another glance at Jason Farrell. "It was just a slip of the tongue."

"I'm sorry," Veronica said. "Go on. I'll have to admit I'm fascinated."

"Well, thank you," said Addie. "As I was saying, our writer has a fresh, exciting handwriting. Emotional, yet capable of keeping that emotion in check. He's..." She stopped, gave a small apologetic laugh, then plowed on. Her own handwriting revealed she operated on instinct. This was a man's handwriting, she was certain of it. Her glance once more sought out Jason Farrell.

He had wandered over to the fireplace. His back was to her. He picked up the poker and began stabbing at the logs, sending sparks flying up the chimney.

"I find a dichotomy in this person. On the one hand he's easygoing, on the other he possesses a certain kind of dynamic energy. Creative, intelligent and sensual," she went on. "But the writer is also quite precise and levelheaded. You can count on him—*her* in a pinch."

"Sensual," Meg cried. "I'll lay claim to that handwriting at once." She looked over and smiled at Jason Farrell, who had turned around, still holding the poker in his hand. "Everyone kindly take note."

"One other thing," Addie said. "The creativity in this handwriting outweighs every other consideration, except," she added with a laugh, "the sensual. And that's about it," she said, "I've reached the end, there isn't any more."

"I don't think you have." It was Jason Farrell, who had replaced the poker and moved restlessly across the room to pick up his drink.

"Twelve guests," she said, "twelve poems."

"Precisely."

"Thirteen," Veronica murmured with genuine distress, "I hadn't even noticed. There are thirteen of us. Good heavens, and I'm horribly superstitious."

"Are you?" Sally Draper asked. "Well, we learn something new every day."

"And have you ever analyzed your handwriting, Addie?" Farrell asked.

"Oh, often, always hoping to find something new," she said.

"And how do you find yourself?"

She was aware of the others watching, of a certain unexpected tension in the room. "That's the delicious thing about handwritings. If you know what's wrong, you can change your way of writing and change your life."

"And have you?"

She stood up, still holding on to the slips of paper. "Definitely. Before I changed my handwriting I was six foot five and had long, blond hair. I was also ice-skating champion of the world. I think we've squeezed all there is out of the subject, don't you?"

"On the contrary," Farrell said with a smile. "I think the subject is as fascinating as our graphologist is slippery."

"Slippery!" She took in a breath, catching herself.

"I mean beating-about-the-bush slippery," he said, smiling. "Hide-and-seek slippery. You know a hell of a lot about us now, and you've given nothing of yourself."

"I know nothing about you individually," she pointed out. "All I'm doing is claiming my fair share of anonymity."

"And so you shall, my dear," said Linus Bishop, who raised his hands and applauded. "A round of thanks for our graphologist. I, for one, was absolutely pleased with what she said. Right on target, Addie."

There was some desultory applause and more congratulatory remarks. Sally Draper came over and took up Addie's hand and held it warmly. "I'm amazed," she said in a whisper. "You were not only on target, but told me a few things I didn't know but that made sense the minute you mentioned them. I guess my third husband was right. I don't even mind telling you which poem was mine," she added.

Addie felt a sudden chilling of her blood but kept silent.

"Chaucer," the woman said with pride. "The lines from Chaucer." She glanced meaningfully down at the slips of paper Addie still held in her hand.

"I remember very well," Addie said, breathing easier. One down and eleven to go. Actually nine since she'd eliminated the Tatlins. Perhaps if she stayed very still, more of them would just come over to her and confess.

Sally put her hand to her mouth. "Oh, but don't say anything more. I'm going to concentrate on changing. Levelheaded but inclined to be bossy. You're right, so right. I don't know why it would be, or even how, but you've made a believer out of me." She hurried away, evidently very pleased with herself.

A believer. A dozen slips of paper and at least one person who'd learned very little about herself, because Addie had fudged the truth.

"You win, you know." It was Veronica West, coming up to her with a glass of wine. "Have some after your long ordeal."

Addie, who wanted nothing more than a good cup of black coffee, shook her head. "And was I on target with you, too?"

"Extraordinarily so. Perhaps it's witchcraft, after all." Veronica drifted away, a languid figure in bright red lacy lounge pajamas.

For a moment Addie stood alone, the uninvited guest, the thirteenth person whose presence had suddenly provoked her superstitious hostess; the one in possession of an incriminating piece of handwriting.

"What didn't you tell us?" George Evans asked, coming up to her. He held a drink in his hand, a good, strong one from the look of it. "You can confide in me."

"Why, George," she said, "I can't. Graphology is the same as the relationship between priest and confessor, lawyer and client."

"Yeah, but still, I've a temper and you omitted that."

"Did I? Must have been an oversight." She tried to think back to the dozen slips of paper, to the ones that had revealed impatience, temper, self-indulgence, all those things she had politely omitted in her reading. This could be game playing of a very sophisticated sort. If George wanted her to believe he was not the writer of the Blake poem then he would pretend some other poem had been his—one in which she hadn't mentioned the word temper. Was George, then, Enigma? She gave him a shaky smile.

"The rest you managed right," he added grudgingly.

Addie took in a light breath, held it, then said, "Which poem was yours? I'll look it over and tell you if the symptoms were there."

He pushed playfully at her shoulder with his finger, then laughed. "Ah-ah, that's not fair. We all agreed on the need for anonymity."

"Can't blame me for trying."

"Hey," he said jovially, "try a little harder, I might just confess."

"You look like a Shakespeare man to me." She waited, watching him closely. A mote of light reflected in his eyes, yet all he did was shake his hand. Whether she had guessed right or not, she couldn't tell. "Although," she added, "I doubt if you'd have quoted a kind of sissy poem from *The Tempest*."

"You're right. I'd have taken something from *Othello*."

"But you didn't, quote *Othello*, I mean."

"You're right. I quoted—wait a minute, you're sneaky." Evans finished his drink, then said, "Hey, where'd all the lovely juice go? What I need is a refill. Be right with you. Can I get you anything?"

Addie shook her head and as soon as he was gone, reached for her bag and slipped the papers into it quickly, hoping her movements wouldn't be observed. Then she followed the scent of freshly made coffee into the kitchen where she found Steven West in deep conversation with the men who had sat over the chessboard, Tim Gruesin and Noah Roberts.

They all looked up when she came into the room. The expression of surprise on West's face and its extraordinarily pale color took her aback. "Oh, I'm sorry," she said. "I smelled the coffee and, and—"

"Come in, come in," West said, recovering himself. "That's what aromas are for, to catch pretty women."

He quickly poured her a mug and she left the kitchen at once, with the odd notion that they'd been discussing her and it hadn't been about graphology.

The coffee turned out to be a savory, dark brew that cleared her head. She stood for a moment and surveyed the crowd then suddenly realized that three or four more guests were not in the room. A trickle of fear slid down her spine.

What had happened to them? Had they gone home? Had she found Enigma only to lose him?

"Just find out who Enigma is. Don't play cop," Pam had warned.

"I'm not a cop," Addie had protested. *"I'm a psychologist with the Department of Corrections and a court certified graphologist. I'm used to dealing with criminals across a wide, wide desk in a well-lit room, with a couple of beefy police officers watching every move they make. Believe me, if I find Enigma, you'll be the first to know."*

And now it was possible Enigma was gone. Then she saw, and sighed with relief, that her three known factors were the very ones to have left, the Tatlins and Sally Draper.

"I think I like you better in your present incarnation." Jason Farrell had appeared at her side, holding two glasses of wine and offering her one, which she accepted out of politeness.

"Present incarnation? What does that mean, exactly?"

"Having gone from a six-foot-five, blond-haired ice skater to a brunette of an absolutely *perfect* size, from where I stand. And all with the stroke of a pen. I'm impressed. And have you put two and two together concerning the rest of us?"

His pointed remark took her aback. "Two and two? They make four as I recall."

"Come on, let's have a talk." He took her arm and drew her over toward the door that led to a glassed-in porch.

"Hey, Farrell." Still holding her arm, Jason turned. Tim Gruesin came up to them. "We've met somewhere, haven't we?"

Jason shook his head. "Doubt it, but could be. I've been on the island for a week, staying at the Island Inn."

"No, we just arrived today. In Boston, maybe?"

There was a slight pause before Jason spoke. "Red Sox game, maybe? Went through Boston a couple of years back and a friend dragged me out on the hottest day of the year."

Gruesin shrugged and turned away.

"Happens to me all the time," Jason said. "I must have the world's most ordinary face."

As they went onto the porch Addie considered that statement. Ordinary? Not ordinary at all.

Night had fallen. The porch overlooked the water, but there was no moon to reflect off the waves. The porch was dark and chilly and smelled strongly of the sea. The furnishings, which were white wicker, had a ghostly appearance under the pale light that drifted out from the living room. Addie went over to the glass doors. They led out onto a stone terrace beyond which the cliff dropped sharply away. Waves rushed against the rocks below and then withdrew only to rush in again—the sound of a soft, endlessly repeated phrase. The blackness was dense, impenetrable. Addie wondered how she'd find her way back home, even with the flashlight Linus had told her to bring.

A lighthouse stood at the highest point on the island, which was to the north, and every thirty seconds its ray swept by high above them and then was gone.

"I'm curious about your answer," Jason said, joining her.

"I'm not sure what you mean," she said, "about putting two and two together."

"Which handwriting matched which character."

"Of course I haven't matched them," she said a little sharply. "I haven't even tried to. It would be a hopeless task since I know none of you at all."

"But you came with Linus Bishop."

"I met him today, by chance. You've been here a week?"

"Vacationing. You?"

"Vacationing. I've rented the Winehart cottage for a few weeks." Even in the dusky light of the porch, she caught sight of the sudden smile he gave and soon erased. Then she thought of the cottage and how deep it was in the woods, and of George Evans who knew she was there alone, and Linus Bishop and now this man who knew it, too. And of the handwriting.

"You fed us pap, after all," Jason said.

She stared curiously at him. Was he the one, then, the quoter of Blake? Is that what he was afraid of, her finding him out?

"You seem determined to challenge me," she said at last, aware of the way the silence had grown between them, and the way he seemed to accept, even want her careful scrutiny. "I'm only going to be on the island for a short time and then—"

"Pity," he said.

"I read the handwritings as I saw them and that's that. Unless," she added lamely, as though the explanation were more for herself than for Jason Farrell, "I believed they might affect my life in one way or another."

"And are they affecting your life one way or the other?"

"You know," she said, "if you feel I've called it wrong, claim your poem and we'll open it for discussion."

Her remark apparently didn't bother him in the least. "Tell me, what degree does one acquire in graphology?" he asked, avoiding her suggestion deftly. "Bachelor of Graphological Arts, to be followed by a Master of Graphology, to be followed by a Doctor of Philosophy in Graphology? I mean, how does one set up graphological shop, so to speak?"

Addie had the distinct feeling he knew precisely what kind of training and court certification was required of handwriting experts. "There are a number of different training methods."

"And what if, for instance, you read something into someone's handwriting, something specious—"

"Like what?" Addie realized that her tone was a little too cautious and would have given anything to erase the flicker of a smile that once again crossed his lips. He was trying to push her to reveal something.

"A person bent on mischief."

"I believe we've already gone into this. Someone's always bent on mischief, even if it's only coveting a neighbor's spouse."

He laughed. "Touché."

They were sparring and, in a way, she enjoyed it. Yet something bothered her about Jason Farrell, something she couldn't quite name, and it had nothing to do with Enigma. There was no denying how attractive Jason was. He was a tall man, a graceful man, although in spite of his slow, deliberate manner, she sensed a restless energy that he apparently kept in check only with difficulty. Her glance went involuntarily to his left hand, but the absence of a wedding band there didn't tell her anything conclusive.

"We were talking about mischief," he reminded her in a surprisingly gentle tone.

"Did I forget to mention the mischief in your handwriting?" she asked. "If so, my apologies."

"Forget it, Addie, you're reading mischief in my eyes, if not anywhere else."

She gave an embarrassed laugh. Was he the writer of Prospero's speech? She rather hoped so. The man with the clearly sensual pressure on pen and paper? "Tell me your favorite poet, I might manage total recall."

"Kipling."

"Really?" She was uncertain whether to believe him or not.

"And Shakespeare."

"I see. A lover of poetry for all the right reasons."

"An admirer of Emily Dickinson, as well."

"Are you an artist, Jason?"

"Hardly. Veronica said it straight. I'm a professor of medieval history. Have you a special penchant for artists?"

"Not at the moment. How come a professor of medieval history didn't quote, oh, Chaucer?"

"How do you know I didn't?"

"It would have given you away."

"Maybe I wanted to be given away."

"You're fresh out of luck," Addie said. "The quoter of Chaucer confessed her sin."

"And you believed her."

Addie sucked in a breath. "Yes, of course I believed her," she said defensively. "And who did you quote?"

"Whoever it was," he said, "your analysis was far off the mark."

"Really? In what way?"

"You really are an amateur at graphology. You read a couple of books on the subject and you were winging it all the way."

She was startled for an instant by the dark, sober look that came over his face and was gone almost before she had a chance to register it. Was it possible he had penned the Blake note, and hoped to find that she was an amateur, hoped she'd read nothing into it?

"Is that what you dragged me out here to tell me?" she asked in a fiercely controlled voice.

"No. I was hoping you'd tell me voluntarily that you have a good imagination and only a cursory knowledge of the subject."

She ought to walk away, let him know just how angry she was. "I'm not a complete ignoramus on the subject. Anyone can miss the more subtle points, that's all."

"I had absolute proof tonight that you can't read your way out of a paper bag," he said.

She waited a moment, then said on a quietly released breath, "Tell me, is Blake also one of your favorite poets?"

There was a long moment while they stood regarding each other. Then he reached for his wineglass and held it up.

"Cruelty has a Human Heart
And Jealousy a Human Face
Terror, the Human Form Divine
And Secrecy the Human Dress.

"Shall I go on?"
"No, I get your point," Addie said.

He saluted her with the glass and drained it quickly, his gaze never leaving hers.

Addie felt a long striation of fear slide down her spine. Without a word, she turned and left him.

Chapter Four

Don't fool around, Addie, don't play cop. Just make the ID and phone me anytime of day or night. Pam's words came back to her.

The only public telephone on the island was purported to be at the Island Inn, which at the moment seemed a million miles away. It was nearing midnight and Addie didn't relish facing that long dark walk to call Pam with the good news that she had found Enigma, but not quite.

She stood at the door to the living room and looked around only to discover that the party had thinned out even more. Kevin Morgan and Meg St. John were gone. Addie had no doubt that Jason Farrell remained on the porch watching her. She could all but feel his gaze ripple along her back and she didn't like the sensation one bit. She moved quickly over to the far corner of the living room where Linus Bishop and George Evans seemed to be having a good-natured but vociferous argument.

Veronica was sitting on the couch trying unsuccessfully to hide a yawn. It was time to leave, to take the handwriting samples to the cottage, to make extra certain the writing of the quote from Blake did exactly match the sample she had brought from Boston. She had little doubt of it, but it wasn't the time to be complacent. At any rate, her hostess's delicate yawn hinted that Addie, as well as the others, had overstayed their welcome.

Steven West was at the fireplace and, like Jason Farrell had done earlier, stabbed away at the logs. A shower of sparks rained onto the floor and the Persian carpet. Addie watched Veronica rush over to Steve's side. She tried to pry the poker from his hand, but he seemed reluctant to surrender it. Then, in another moment, he handed it to her with an apologetic grin on his face.

Addie determinedly went over to the Wests. "I'm surprised how chilly it becomes on Galbraith," she said in an offhand way.

Steve West seemed relieved by the innocuous remark. "You should be here when the fog's in and waves smash a hundred feet high against the cliff," he told her. "They come so high you can actually see them from the porch, even feel their spray."

"It's a little frightening," Addie said. "The cliff being so close to the house. What if you walked in your sleep?"

Steve gave her a surprised look and then laughed. "I've been coming here since I was a child. I know every inch of Galbraith by heart."

"I don't even know one inch," Veronica said. She examined a fingernail. "It's incredibly boring, Galbraith, your company excluded," she added with a dazzling smile that made Addie want to forgive her at once. "Steve insists upon coming here, year after dreadful year, smack in the center of the summer, which breaks it up so ignominiously."

"Veronica's idea of a vacation is shopping Harrods in London from top to bottom," Steve remarked dryly.

"I hate it when you make out to strangers that all I'm interested in is spending your money, Steve. My idea of a good time is going to the theater. Addie, does Steve's handwriting prove him a tightfisted bore?"

Addie moved uneasily, unwilling to answer Veronica's question, even if she could. Instead of showing anger, however, Steve said, "Her analysis came uncommonly close, Veronica. And it said nothing about my famous cautiousness concerning money. I'd be interested in hearing more, Addie. Let's see. Where are those samples, anyway?"

Addie's heart began to beat unnaturally fast. She said carefully, "I put them down...now where, that's the hundred-dollar question. Never mind, I'll take a new sample if you'd like." She glanced past her host to find Jason Farrell standing not ten feet away. She experienced a curious feeling of certainty that he knew she was lying, that he knew precisely where the samples were.

"Really, Steve," Veronica put in, "the woman's on *vacation*. Give her a break. And I thought we all agreed to anonymity."

"She's perfectly right," Steve West said to Addie. "I should've known better."

Linus Bishop came over. "Midnight's my limit," he told Addie with an exaggerated yawn.

"I was just about to leave, Linus."

"Hold it," George Evans said, coming up close behind Linus. "I'll see she gets back safely."

Linus frowned, his gaze catching Addie's. He didn't need to warn her, however. She had no intention of being alone with George Evans at any time. "Sorry," she said, "Linus is my date tonight."

George gave an exaggerated bow. "I defer to extreme old age."

Linus merely laughed, but the word *boor* slipped out in a whisper that only Addie caught.

Once they were outside West Wind, Linus took her arm. "Enjoy yourself tonight?"

"Immensely. Your friends are nice."

"Not all nice and not friends in any real sense of the word," he reminded her. "Summer residents on a small island bound by time and the ocean. When the cold weather comes, and our revels are ended, we part company with nothing more than 'See you next summer.'"

"That's a pity."

"Not at all. By the end of the season, we're all heartily sick of each other. But," he added, "while we're here, we stick together like orphans in a storm."

"You mean as in protect each other?"

"You might say that. Accept each other's peccadilloes, that sort of thing."

Linus's gait, like his speech, was slow and steady. Their flashlights played the air, his a strong circular beam that bobbed along the gently curving road that led into town. The silent, relentless beam from the lighthouse swept high above them, piercing the gloom and, as if not finding what it was searching for, sliding away again.

"We go left here for a couple of hundred feet, then take the first turnoff," Linus told her. "Watch that pitted hole. I'll see the day when the highway department—"

"Highway!" Addie laughed at the notion.

"We're under the aegis of the highway department out of Port Clyde on the mainland. Just like everything else, police, schools."

"Ah, of course."

"Money for every damn pothole over there, and none left for Galbraith."

"For the one vehicle on Galbraith?"

They found a bare spot among the trees that held a vista of sky and the rising moon, partially hidden at first behind a slow moving drift of clouds, which teasingly offered some light and then pulled back. "Isn't Galbraith beautiful," Addie said spontaneously.

"Admire it, but don't quite trust it," Linus told her.

"In what way?" She looked at him in surprise.

"Just don't go walking in your sleep, and above all, stay away from the east end of the island at night. It's a long trip down to the sea when you miss a step."

"You're scaring me," Addie said.

"Meant to. You're much too pretty to turn up floating facedown in the water. We have them occasionally, you know, the visitors who know nothing of dangerous undertows and who end up quite dead. Here we are, the turnoff to Winehart.''

Addie stopped and looked down the narrow, gloomy path to her cottage. ''Linus,'' she began but didn't go on. She wanted to talk more about the evening at West Wind and the handwriting she had come across, but she couldn't. The Blake poem might just as easily have belonged to Linus Bishop as any of the others.

''I think I can go on from here,'' she said at last and extended her hand. ''Thanks for bringing me back to the Wests.''

''You went easy on them,'' he said. ''Jason Farrell was right. You knew you were feeding a bunch of egos.''

''Was I truly on target for you, Linus?''

''I'm afraid so, my dear, just as I said.''

''Who's your favorite poet?''

He laughed. ''Uh, uh. Scout's honor. I live with these people. Some of them wanted anonymity, and I have to respect that wish. Look, Addie,'' he said, suddenly turning serious, ''it was a game, an amusing one. Next time we'll play twenty questions or charades. They're a lot safer and far less ego busting.'' He took her arm and drew her down the path to the cottage. A fresh breeze had started up. The moon cast a sliver of light through the trees and Addie knew she had to shake her depression. The beam from the lighthouse swept overhead through the canopy of branches, exaggerating the silence. After a moment or two of dragging her feet, Addie fell into step with him.

''What I believe, Addie, is that your curiosity was piqued by what you read tonight. You want to fit a lot of square pegs into a lot of round holes, which should give you the advantage over the rest of us. My favorite poet,'' he said, ''happens not to be the one I quoted, and I saw you tuck those slips into your bag. Why?''

She felt her apprehension deepen but managed a light laugh before answering. ''Force of habit, I suppose.'' She wondered if anyone else had seen her.

Their flashlights picked out the small, gray-shingled cottage, with its front porch framed by climbing roses. Addie held out her hand. "Thanks for walking me back, Linus. I enjoyed myself very much and hope I didn't offend anyone."

He placed his hand warmly over hers. "I learned a long time ago that it doesn't pay to know too much about people. If you want to enjoy yourself on Galbraith, my advice is to take those slips of paper and stoke the fire with them."

She frowned. "Maybe you're right."

"I'm right." He released her hand. "Take a walk over to Gull Rock tomorrow. I'm working on a watercolor and I'm usually there at two to catch the light. Gull Rock has two outstanding things about it. It's an interesting area for tidal pools, and it's dangerous as hell because there's a terrific undertow when the tide's coming in. So watch your footing."

"I'll come, I promise. I'd like to see your work."

"Good night, Addie. Sleep well."

"Good night, Linus, you, too."

She hurried up the wooden steps and unlocked her door. She heard his footsteps fading as he walked down the path and when all was finally silent, she went in and closed the door behind her.

Her flashlight picked out the kerosene lamp on the hall table and she hastily lit it. She took up the lamp and went into the living room, finding the shadows cast by the light not quite as quaint as she had imagined they would be. The dark shape that moved on the couch opposite her drew a small cry from Addie until she realized it was just Fitzgibbon. He jumped off the couch and followed her back through the kitchen, rubbing against her leg. She wondered idly how George Evans could own such a sweet, good-natured animal. She opened the door and he went out to the porch.

"I'll wait for you, Fitz." For a while she remained staring at the rather gloomy mix of trees and undergrowth, a tangle of wilderness that made the night blacker than it was.

The lighthouse beam swept the sky and disappeared. When the first, faint tear started to her eyes, it took Addie several seconds before she recognized the symptom. Fitzgibbon had triggered her ancient allergy to cats. She heard a rustle in the leaves and a soft meow. Fitzgibbon had come back and he sauntered up the steps, head held high.

Addie retreated behind the kitchen door, closing it between them, but when the cat stood there and looked up at her, she relented and let him in. "I shouldn't, you know."

She locked up carefully behind the cat, went into her bedroom and took up her favorite old flannel nightgown. She checked all the doors and windows before getting ready for bed, cursing her jumpiness and knowing it had to do with the sample of handwriting tucked into her bag.

Ten minutes later Addie was in the canopied bed, her only light the soft yellow glow of a kerosene lamp.

"Cruelty has a Human heart." Farrell had known the poem; he hadn't missed a comma when he'd recited it. She held the two pieces of paper she had to compare and carefully ticked off the matching elements in both: the heavy, muddied weight of strokes, yet the clear sign of intelligence in the formation of the m's and n's. Enigma wasn't crazy so much as full of appetite, with a short temper. He was always a hairsbreadth away from an outburst, and once it began he couldn't stop it.

She gathered the slips of paper from the party together, tapping them so that their edges aligned perfectly. Then she slid them under her mattress. She slipped her copy of the original sample back into her wallet. No one could fault her for having taken the party samples, yet she had lied to Steve West about it. She closed her eyes and leaned back against her pillow. The image of Jason Farrell came to mind, his smile dismissive and mocking. Damn the professor of medieval history, anyway. Medieval history! How far out of this world did he live?

She reached over to the lamp and turned it off. The scent of hot oil drifted on the air as the room was plunged into blackness. There was a sudden soft movement and after a

moment of dead shock she realized that Fitzgibbon had
jumped onto the bed, purring.

Addie rubbed her eyes. "Fitzgibbon," she said, "how
about sleeping outside?"

He circled several times and at last settled down, press-
ing against her right leg.

George Evans's remark about his cat came back to her.
"I'll know where to find him if I want him."

She shivered and closed her eyes. Tears or no, she was
unable to fight sleep. Her last thoughts were of Jason Farrell and his patent disapproval of the way she analyzed
handwriting. Oh, she had read them correctly, all right.
That was the trouble.

IN ANOTHER ROOM, in another place on the island, stood a
solitary figure, quietly looking out the window toward the
sea. The only light in the room came from the dying fire.
Outside the window the night world was pierced by the
lighthouse beacon whose beam swung ceaselessly above the
ground. The moon, at its fullest, lit a path along the ocean
straight to the horizon.

The figure at the window expelled a harsh breath; anger
fueled by the fact that such a moment had been spoiled by
thoughts of the most banal kind.

From almost every point on the island one could catch
sight of the ocean, see the white-topped waves seething toward shore. It was beauty of a primordial fierceness and
then, just when one should be most at peace, should be able
to reach into one's soul and extract the meaning of life,
reality intruded.

Another harsh breath was expelled into the charged air.
Too bad there was so much at stake. Murder did not belong in such an atmosphere, but Addie Cordero simply
must die. She must depart this vale of tears for much the
same reason as the messenger bearing bad news died. She
possessed information that could ultimately prove damag-
ing. One could only speculate on why she had really come
to Galbraith or who had sent her.

Of course joining in the game of graphology had been a risk but to have refused would have been worse. The idea of anonymity had made everything seem all right. And Addie had been willing to go along, which had made her seem amateurish. So much to the good. For a proper script analysis one needed charts, physical information, a host of aids. Joining in had seemed harmless. It had almost paid off.

That is until Addie surreptitiously tucked the batch of handwriting samples into her bag. It could, of course, have been a reflex action. But no, Addie had cast a glance around the room; her actions had been furtive, although only someone curious about her would have paid attention.

Cruelty has a Human Heart
And Jealousy a Human Face
Terror, the Human Form Divine
And Secrecy, the Human Dress.

Addie Cordero must die for that little reflex action. Her death must be carefully planned. It must be clean, quick, accidental, and the phone line must be cut to prevent a call for help before it was time to move.

The figure turned away from the window, went over to the desk and took out a pen, then threw it down with a hard little laugh. No lists of things to do. No revealing scraps of handwriting. One had to think, to try to figure out whether they had sent Addie Cordero to Galbraith in the first place. What clue had been left behind? First find out, then get rid of her, that was the way to do things and do them right.

All the other murders had been well thought-out and cunningly conceived. Dealing with the unexpected, however, could be an exhilarating experience. Pitting one's intelligence against adversarial forces, both of nature and of man.

The killer bared bright white teeth and knew an odd contentment.

EARLY MORNING brought with it fog and the lugubrious, persistent groan of a foghorn. The mist fingered every rock and hiding place in Squeaker Cove; it was a ghostly world that Steve West materialized into and where Jason Farrell already awaited him.

"Damn fog," Steve grumbled, coming up to Jason. "That's all my sinuses need, this fog. I've hated it since I was a child. And the wretched foghorn's worse. And what were you doing at my house last night, anyway? I thought we were going to steer clear of each other for the duration. I know, I know," he said, waving his hand about, "my wife insisted. And where did you happen to meet my lovely bride, anyway?"

Jason laughed, shaking his head, and sighting through his camera's eyepiece. The combination of fog, rock and the roiling waves coming into the cove was ideal for black-and-white film. He released the shutter and caught a wave as it smashed against rock and sent a fountain of white water into the mist. "I'm afraid your wife picked me up in line at the post office. It would've seemed positively ungrateful of me to have refused her invitation."

"She's too friendly by far. All I need right now," Steve added, "is for them to figure you're not a professor of medieval history. And Linus bringing in that psychologist who reads handwritings," he went on, "the fool."

"You'd never met Addie Cordero before?"

"You know I hadn't," Steve said. "And the trouble is I believe strongly in graphology."

"What banker wouldn't," Jason said, "considering your dependence upon the truth of signatures. What are you worried about, anyway? That lady had no idea what she was talking about. She was faced with the specimens of a couple of dishonest characters and said nothing."

Steve shook his head and said angrily. "I suppose you mean my handwriting as well. She came damned close. Anyway, what did you want her to say? Just because she kept quiet doesn't mean she didn't pick up on a few of our negative traits."

Jason was silent for a few moments. He had considered the possibility she'd been holding back, although using his own handwriting as an example, he had decided the lady was a fraud, pure and simple.

"She knows something," Steve said. "Last night's demonstration was a parlor game. I'm not certain if the lady knows the players, but she does know the game. Where did those slips of paper go, anyway?" he added. "I looked for them after everyone was gone, but they weren't around."

Jason shrugged. He knew perfectly well where Addie Cordero had put them, but something told him to keep the information to himself. Or rather between himself and Linus Bishop. A quick glance around the room the night before had ascertained that the artist had possibly also caught her surreptitiously tucking the samples of handwriting into her bag. "She was at the fireplace," he said to Steve. "Probably sent them up the chimney."

"I don't like it," Steve said. "I don't like any of it."

Jason ignored the outburst. Instead he extracted a small leather case from his camera pack and handed it over. "You know how to use it, or should I take you through a fast course?"

Steve gave him a look of disgust. "I'm the director of a large bank in Boston, Farrell, or have you forgotten? I think I can handle this contraption. Any more of these?" he asked after a slight hesitation. "In case this one breaks down."

Jason stared at him unblinking. "It's the best equipment. Believe it. But I never travel without a spare. Set up the meeting and go ahead as planned. This little item is glitch proof and that's just how I want the meeting to go."

Steve raised his hands in a gesture of supplication, which Jason didn't quite believe. "I'll try to arrange the session for tomorrow afternoon. At the moment my guests are oversleeping and overindulging themselves at my expense."

"And the condemned ate a hearty supper," Jason said without the trace of a smile. "Incidentally, your pal Gruesin claimed to have met me somewhere."

"I know about it. He quizzed me in the kitchen. I told him I never saw you before tonight and figured you were a friend of the wife's. He tried hard to swallow a laugh at that and if it were any other time I'd have smashed his face in."

"That day I came out of your office," Jason said. "Is it possible Gruesin was visiting you?"

"I'd have to check my calendar and that's in Boston. Damned foghorn, is it ever going to stop?" Steven West turned from Jason and made his way over to the path that led up the cliff, the fog washing around his figure. "Incidentally," he said in a low voice, but one that carried clearly over to where Jason stood. "You're not planning anything with my wife, are you?"

Jason laughed and shook his head. "I'm on Galbraith for a holiday, Steve, just a professor of medieval history who takes the odd, occasional photograph. One thing I don't do, besides windows, is fool around with other men's wives. I want this thing over and soon. If Gruesin starts getting suspicious you'll have nothing on that tape but the sound of the sea."

As Steve West grunted and continued on up the cove, a small stone broke away beneath his foot and tumbled noisily down.

Jason waited. The fog would burn off in another hour. The day promised to be a scorcher, even on that island around which the Atlantic bumped and washed, an endless, moving mass of blue that seemed headed nowhere.

His mind went back to Addie Cordero. He surprised himself with the clear picture he had of her, the short dark hair with the lock that fell over her eyes and her way of pushing it with a graceful yet impatient gesture. He was still uncertain of the color of her eyes. Brown, or possibly hazel.

One thing he knew for certain: Addie Cordero didn't like being called a fraud, and while Jason hated to admit it,

Galbraith was a tight little island. One made friends and influenced people by flattery. She'd be worth thinking about if it were any other time, any other place. But his whole life was a series of encounters that were never what they seemed. His life was like a distorting mirror in a fun house, reflecting back a reality bent out of shape. Most of the time he lived exactly the way he wished. For some reason, now that he was on this small, solitary island where even in the fog clarity was the order of the day, he wished he were plain Jason Farrell, a man with a nine-to-five job and a permanent address.

AT THE ISLAND INN, where Addie treated herself to a very late breakfast, the jam was marmalade, served with blueberry muffins. She consumed two muffins and two brimming cups of coffee before coming fully awake. From her vantage point on the open veranda facing the dock, she watched the late morning ferry coming in. Passengers disembarked, including a good dozen day-trippers from the mainland who would make the trip back in the afternoon. Although she had been on the island for no more than twenty-four hours, Addie watched them straggling off with the air of a Galbraith native. Then, when a sea gull alighted on the porch railing, Addie broke off a piece of muffin and threw it over the side, which invited a flock of sea gulls to come feast on the grass below. Addie obligingly crumbled up the last of the muffin and tossed it to them, as well.

"I don't know why people come to places like this."

The voice, which at first seemed disembodied, issued from the man sitting at the table opposite hers. He was plump and middle-aged and wore a rumpled wool business suit. There was a battered briefcase on the floor beside his chair. She recognized him as one of the passengers who had come off the morning ferry.

"Excuse me?" Addie said.

The waitress placed a serving of eggs and bacon before the man, and for a while he busied himself with buttering a roll. "I said I don't know why people come to a place like this." He didn't quite look at her but allowed his gaze to come to rest on a spot over her right shoulder.

Addie wasn't certain how to answer that, but after a moment ventured, "For peace, quiet and solitude."

"They're in for a surprise then," he said, at last gazing directly at her and waving the roll about for emphasis. "Treacherous, this rock plopped in the middle of the ocean. What is it? It's the top of a mountain, that's what it is. And it's a long way down to the bottom." He reached for his napkin and dotted it across his damp forehead. "Dangerous, a place like this, take my word for it. Worse than the city."

Addie glanced at his suit once more, shaking her head slightly at the incongruity of wearing wool in the summer. "Are you talking about crime?"

"Worse than crime," he said, pulling in a wheezy breath. "Crime you can see and handle. Things here catch you by surprise."

"Really?" She asked the question politely, but thought he had a point. The island of Galbraith had been a surprise to her from the very beginning. "Are you a resident?"

He laughed briefly. "Me? Never been here before in my life, and I'm leaving again as soon as I can. But I know about these things. Take the rocks. They look okay, solid as Gibraltar but when they get wet, one wrong step and splat, right into the ocean. And dusk around here," he added. "They'll tell you it's romantic, don't believe a word of it. You think you know where you are but when it's dusk everything changes. The water in these parts, icy, *icy*," he continued, "don't even try to swim. I wouldn't give you three minutes in it."

Addie stared at his briefcase. It was bulging and she noted that one clasp was open. "And you're here on vacation, I take it."

"You kidding?" He dug into his eggs and bacon and was quiet for a few moments while he concentrated on eating. "Vacation. I take a vacation it's in Florida at the racetrack. Horses on one side of the fence, me safe on the other. No, business, that's why I've gone a couple of hundred miles out of my way to end up here. Soon as that's done, I'm off this island.''

The Port Clyde boat sailed at four-fifteen that afternoon. Addie had every intention of being at the dock to make certain no one from the party at West Wind got on it. She had a sense of time moving too fast, of not being able to hold on. Addie stood up and smiled helplessly at a sea gull sitting at attention on the porch railing. She was out of crumbs. "Well, good luck," she said to the stranger while reaching for her bag.

"That boat ride back. When does it leave? Four-fifteen, that's what they said." He shuddered. "Freezing wind. I suppose it'll be worse than on the way in."

Addie waved at the man and went into the hotel's cool interior to pay her bill. She noted the public telephone in the lobby but decide she would wait to call Pam at home after work. They had agreed on a coded message. It wouldn't do to speak plainly with the island telephone operator monitoring their calls.

Addie reasoned that Linus was still her best contact on the island and he'd said he'd be at Gull Rock at two. It was too early in the day to head straight out there so she made her way over to the general store to pick up some postcards. A brief conversation with the owner ascertained that he was born on Galbraith and seldom went off island. He professed to know everyone who stepped on the island if not intimately, then by sight, with the exception of the day-trippers.

Addie hadn't quite formulated the kind of questions she might ask about Enigma. Was he a stranger to the island or were his ancestors buried there? She needed clues, and she had none but that muddied scrawl.

She returned to the dock and sat there with her feet over the side, doing what legitimate vacationers do, writing postcards to her friends and enjoying the cries of the gulls.

She mailed the postcards from the post office, meeting no one from the party of the night before.

Afterward she spent a half hour exploring the western shoreline of Galbraith, which interspersed small streets lined with cottages and lobster shacks. There was a tiny beach of shells crushed by the tide just beyond the dock and she watched the fishermen scaling their catch and preparing it for market.

Once back on the road, she pulled her map from her pocket. She easily located Gull Rock on the east side of the island, near a narrow promontory called Gertie's Nose. She noted the absence of houses and then saw that both Gull Rock and Gertie's Nose were part of the Galbraith Nature Preserve.

The noon sun was high and hot as she started out, and Addie, who had left her house with a sweater over her T-shirt, soon pulled it off and tied it around her waist. The town road meandered past a dozen houses set back among flower gardens and ended in a wooded area that her map grandly called Cathedral Woods.

Once in the cool forest, she passed several people who were perched on tree stumps or rocks, with watercolor blocks or sketch pads in hand. None, she determined quickly, had been guests at West Wind the night before, yet a nagging fear remained. What was Enigma's reason for being on the island? If he had come to see someone, it might be any of the artists she passed on her way to Gull Rock.

Farther on, when she began to hear the sound of the ocean, she came upon Meg St. John sitting at the base of a tall pine, a notebook in her lap.

"Hi," Meg said, waving her over. "You were right, of course. About me, I mean."

Addie looked longingly at the notebook and contemplated sitting down next to her, but Meg slammed the book shut and stuffed it into a knapsack. "Well," she said, standing up, "I'm off. It's well past lunchtime. The stomach calls. Come see me at Dandelion Cottage."

"Thanks, I will." Addie waved goodbye and within a few minutes found herself in the bright sunlight high above the glittering ocean.

Addie pulled her map out once again and marked where she stood. Dandelion Cottage was halfway up a hill on a path that snaked off the main road. She'd stop by on her way back from Gull Rock.

Gull Rock was somewhere off to the right. From her vantage point she could see the steep drop of cliff to ocean, perhaps a hundred feet. Times Square was her first thought. She had exited the forest at a beautiful and busy spot. Even under the noon sun, which reflected heat back from the rocks, several artists worked at easels. Off to the right a group of bird-watchers had set up their equipment to catch cormorants and terns in their lenses. And coming from the direction she was headed were a couple of hikers in sneakers with sensible walking sticks. She exchanged hellos and waves as she moved along the crest of the cliff, taking the rifts and hollows easily as they came. As the land sloped down to the ocean, however, the path became more difficult, the huge rocks treacherous to maneuver around and empty of artists and sightseers alike. Addie reached Gull Rock early and Linus Bishop was nowhere in sight. She discovered a narrow platform directly below, no more than six feet in length. Years of rough winds and pounding storms had smoothed the ancient rock, giving it a silky appearance. To reach it Addie had to cross a bed of wild grass and stunted bushes, then climb down a tumble of crags and rocks that looked as if they'd been thrown around by an angry, willful wind.

"Oh, damn." Caught in a narrow passage between rocks, she skinned her arm and, for a moment, had to balance there while she staunched the blood. She hadn't realized how treacherous the climb down was until she reached the point of no return.

It was as dangerous going back up, as down. "Okay, genius," she told herself. "Keep going. Once you're on the ledge, it looks an easier climb down to the waterline. Maybe."

A misstep loosened a small stone that bounded away, crashing into the water below. When Addie reached the ledge she discovered that it sloped slightly outward and was slippery with algae. "Oh, lovely," she said out loud. With a careless movement she could go sliding down to oblivion.

Well below and to her right was an oval of rounded, pitted rocks forming a tidal pool that was washed by the ebbing high tide. The ocean was rough and the waves a deep blue capped with white. A ship appeared to be anchored on the horizon, and only when it disappeared from view did Addie realize it had been moving all along.

Off to her left at the cliff's edge was a rock outcropping. There was a sudden movement nearby—a shadow that might have been a reflection, or nothing at all. She was distracted by the swooping motion of a gull and when she looked back she wondered whether she had been imagining things.

"Don't move." The words from above rang out deep and clear.

For a moment Addie remained absolutely still, her mind a near blank. When nothing further happened, she turned and looked up, shading her eyes.

"You moved."

He was above her, silhouetted against the sun, but she knew perfectly well who it was. Jason Farrell, with his camera again.

"You scared the daylights out of me," she called up to him.

"Did I?" He scrambled down a lot less cautiously than she had to join her on the ledge. "I didn't mean to."

She retreated a step, which on the narrow, sloping ledge, still left very little space between them. If Jason were Enigma, and if he knew she was looking for him, then the simplest push could well dispose of her forever.

"Are you following me?" she asked. "Every time I turn around there you are clicking away."

"Hey, blame my camera. It's on automatic. Sees something beautiful and rears up. Result? Lights, camera, action."

"I'll want a signed copy of every one of them."

"Signed and numbered. This is a dangerous spot," he added, looking around. "What in hell possessed you to come down here?"

"I'm waiting for Linus Bishop to show up, as a matter of fact. He'll be here soon. He said he's been painting Gull Rock. Do you suppose that's it, Gull Rock? That long black bit jutting out of the water?"

"The one with all the gulls on it? I expect so. Clever name. I wonder who thinks them up. I believe Linus also paints tidal pools. There," Jason said, pointing to the oval of porous rocks below. "The tide's ebbing now and soon nothing will be left but a quiet pool of water with all manner of ocean creatures visible to the discerning eye; snails, barnacles, seaweed, anemones."

"Instead of photographing me, why haven't you been photographing tide pools?"

"I work in black-and-white. Wouldn't pick up the color and diversity of sea life very well. But you ought to take a closer look."

She turned to him. "Yes, I'd like to. I guess I have time before Linus gets here." She glanced at her watch. A quarter of an hour to go.

"How'd you shin yourself?" His hand was on her bare arm.

How'd he gotten so close? "I slipped coming down. I'm usually a better athlete than that."

He touched the wound. "Hurt?"

She pulled her arm away. "What do you think?"

"You ought to take care of it."

She thought a moment before answering. The look of concern he gave her was disquieting and unexpected, but then she hadn't any doubt of Enigma's charm. "I'm not a baby," she said.

"No, I don't think you're a baby at all. I think you're a beautiful but tough lady. Come on, with the ebb tide you'll see the tidal pool at its best. Then it's off to the Island Inn for a bandage and a bit of first aid."

"First aid at the Island Inn? You mean there's a doctor on Galbraith?"

"My hotel room. I always travel with a first-aid kit."

"Hold on, Jason. I'm not going anywhere with you."

"Sure you are. I have you at my mercy." His eyes, she thought, were the fascinating soft gray called dove. Sensuality seemed to flow effortlessly from him. She was standing there on a dangerous ledge with the most attractive man she had ever met, and she was, quite simply, scared stiff. He reached out and took her hand.

"Come on, toughie, I can see you had trouble on the way down, and I'm not about to leave you until you're safely back on *terra firma*."

She glanced at her watch once again but his slight tug at her hand told her she had no choice but to go along. The way down, however, turned out to be remarkably easy. The ledge led to a series of rock steps, impossible to see from above, which led right to the water's edge. Jason hadn't relinquished her hand although she had tried to pull away several times.

"There's your tidal pool," he told her once they were down.

Close up, the rocks surrounding the pool were larger than she had imagined. She had to climb up on one to get a closer view of the pool. What surprised Addie wasn't the color of the pool, nor the algae clinging to the surface of the rocks. It was the large, puffed-up shape riding at the edge of the pool, scrubbed and pushed around by the water still flooding back and forth over the rocks. Before she could even make out the shape, her heart began to pound. She knew she wasn't going to scream, but what surprised her was that she couldn't utter a sound if she wanted to. She bounded along the wet surface of the rocks until she came close to the body lying in the pool.

Chapter Five

He lay on his stomach, his face turned to the side, one foot wedged between two rocks. His mouth was open. A thin line of blood had oozed out on the side of his face. His eyes were vacant and told of death.

Linus? No, it couldn't be. In another moment Addie knew exactly who was lying there. The shock was so great that she didn't even hear Jason Farrell come up behind her.

"What the devil..." He bent quickly and expertly over the body and examined it for signs of life.

"But that's..." Addie began, then stopped.

Jason was on his feet again. "Do you know him?" His eyes were hard and quick.

She shook her head. "No, I don't know him."

He took her by the arms, gripping her tightly. "You know him."

"I don't." She couldn't take her eyes from the water and its burden. "I just had a few words with him this morning at the Island Inn at breakfast. He came over on the boat from Port Clyde. I don't know who he is. And you're hurting me."

Jason Farrell regarded her through cold, narrowed eyes. "The boat comes in from Port Clyde at eleven. According to you, he stepped off it and now, one and a half hours later, he's dead. And when I arrive at Gull Rock, who's overlooking the murder scene, but our clever psychologist." His face was just inches from hers when he said,

"Just who the hell are you anyway, Addie Cordero, and why are you on Galbraith?"

"I don't know what you're talking about." Addie felt a tightening in her chest. She could have kicked herself for reacting so badly, yet instinct told her it wasn't too late. When attacked, attack back. "I might ask the same of you, Professor Farrell. You dragged me down here, remember?" She was startled by the look of surprise he gave her.

"My apologies," he said with a self-deprecating smile she didn't quite trust. "You've made your point." He gazed back down at the body and said so quietly she almost didn't hear him, "You said you knew him."

"I told you we talked briefly at the hotel, that's all. The way he went on...." She stopped, aware of the manner in which Jason was listening, as though measuring each of her words. "Just some nonsense about how dangerous the cliffs are, that sort of thing. I had the impression he wasn't going to move from the hotel veranda if he could help it."

"Something obviously made him change his mind."

"I wonder what happened to him." Addie had seen dead bodies before, victims of crime, accident or misadventure and yet it never got any easier. And the worst of it was that the poor man's fears had somehow been transformed into reality.

"Fell, I'd say," Jason said. "Perhaps broke his neck." He bent down and examined the back of the man's head. "Nasty head wound." Then he slowly took in the surrounding scenery. "Damn, an island full of people and nobody around when you need them. Addie, I'm going to stay here, baby-sit the body."

"You think it's necessary?"

"I want to make sure nobody comes along and decides to rearrange the scene. You head for town, find out who or where the sheriff is."

"You're not talking about murder?"

"I'm not talking about anything. Get hold of the sheriff, Addie, let him do the worrying."

Addie knew there was no sheriff on the island and that the nearest police facility was in Port Clyde, but she also knew it was information she shouldn't admit to having.

"My guess is you'll find him on the mainland," Jason went on. "Galbraith is actually part of the township of Port Clyde. Place a call and tell him what we've found. Incidentally, I wouldn't let anyone in town know what's happened."

"Thanks for the advice," she told him curtly. "I was thinking of shouting it from the top of the lighthouse."

"Addie." He stopped, then reached for her hand and held it for a moment. "You all right?"

She could not take her eyes from the body. "I wonder what his name was."

"We'll find out soon enough."

"Yes," she said slowly, "of course we will." Still she lingered, reluctant to leave Jason alone. His manner suggested he didn't believe for a minute the victim had taken an unexpected fall. He was on a murder scene and knew precisely what steps needed to be taken. But then, so did she.

She gazed out over the horizon. The ocean was a hard blue-gray dashed with whitecaps. A ship that looked like a blip on a screen broke the edge where water met sky. Birds screamed overhead. Waves curled up and flew against the rocks. Life went on mindless of the crumpled body disturbing the diurnal activities of the tidal pool.

"I'll wait for the sheriff and bring him back," she said at last. "I haven't any idea how long it'll take."

"You won't have to come back with him, Addie. Tell him I'm at Gull Rock. I've no doubt he'll know where it is."

Addie knew she had no choice but to leave him there. She had the uneasy feeling he'd go through the man's pockets once she was gone. There was nothing she could put her finger on about why she might distrust Jason Farrell. Not even his easy quote of Blake gave enough reason to warrant her suspicions. He gave every appearance of being good, strong, competent, and a professor of medieval history. She was already halfway back up Gull Rock when he called. "Addie."

She turned. "Yes."

"Get that arm attended to."

"Right." She smiled bravely. "I forgot about it."

"Wait for me at the hotel."

She didn't answer but continued on her way. Once on the cliff, she glanced back. Jason crouched at the water's edge, but his head was raised as though he were peering out to sea.

As for the dead man, Addie had spoken briefly with him, but would have wagered on his never straying from town. Once in a while Addie came across patients who tested themselves constantly. Afraid of heights, they'd go to the top floor of a skyscraper to stare out a window, fingers gripping the edge in white-knuckled dread. They'd confront their fear of cats or horses or elevators just for the terrible shot of adrenaline it gave them. Something told Addie, however, that the victim in the tidal pool wasn't the type to make a bargain with the devil. He knew what frightened him and he steered clear of it.

He'd said he had business to take care of on Galbraith and would then head back to Port Clyde. Gull Rock was out of the way and part of the Galbraith Nature Preserve. There were no houses in sight. Business with whom there? Enigma? It was a pretty frightening thought.

Forty-five minutes later, Addie scrambled back down the cliff. She found Jason facing the sea away from the tidal pool and he didn't hear her at first over the crashing of the waves against the rocks. The tide was beginning to ease around the body. Jason held his camera in his hand and she had a feeling he'd been taking pictures of the dead man. Impossible, she told herself, it was a ghoulish idea.

"You were right," she said, sitting down beside him. "The sheriff is in Port Clyde. And he knows where Gull Rock is. It'll take him a while to get here so I came back."

"You didn't have to, Addie."

"I think I did." She had analytically, even coldly, decided it was in her best interests to come back. She wanted to remain in the middle of the inquiry. And there was another reason, purely a business judgment. Even if the dead man had nothing to do with Enigma, Addie reasoned that finding the body would make her an inadvertent center of attention on the island. Another ghoulish thought, perhaps, but she needed to keep up the impetus that began the night before at West Wind. She had to find Enigma. She had to examine the handwritings of everyone who had been at the party, and she'd use any method at her disposal to do it, including becoming the town gossip.

"Incidentally," she said, "I didn't talk with the sheriff, I talked with one of his deputies. The sheriff is out chasing a couple of kids who were in the bay cutting some lobster traps loose. Oh, and I made the call from the public phone at the hotel. It goes through the hotel switchboard, however, and for all I know the news could have been spread over the island by now."

"Well, our friend isn't going anywhere and I doubt he'll worry about the notoriety."

"Spent any more time figuring out what happened to him?" She asked the question quickly, hoping to throw him off guard.

"I'm a professor of history, not Sherlock Holmes. However, reason tells me he was either pushed or fell, and he drowned."

"Clever deductions, Sherlock. Look," she said, moving away, unwilling to be any closer to the body than she had to, "I think I'll wait up above after all."

She climbed over to a rock overhang, which was an effective barrier to her view of the tidal pool. She sat down to wait and didn't even turn when Jason came and quietly sat down beside her. The sun sent shadows along the rocks and their shared silence seemed every bit as deep and dark as the shadows. When they at last heard voices and saw the heavyset man in a brown uniform carefully making his way toward them, an hour had passed.

He was of medium height, clean-shaven and had pale blue eyes that were direct and serious. When he stopped in front of them, he wiped his brow with a damp handkerchief. "Never liked this climb," he said in a surprisingly deep, warm voice. "I'm Sheriff Clayborn. You Addie Cordero?"

Addie nodded. "This is Jason Farrell. He was with me when I found the body."

The sheriff was followed by several other men, all cautiously making their way down Gull Rock.

"Okay," the sheriff said, after briefly introducing his deputy, the coroner, a photographer and two local firemen, who carried a folded stretcher. "Where's the victim?"

"Down below, other side of the overhang." Jason rose and led the way down to the tidal pool.

"That just the way you found him?"

"I checked his heart and pulse to see if he was still breathing," Jason said.

The coroner, carrying a worn leather physician's bag, stepped gingerly onto the rocks. They were slippery with wet algae. Addie's mind went briefly to the worn briefcase the dead man had carried in town. She hadn't seen it anywhere near the body, but then she hadn't been looking for it.

"You have no idea what happened, who he is?" the sheriff asked.

Addie and Jason both shook their heads. Sheriff Clayborn regarded them with cool appraisal. "You live on the island permanently?"

Addie decided he knew just who the island's permanent inhabitants were.

"I'm here for a couple of weeks," Jason said. "Staying at the Island Inn. Miss Cordero is renting the Winehart cottage."

"Tell you what," the sheriff said, "why don't you two go on back to the Inn and wait for me there? I'll want to talk to you again."

Jason seemed about to say something, then clearly changed his mind. He gathered up his photography gear while Addie made her way along the rocks, searching without success for the briefcase belonging to the dead man.

Only when they were well on their way into town did Jason speak. "My guess is the sheriff probably stopped the ferry captain from carrying passengers back to Port Clyde." He made the remark with a certain amount of bitterness in his tone as of someone thwarted and unable to act on his own behalf.

"What about the day-trippers?"

"I don't even want to consider the logistics of the island putting up an additional dozen or more visitors."

"A ten-mile swim to shore," Addie mused. "I wonder if anyone's done it."

"Not in that freezing water."

"Trouble in paradise," Addie said. "And to think I wanted to get away from the world's troubles by coming to tiny Galbraith."

"Believe me, Addie, it's a microcosm of the world's troubles."

"Someone should have warned me."

"You didn't notice it last night, while you were acting the part of graphologist?"

She whipped around. "Jason, I'm really quite tired of your innuendos. Just because what I said about you, whatever that was, doesn't jibe with your excellent opinion of yourself, doesn't mean I'm wrong."

She walked briskly ahead of him, not wanting him to catch up with her, but in a few steps he had. He took her arm in a strong grip. "And where do you practice psychology?"

"Reading bumps on people's heads, you mean."

"That, too," he said with a laugh.

"In Boston. In my office, which is on the first floor of a brownstone. I have the garden apartment." The answer wasn't a lie. Her job with the state allowed her a part-time private practice. Part of her day was filled with people caught up in the criminal justice system. The rest was filled with the contrast of middle-class patients concerned with problems of career and marriage, of family and love. She traveled in two different worlds, one balancing the other; in both she was able to contribute.

"Can you tell if someone were contemplating a crime, murder for instance, or grand theft?"

"Are we talking about graphology again?"

"We're talking about your practice."

"You seem awfully fixed on my ability to ferret out criminal behavior. You asked me the same question at West Wind, only then it concerned handwriting."

"So I did. Nasty turn of mind, I guess."

"I deal with a very bland clientele," she told him. "Most of my patients are more concerned with their love lives than with doing away with anyone."

"That sounds like a cop-out, Addie. What do you do, advertise for nonviolent patients?"

Her back stiffened. He was forcing her to prevaricate and she didn't like it one bit. What was worse is she wasn't any good at it. "Most people who come to therapists are troubled by personal problems. All they want to do is get their lives in order. They certainly don't want to attack the one person who can help them."

"Still, you're alone with someone who might be more disturbed than he lets on initially. You take precautions, I gather."

"What are you trying to get at, Jason? Do I pack a gun? No. Do I expect my patients to become suddenly violent? No. By studying their handwriting can I discover certain volatile tendencies? Yes. If you show me your handwriting, I'll tell you whether I should run away from you right now, or continue on into town in your company. I can probably also tell whether you're an awful liar."

Jason laughed and picked up his step. "Me? I'm the most readable man in the world. All you have to do is ask me a question and I'll answer it."

"Funny," she said, easily keeping up with him, "I can't think of a thing I want to know."

She had meant to get back to town in time to see which of the guests from West Wind embarked on the ferry and which remained on the island. When they reached town, Addie saw at once that the Port Clyde boat had left, but whether with or without passengers it was impossible to tell. She found the answer almost at once when they were accosted in the lobby by the hotel manager.

"You found him out at Gull Rock, did you say?" he asked in a distracted voice.

Jason's answer was brief. "I think we'll wait until the sheriff gets here before we talk about what we found and what we didn't find." The lobby desk was surrounded by day-trippers, people loaded down with cameras and drawing equipment, but no luggage.

"Sheriff sent the Port Clyde boat on its way without passengers," the manager said, looking thoroughly harassed. "Nobody new to step on the island and nobody to step off. He's treating a simple drowning like murder, but Sheriff Clayborn always was a careful man. Meanwhile we're short of room space and the day-trippers are already grumbling about suing."

Addie was relieved. At least no one had left the island, which meant Enigma was still around for the time being. She'd have to find out which of the half-dozen private launches at the dock belonged to the Wests or anyone else who was at the party the night before. Meanwhile there was a more important matter to consider. She detained the hotel manager a moment longer.

"The victim came in on the Port Clyde ferry this morning," Addie told the manager. "Do you remember him? He was plump, middle-aged in a rumpled wool suit. He carried a kind of battered briefcase. He had breakfast on the veranda." Jason put a warning hand on her arm but she pulled away.

The manager nodded and absentmindedly consulted his watch. "I remember him."

"Did he tell you his name?"

"Said he wasn't staying and I wasn't a bit curious about him."

"He didn't happen to ask how to get to where he was going?"

"I was at the desk when he came in. He asked for a map of the island. Funny buzzard. He seemed annoyed that he had to shell out some money for it. I explained about the Galbraith Preservation Society. He said preserve it for what? I didn't bother answering him."

"And that was all?"

"He asked directions to the general store." The manager began to exhibit signs of impatience and Addie knew she had to back off.

"Thanks," Addie said, and led the way to the side veranda.

"Playing detective?" Jason asked, once they were out of earshot of the manager.

"Just curious. Aren't you?"

"I've run out of all the curiosity I've had with respect to our friend out there at Gull Rock. I suggest, Miss Cordero, that you consider the same."

"He was sitting over there," she remarked, pointing to a table at the railing.

"We must mark it in bronze."

"The man's dead, Jason. You have a macabre sense of humor."

"Maybe it's the only way to get through the day."

When Sheriff Clayborn found them there an hour later, the sun was low on the horizon and the sky and clouds were tinted with pink and pale green. While waiting for him, they had disposed of a pot of coffee and plateful of donuts between them. Addie was surprised. She hadn't thought she could eat a bite. Clayborn grabbed a chair, sat down and began wiping his brow.

Addie asked the question while he ordered himself a tall iced soda. "Did you find out his name? Where's he from?"

Clayborn regarded her for a few moments, then shook his head. "I was hoping you'd tell me."

"No, I'm sorry. I met him here at the inn, just briefly. You couldn't even call it meeting. He never told me his name and I never told him my name."

"Strangers that pass in the morning," Clayborn said, "that sort of thing."

Addie glanced quickly at Jason and, noting the particularly bland expression on his face, decided he was quite possibly capable of having palmed the victim's wallet.

The deputy sheriff came up the veranda steps and joined them at the table, removing a notebook from his back pocket. Addie knew with a sinking heart that he was about to take notes. She wondered why she had to account for having spoken politely to a stranger when at the time reason had told her not to bother.

"He was really talking to the air," she said, glaring at the notebook as though it were an open microphone. "I happened to be within listening distance. The only odd thing was the way he raved about the physical dangers of the island. I thought he lived here but it turned out it was his first trip. At least that's what he claimed. And, from the way he sounded, it was certainly going to be his last, which," she added with an uncomfortable laugh, "seems to be the way it turned out."

"Go on."

"Well, it was very strange. I had the feeling he was the sort who'd be afraid to cross a street at a busy intersection. But he said he knew all about the dangers of Galbraith and I took his word for it."

"Say anything about why he was on Galbraith, or whom he wanted to see?" The sheriff's manner was slow and deliberate, far different from the Boston cops Addie knew. She'd bet he didn't miss a thing.

"He said he had some business here and would leave in the afternoon on the Port Clyde ferry."

"You had the impression he was afraid of something, then."

"No, not something. I think he spoke more as a man with a vast experience of being afraid of his own shadow."

"Tilly told me you seemed quite matter-of-fact about making the call, Miss Cordero," the sheriff remarked. "Didn't even tell her about finding a body."

"But she knew anyway, Tilly being the lady behind the reception desk?"

The sheriff nodded.

"Does she listen in on every call?"

With a smile the sheriff said, "They all go through the switchboard. You never answered my question."

"I'm sorry," Addie said. "I wasn't aware you wanted an answer. Jason and I thought it best to keep quiet about the accident until you came." She was now certain of one thing, she'd have to be very careful about using the telephone, day or night.

The sheriff turned to Jason. "And you, Mr. Farrell, did you know the victim?"

Jason shook his head. "Sorry." To Addie he seemed a little distanced, as if he had stepped into somebody else's parade and was waiting for the opportunity to quietly step away.

"Want to tell me how you came on the scene?"

Jason recounted the details succinctly and when he was finished, the sheriff asked Addie why she thought the dead man was wearing a wool suit on such a hot day.

"I wondered about that, too, but he said the waters were icy and complained about the sharp wind on the trip over from Port Clyde."

"Didn't mention any names at all, introduce himself, try to make a date?"

Addie gave him an annoyed smile. "No. I told you everything that happened. We had a few words at breakfast. He sat at his table. I sat at mine. I left him sitting there and went on my way. Only—" She stopped. It still bothered her that he had gone all the way to Gull Rock.

"Only what?" the sheriff asked.

"If he was so afraid of...of..." She stopped and shrugged. "*Everything*, what was he doing in such a treacherous spot?"

"Perhaps he didn't know it was dangerous until he got there. Incidentally, was he carrying anything when you met him?"

"He had a black, kind of battered briefcase with him at breakfast. I presumed it was his. It was stuffed to the gills. I remember one clasp hadn't been closed properly. But he had no proper suitcase that I remember."

"You have a good memory, Miss Cordero."

"Well he *was* acting a little odd." She caught a quizzical expression on Jason's face and wondered whether he was surprised at her ability to remember details.

"Where are you from, Miss Cordero?"

"Boston."

"Here on vacation?"

"Yes."

"What do you do when you're in Boston?"

"I'm a psychologist."

"Private practice?"

She hesitated a moment before answering. "Yes."

The sheriff exchanged a glance with his deputy, then turned to Jason and proceeded to question him closely in a similar vein. Addie knew that if the death was ruled accidental, she'd be free to go about her business. If it turned out otherwise, she had no doubt the result would be to abort Operation Enigma.

"One other thing," the sheriff said when Jason had answered all of his questions. "Were you two together all morning?"

"No," Addie said, a little affronted.

"Ah." He waited.

"We met at Gull Rock, as a matter of fact."

"Above or right at the tidal pool?"

"I found Miss Cordero headed down toward the water," Jason said.

"Going down. Not coming back up."

Jason looked quickly at Addie. She felt her heart sink. It was obvious she wouldn't be able to stay in the center of activity here without having trouble stick to her like glue. "I was going down, Jason, looking for Linus."

"Linus?" The sheriff raised his eyebrows. "I take it you mean Linus Bishop. You were supposed to meet him there?"

"Informally," she said, "it's all so casual. I was looking for him. Going down. You were photographing me," she said in a furious voice to Jason, adding irrelevantly, "and without my permission."

He grinned. "So I did. But that doesn't mean I'm sure if you were coming up or going down."

The coroner appeared, climbing onto the veranda with slow, heavy steps. "Got to get something cold to drink," he said. "That trek over to Gull Rock and back works up a thirst. Must have given you folks a shock," he said, summoning the waitress and addressing Addie and Jason at the same time.

"Not the sort of thing you expect during a nature walk," Jason remarked.

"Apparently our mystery man didn't expect it, either."

"Well," the sheriff said to the coroner, "got an opinion?"

"From the looks of it, the victim stumbled on something or slipped on the algae, lost his balance and broke his neck when he landed in the tidal pool. We'll have to wait for the autopsy to confirm. They're bringing the body down," the coroner told him.

"I'm going to station a deputy on the island till I get the chance to talk to everyone," the sheriff told Addie and Jason. "I don't want anybody to leave Galbraith unless I know about it. No doubt the victim died of a mishap." He smiled unexpectedly. "Don't let what happened ruin your vacation, Miss Cordero."

"I'm afraid it already has," she said and hurried off the veranda without looking back. One thing was certain, if the sheriff's orders were being followed, at least Enigma was stuck on the island like everyone else.

Jason caught up with her as she turned onto the town road. "Come on, I'll walk you home, if that's where you're headed."

"No you're not, traitor. Trying to save your own neck at my expense, thanks a lot."

"I'm a stickler for the truth, Addie."

"Spare me your truth, then. You know perfectly well I wasn't headed up from the tidal pool."

"If that's what you say, then I believe you. How's the arm, by the way?"

"You couldn't be in the least interested." The wound had been taken care of at the general store, where she had purchased a first-aid kit.

"How about dinner tonight?"

"Jason, I'd rather not be seen in your company. It could land me in jail. Goodbye." She went briskly down the road toward the general store. She had no intention of going back to the Winehart cottage quite yet. She planned to visit Meg St. John after she'd stopped at the general store, then she'd come back to town to see Linus Bishop, to find out why he hadn't been at Gull Rock as he had promised.

"No, I don't remember him," the owner of the general store said when Addie questioned him about the dead man. He was behind his delicatessen counter, slicing some of the local cheddar cheese for a customer. "Wool suit, you say? No, I was here all morning."

Addie looked closely at the man. He sliced the cheese in quick, short strokes. Was everyone on Galbraith hiding something, or was her imagination stuck on overtime?

"Wool suit?" The girl waiting for her order was the same college student who had served drinks and canapés the night before at West Wind. "I saw some guy this morning in a wool suit. Kind of baggy pants?"

"With a beat-up briefcase?" Addie asked.

"I think so. He looked weird."

"Where'd you see him?"

The girl drew her eyebrows together. "Trudging up the town road."

"Toward Gull Rock?"

She shrugged. "I just glanced at him. I was on my way to work. He could have been going anywhere."

"And that was the last you saw of him."

"Yeah."

"And what time was that?"

"I don't know. Before lunch, I suppose."

"Thanks," Addie said, even though she had come up empty.

It was nearly five-thirty when Addie found the short lane leading to Dandelion Cottage. The sun had withdrawn some of its heat and there was a promise in the air of a cool evening ahead. Perhaps *she'd* need a wool suit. Addie suddenly realized she was hungry and hoped Meg St. John wouldn't think she was trying to cadge a dinner invitation.

Dandelion was a tiny cottage at the edge of town, next to a shack decorated on the outside with a dozen colorful lobster buoys. There was a skylight cut into the roof to let in the north light. The shrubbery around both house and shack was neatly trimmed. Most of the houses on the island, she had noticed, were graced by flowers and shrubs as rangy and charming as those in English cottage gardens.

As Addie neared the cottage, Meg appeared at the open door. "Wonderful, you've come. Saw you through the window. I love visitors arriving out of the blue." Her face darkened for a moment. "I've just heard, you've had a terrible initiation to Galbraith. Who was he, anyway? Any idea? Come in, come in," she said, standing aside.

She was dressed in a short cotton dress, which showed off her shapely legs, and wore a pair of eyeglasses on a string around her neck. "I don't know why they don't warn visitors about the dangers of Galbraith on the boat coming over," she said. "I mean, Gull Rock has always been hairy. Just come out and say it. Then people don't run scared, they pay attention."

"I'm not so sure about that," Addie said. The dead man, of course, had been forewarned, either by his own fear or by someone else. "I'm always tempted by the word danger," she said to Meg.

"Really? How fascinating. Come on, join me, I was just about to mix myself a drink," Meg said, waving her into the kitchen. "Tell me everything that happened. And with the divine Professor Farrell. The last I saw of you, you were in Cathedral Woods *toute seule*. Bump into him on Gull Rock?"

The kitchen was a small rugged room charmingly furnished in early American pieces. There was a typewriter on the table, which Meg pushed aside, smiling apologetically.

"News certainly travels fast on Galbraith, even if information about the dangers of Gull Rock doesn't," Addie commented.

"Addie, dear, nothing happens around here that isn't instant news. I keep wondering if all my secrets are floating on the wind."

There were some typewritten pages on the table, clearly a play. Someone, presumably Meg, had scribbled notes in the wide margins in tiny handwriting. Addie was mesmerized by the possibility of reading it upside down when Meg scooped them all up. "Comedy," she said. "Hardest thing in the world to write, therefore, the ultimate challenge. You know, the angst beneath the laughter."

She slipped the manuscript into a white folder and put a paperweight on top of it. Then she went over to her icebox for a tall pitcher containing a liquid the color of pink candy. She poured some into a glass over shaved ice for Addie. "My special brew, you'll love it. Let's go into that small space over there I euphemistically call my living room." Just beyond the kitchen door was a small room with a stone fireplace, a couple of Shaker chairs and a sofa upholstered in a soft flowered print.

"I'd love to see some of your writing," Addie said. She tasted the drink and although she had no idea of the contents, found it tart and delicious.

"Terrific, anytime." Meg joined her on the couch.

"Right now."

Meg laughed as though she thought Addie were joking. "You saw my writing last night."

"Yes, of course I did, although I meant your plays, not your handwriting."

"Said I was creative. Intuitive. Oh, self-assured. You were very nice. Best of all was the reference to my sensuality."

"Aah," Addie said. "I remember now but I can't quite recall the poem."

"The truth is, I made it up but pretended it was by—"

She was interrupted by a loud voice calling her name from the front door. "Meg, you in there?"

Addie recognized George Evans's bellow.

"In here, George, with Addie Cordero."

Addie caught a tone of warning in her voice. The artist came in, dwarfing the room and its furnishings. His first glance seemed to hold a hint of irritation, which was quickly turned into a smile. "Well, you do get around, Addie. The last I heard you were out on Gull Rock discovering dead bodies."

"Don't be crass, George. She's still shaken up about it."

"It isn't the first time it's happened," he said grudgingly.

"It's the first time I've discovered a body out at Gull Rock," Addie said.

"You know what I mean. Over the years there've been a couple of accidents out that way. It's no place for timid souls."

"You knew the dead man, then," Addie said.

George looked sharply at her. "What the hell does that mean?"

"You said he was timid."

"No," he told her with a level gaze. "That's what you said."

His remark stunned her. She raised her drink to her lips with a shaking hand. "I only made that remark to the sheriff." And to Jason. What kind of game were they all playing?

George grinned and took the glass Meg handed him. It clearly contained a good slug of whiskey. "Listen, Addie, how about dinner together, the three of us," he said with unexpected jocularity. "That's what I like, a ménage à trois with the two most beautiful women on Galbraith."

Addie made a face. "Ménage à trois!"

"Kidding, kidding, how about it? I'll pick up some lobsters in town and cook them over at my place."

The idea was distasteful but Addie knew that if she were to make any headway in finding Enigma, she should agree to go along. But then she caught the spiked look Meg threw at George. Alienating the locals was not what Addie had in mind. "Sorry," she said, "I'm heading home. It's been a long day and my nerves are shot."

"All the more reason why you shouldn't be alone," George said.

"I've got Fitzgibbon, remember?"

"I haven't forgotten."

"That cat," Meg said disdainfully.

Addie had struck out badly and was about to take reluctant leave of them when she noted a pad of paper on a small desk near the window. From where she stood she could see some writing on it. She finished off the last of her drink. "What's in this drink, anyway? It's fabulous."

"Not complicated at all," Meg said, looking pleased. "Cranberry juice, bitters, lime, touch of cassis, spot of sugar and last but not least, a huge splash of vodka."

"Cranberry, vodka and what else? Damn, my memory's on vacation," Addie said. "Mind if I write it all down? Oh, there's a pad and pencil on your desk. Would it be all right?" She headed for the desk without waiting for an answer.

As she bent toward the spidery handwriting on the pad she felt a heavy clap of hand on her shoulder. George Evans, standing too close, was likely to spoil everything. She whipped around to face him and found him grinning at her.

"Cranberry juice and vodka," he said, his face close to hers. She could smell the whiskey on his breath. "Don't ever try to serve it to me."

Addie closed her eyes briefly. All she had taken in of the handwriting on the pad was its open, forward slant, its clear garlands indicating a generous nature. It wasn't Enigma's, but then it might not be Meg's either. And even if it were Meg's, she could still be the reason for Enigma's presence on the island. If she was Enigma's victim she still wasn't entirely off the hook.

As with Sally Draper, who had admitted at the party that she was the writer of the Chaucer poem, Addie could only tick a *maybe not* next to Meg's name. The returns were definitely not in.

After she left the house she headed back to town to confront Linus. She needed to reassure herself that he was exactly who he seemed to be, a charming and talented artist absorbed in recording the natural beauty of Galbraith Island.

JASON FARRELL adjusted the tinted aviator glasses he wore and watched Addie Cordero as she turned down the road leading away from Dandelion Cottage. It hadn't taken her long to leave after George Evans showed up. There was something going a little haywire here. The one thing he always paid attention to was that itch that clued him into anything off track. Out of nowhere, a psychologist-slash-graphologist arrived on Galbraith and appeared the same day at West Wind. It might mean something or nothing, but he was too close to success with Steve West to take any chances.

If Addie hadn't surreptitiously tucked the handwriting samples into her bag, he might have fallen for her line of pap, or at least excused her ignorance. But when a man ostensibly steps off the boat from Port Clyde, has a few words with the lady and an hour and a half later shows up dead, it was time to watch his front, rear and sides. And only

Addie Cordero knew what the man had said, and maybe who he'd come to see.

Perhaps Steve West was right. Perhaps his banker friends were on to something and were taking their own precautions. A beautiful diversion named Addie Cordero might be the bit of insurance they'd bought themselves. Then again, perhaps she was a free agent who'd cottoned on to a deal and saw a way of making a hit. Or maybe none of the above.

He had lived so long in a world where paranoia was the norm, it was sometimes difficult to just look at an attractive woman and enjoy the view.

As he watched Addie walk along the path that would lead her to town, Jason wasn't quite certain how to handle her. The only thing he knew was that he liked the way she moved. It would be a shame if she weren't as innocent as her dark eyes promised.

Chapter Six

"Oh, Linus, I was just looking for you."

Linus Bishop, in the act of locking his front door, turned around and smiled at Addie. "Ah, our little detective. Come along, I'm about to have dinner at Mrs. Oliver's. Hungry?"

Addie was feeling light-headed from the drink Meg had served her and the idea of dinner seemed fine. "I am, but I just wanted to talk to you for a minute."

"Come along, come along." He drew her toward the town road. "Had dinner at Mrs. Oliver's yet? No, of course, you couldn't have. You weren't there yesterday and you've only been here a day and a half."

She remembered now that the Wineharts had suggested Mrs. Oliver's small boardinghouse, where she served dinner and took in a few guests. "True, I've only been here a day and a half," Addie said, "but frankly, with the way things have been going, it feels more like a month."

"What was this about you finding a body out at Gull Rock?"

"I'm afraid so. I'd come looking for you and instead turned up a body. I wasn't alone, though," she added hastily, "Jason Farrell was with me. Linus, I thought you said you'd be painting at Gull Rock around two."

"Ah, forgive the memory of an old man," he said, laying his hand over hers and patting it apologetically. "A couple of day-trippers from Port Clyde stopped by to see my work. Friends of friends, with a commodious wallet between them. They bought a sketch and in the time-honored tradition of completing a sale, I offered them a glass of wine. By the time they had to leave for the ferry to Port Clyde, the sun was in the wrong position for my Gull Rock piece, and I decided not to go out painting."

"They never left for Port Clyde," Addie told him. "The sheriff sent the boat back empty. Apparently he wants to take statements from all the passengers who came over to-day. Meaning the day-trippers are all stranded here over-night."

"Are they?" He looked nonplussed and came to a standstill in the middle of the road. "I suppose I'd have to put them up if I went looking for them. They're probably trying to book a room at the Island Inn." He gave Addie a conspiratorial smile. "Come, haste makes waste. Mrs. Oliver's is right over there, and she's definitely booked to the hilt." He pointed to a wide-verandaed house of brown shingles that seemed to be hiding behind a riotous garden of flowers and shrubbery. "She has all the amenities including an electric generator," he added.

The dining room was long and narrow and filled almost to capacity. In the living room opposite, some people lounged around, apparently waiting to be seated. A television set was on in the corner and a couple of kids sat cross-legged in front of it. Linus dragged Addie quickly past the room, apparently afraid of meeting up with the day-trippers who had purchased the sketch from him.

Linus, who was a regular, had his table waiting for him in a corner of the dining room. "In spite of the occasional addition of an electric generator, nothing changes on Galbraith," he told Addie, holding her chair for her. "Sunday nights at Mrs. Oliver's, for instance. She serves lobster salad. I haven't missed a meal all summer."

There was no menu offered, and a bowl of thin bean soup was brought out almost immediately. There was a salad of lettuce and tomatoes, followed by another salad, this time the promised lobster with a small baked potato.

Between courses, Linus asked for details of the discovery out at Gull Rock, which Addie gave willingly.

"They still haven't found out who he was?" Linus asked her when she finished her recitation.

"You didn't happen to see him sometime around noon?" she asked. "Plump, middle-aged, wore a wool suit and carried a battered briefcase. Sort of looked as if he were, well, discombobulated."

Linus reached into his jacket pocket and pulled out a tiny sketch pad. He flipped through a dozen pages. She could see various sketches in pencil—of people, birds, flowers. He stopped, gazed down at a drawing and handed it across the table to her. "This the one?"

She held in her hand a tiny, beautifully rendered drawing of a man, his face barely indicated. There was something sad and resigned about the figure. His slightly stooped posture, the ill-fitting suit and the way his hand gripped the briefcase captured every nuance of the man she had spoken to that morning—and found dead at Gull Rock that afternoon.

"Yes," she said, unable to take her eyes from the drawing. With such delicate and consummate drawing skill, she believed Linus would possess an equally careful, dispassionate handwriting, but then anything was possible on this strange, isolated island.

Linus said, "I saw him standing in front of the general store."

"Was he going in or coming out?"

"No idea. I'm like a camera. Something strikes me, I pull out the pencil and do a quick drawing."

"Did you show it to him?"

"I never do. They tend to want to be paid for posing. Or else they expect the drawing as a gift."

"Did you show this to the sheriff?"

He shook his head. "Never made the connection."

"May I?" She flipped back to the first page of the pad.

"Go right ahead," Linus said with a pleased look.

Addie began to go through the pages carefully, hoping to come across some writing in his hand, but she was out of luck. There was no name or address on the pad, and no identifying notes about the birds or flowers he had sketched.

She handed the sketch pad back. "Your drawings are beautiful. Aren't you afraid of losing the book? No name, no return address?"

His expression was good-humored. "If you found this sketchbook, even with my name and address on it, would you return it to me?"

Addie laughed. "No, of course not."

"Come on, let's have coffee," he told her, finishing the last of his salad. "And I recommend the rhubarb pie."

She took an exasperated breath. "Rhubarb pie is fine. But tell me, Linus, you know I have those handwriting samples. My curiosity is piqued. I'd have guessed you wrote the William Blake poem. After all, Blake was an artist."

Linus made a face. "Always liked his poetry, but can't say I thought much of him as an artist."

"Which poem was yours?" she asked, offering him an interested smile.

"Addie, Galbraith is a tiny island. The pack you met at West Wind, at least the creative portion, Veronica West included, forms a tight little community. We may not love each other, but I believe I told you this before, we're voyagers on the same ship, summer after summer. Curious strangers never get very far with us, believe me."

Stymied again, she thought. She put her elbows on the table, and with her chin in her hand said, "Rhubarb pie, Linus, and coffee, very black."

IT WAS NEARING SEVEN-THIRTY when Addie reached the path leading to her cottage. The dusk folded in on itself. She remembered putting her flashlight on the hall table when she'd left that morning. She hadn't expected to be gone all day.

In the half-light of early evening the path looked eerie, dark and uninviting, and she found herself reluctant to go on. After hesitating a moment, she made her way slowly, keeping her step light, making scarcely a sound. Fitzgibbon sat beside the door like a statue, his huge tail curled around him. As she approached, he lifted a paw to lick it gently. He didn't seem in any hurry to join her. She crossed to the front door, found the key where she had left it—above the lintel—and breathed her first sigh of relief.

It was a premature sigh. A second later she stared at the lock in puzzlement. The key turned to the right, which meant the door had been unlocked. She switched the key to the left, then again to the right, carefully jiggling the lock, trying to remember how she had left the cottage that morning.

Probably unlocked, she decided. Galbraith wasn't exactly a den of crime. At least it hadn't been that morning when she'd closed the door behind her.

Addie pushed the door open and stepped inside. She heard a faint footfall as Fitzgibbon joined her. She closed the door softly behind them both and made her way over to the foyer table. The foyer was shadowed but she could see her flashlight and was about to reach for it when she realized it was standing up. She remembered very clearly putting the flashlight on its side that morning. She'd been afraid it would fall over.

A sudden rustle in the living room stayed her. Why the devil had she tiptoed in? She had no desire to meet up with anyone unexpectedly, friend or stranger, in the dark house. Well, it was too late to change tactics now. She grabbed the flashlight and made her way quietly over to the living-room door, her heart beating rapidly. She peered in. No one was there.

She was just about to beat a retreat when there was a sudden noise of heavy, running footsteps in the kitchen, followed by the sound of the back door being opened and closed. Then there was a clatter of footsteps on the back porch and down the wooden stairs. She raced through the

kitchen and found the screen door hanging on its hinges.
Without thinking of her safety, she took off after the intruder, pushing crazily through the prickly, dense undergrowth that covered the hillside. Then Addie came to her
senses. In the early dusk everything suddenly seemed tangled, mysterious, and worse, dangerous.

The handwriting samples! She raced back into the house,
and sighed with relief when she found them just where
she'd left them, hidden under the mattress. But then Addie discovered a chewing-gum wrapper on the floor next to
her bed and a few feet away, carefully balled up, its silver
foil.

Her dresser drawer wasn't quite closed; the one that held
her lingerie. A slow wringing out of her insides seemed to
hold impending panic at bay. Her hand shook as she
reached for the drawer. When she pulled it out, she discovered that her panties and bras had been sifted through.

Nothing had changed, nothing had been added to it or
taken away. She still held the gum wrapper and silver foil
she'd found in her hand. She relaxed. There was no doubt
about it: some crummy little voyeur, a kid—a gum-chewing
kid—had decided that a single woman living alone in a
isolated cottage deep in the woods, was an object worth
spying on, even when she wasn't there.

Her panic subsided as quickly as it had come. She began
to straighten out the drawer almost methodically, as though
her action obliterated the deed. She had met that kind in her
work, young, smart-aleck, harmless. Her coming back so
suddenly had also obviously scared him off. For good, she
hoped.

THE MORNING SUN crept in through the gauzy curtains
stealthily, like an animal in unfamiliar terrain leaving tiny
paw prints of light upon the ceiling. Addie lay for a while
thinking about her intruder of the night before. Some kid
from town, probably. Maybe a couple of them, even, on a
dare, sneaking around the house laughing, then running
scared when she'd come quietly, unexpectedly back.

Not Enigma, certainly. If Enigma had come it would be because he knew she had the samples and he would have been able to find them easily. They weren't very well hidden. No, not Enigma, definitely not Enigma. Her adversary was clever but he still had no idea she was on the island looking for him. None at all.

The night before, when Addie had given up trying to sleep, she had gone carefully through her samples and at last had come upon a poem in a hand similar to the one she had espied on the notepad at Dandelion Cottage. Lord Byron was the purported author. She remembered Meg's unfinished sentence, "The truth was I made it up but pretended it was by—"

When we parted there were no goodbyes,
It was see you anon. Another time,
Another place, another greeting.

Definitely not Lord Byron. Meg St. John had suckered them all, including the poet Sally Draper and Jason Farrell, the putative college professor.

Unable to get back to sleep, Addie dressed hurriedly in a blue cotton shirt and pants of a slightly darker hue. She decided on a minimum of makeup, a dab of mascara and some lipstick. She was about to make herself a cup of coffee when she heard a scratching sound on the front path. In two swift moves she collected her cache of handwriting samples. If her visitor was George Evans, she didn't want him to see them. She didn't want to see him, either. Ménage à trois, what nerve. It was a wonder Meg hadn't thrown him out on his ear. She shoved the samples into a large art book on the cocktail table, which was devoted to the works of David Larimee, who had summered on Galbraith around the turn of the century.

Then she went to the front door, opening it to a surprised-looking Jason Farrell. He wore a tan sports shirt and chino pants. He was well muscled, lean and broad shouldered. When he gave her a lazy grin she thought again, with a little intake of breath, how good-looking he was and how, against all reason, she was happy to see him.

"I hadn't even knocked yet," he said. "You telepathic, too?"

"I have a finely honed sense of encroachment. Get too close to my abode and all my receptors fire up."

"I'll have to remember that. Wouldn't want a conflagration."

His camera was slung around his neck on a leather strap. And he carried a small pack of camera equipment. There was a rubberized, waterproof flashlight dangling from one belt loop and a small leather case from another. He appeared rested and carefree, just an overworked professor on a holiday.

He held up a paper bag. "The freshest blueberry muffins on the island and black coffee that's a great eye-opener. Get a move on, we haven't much time."

"What in the world are you talking about?"

"May I come in?" Without waiting for an invitation he moved past her into the living room.

"No, I'm busy."

"I thought you were on vacation."

"I am."

"Then you can't be busy. That's an oxymoron, meaning two words that don't go together." He put the bag down on the coffee table. His eye lit upon the art book. "David Larimee. I heard there was a very handsome book around covering his work. Sensational." He reached for it.

"No," Addie said, jumping forward. "I mean, that bag. It's leaking coffee, I think."

"Is it?" He put the art book down and took up the bag again.

Addie grabbed it out of his hands. "Come on, I'll serve it up in the kitchen."

"Not quite what I had in mind," he told her, following her nonetheless.

She faced him sharply. "All right, what did you have in mind?"

"Anemones, as a matter of fact."

"For breakfast?"

"Below White Head, brilliant one. I thought you might like a distraction from thoughts of yesterday. There's a cave you can get to by walking along the edge of the cliff from Gull Rock."

"Gull Rock," she exclaimed. "No way."

"Rare anemones, not your ordinary kitchen varieties. They're found in a cave that's accessible only at certain times of the day. We'll get there early, tank up with coffee and blueberry muffins, then go down."

"Farrell, hasn't it occurred to you that I don't want to have anything to do with you? You were perfectly willing to sacrifice me in front of the sheriff yesterday, as long as you came out smelling like a rose."

He shook his head slowly and gave her a crooked grin. "You have me all wrong, Addie. The sheriff's question caught me by surprise, that's all."

"Somehow you strike me as a man who's never caught by surprise."

"You never did tell me. Were you on your way down to the water or back up?"

"Goodbye, Farrell. Close the door on your way out."

He pulled a map out of his pocket and spread it on her kitchen table. "Here's a solution, right here. We can avoid Gull Rock if we go down Gertie's Nose. It's a little tougher climb. Think you can do it?"

"I'm not interested in anemones. I saw all I ever needed to at the tidal pool below Gull Rock."

He gave her a look of chagrin. "Hey, there are anemones and there are anemones. A trip to Galbraith isn't a trip unless you've seen the ones in the cave below White Head."

"I'll survive." She caught his gaze straight on and then smiled. "No, maybe you're right. Someone's bound to ask me when I get back to Boston, then where will I be?"

She had spent some time the night before looking over the handwriting sample of Prospero's speech from *The*

Tempest. She knew enough not to speculate but had anyway. Perhaps she wanted desperately to believe that intelligent, sensual, creative hand belonged to Jason Farrell, or perhaps she was just operating on instinct. She wanted a sample of his writing for more reasons than one, and if visiting the cave at White Head was the only way to get it, she had little choice. It seemed harmless enough and maybe even pleasant. "Let me get a sweater," she said, heading back to the bedroom. "Oh, could you do me a favor? Write a note for George Evans. I'll stick it on the front door. His cat Fitzgibbon rooms here part time and I overfed him yesterday. I haven't seen the animal this morning, and if he's sick, I want George to know the reason."

She smiled at her cleverness. Just a sentence or two was all she needed. She took her time rummaging around a drawer before finally returning to the living room with a pink sweater slung over her shoulders.

Jason handed her a pad he had found on her desk. "You write it. He'll want the note in your hand. It'll show you really care."

"You're an untrusting soul, aren't you?" she said in response to his sly grin. He had outmaneuvered her again and she had no choice but to pen a note that was patently untrue. On her way to the front door, she caught a glimpse of the art book on the cocktail table. It had been moved from the center to the right. Jason might have come across not only the samples she had tucked within, but also the careful notes she was making about them. She pressed her lips together, worrying. Well, if he had been nosing about, the damage was already done. She decided to leave the samples in the art book, however, rather than call further attention to them by trying to move them.

She tacked the note to the front door and then checked the lock twice and slipped the key into her pocket. As they went down the front path, Fitzgibbon appeared. He pounced on something small, a furry little creature that darted out from between his paws.

"Looks like Fitzgibbon *has* slowed down a little," Jason said, the sarcasm clear in his voice. "Overeating can do that, you know."

"Fitzgibbon is very single-minded," Addie said. Like Enigma. "And unfortunately," she added, remembering the present of a dead shrew the cat had left her the morning of her arrival, "I've already seen the evidence of what he can accomplish."

WHEN THEY ARRIVED at Gertie's Nose, the origin of the name long ago lost, the early morning sea fog, still low on the water, had not quite lifted. Gertie's Nose was a narrow promontory, leading on the right toward Gull Rock. To the left, past Squeaker Cove and over successive layers of huge boulders, lay the way to the cave beneath White Head.

"This is a stunning spot," Jason said, looking around in a very self-satisfied way. "The light, the angles, the rocks, the sea. I've photographed it at every time of day, but I think the early morning light is best when the sun hasn't burned off the fog. Ready for breakfast? Let's hope the coffee is still hot. I had it put into double Styrofoam cups."

They settled down at the promontory as though they were riding fore on a ship breaking through heavy seas. Beside the muffins, still warm to the touch, Jason produced little tubs of jam and some small packets of cheese.

"It's wonderful," Addie said, genuinely pleased. At that moment she was ready to forgive him anything.

After a first sip of the coffee, Jason took his camera and snapped several shots of the way the morning fog still resolutely fingered the edges of White Head.

"You never stop, do you?" she remarked, when he came back and sat down beside her.

"Not when I'm offered such splendid scenery." He looked back out to sea. Addie decided she liked his profile. His chin was strong, and there was a touch of humor in his eyes that softened his expression. She thought she would like to know more about him, beyond a graphological portrait, yet she didn't dare ask. She wanted no lies that

would ultimately disappoint her. She was also afraid to ask
him too many personal questions for fear he would turn the
tables and demand some answers from her. She had already learned he was likely to do that and she wasn't really
a very good liar. She had been told that something in her
eyes invariably gave her away.

She liked his hands, too, his long fingers with their neatly
clipped nails. Surely they were not the hands of a killer.
Surely she'd know, something in her soul would tell her.

"Have you managed to put names to those handwriting
samples?" Jason asked the question casually enough, yet
in so pointed a manner he had to know for certain that the
samples were in her possession.

"I'm not sure what you mean," she said after a moment
of silence.

He turned and gave her a long, studied look. "You're
right, of course. It was a parlor game, wasn't it? Nobody
remembers parlor games five minutes after they're played."

"You're absolutely right. Exactly why do we play them,
then? Twenty questions. Charades. We test ourselves
against each other, I suppose."

"Conviviality," Jason said. "Strangers and friends acting in unison. A shame about the need for anonymity, under those circumstances, wouldn't you say?"

Addie shrugged. "Didn't matter to me, if you're talking
about what happened at West Wind. I don't know anyone
there, anyway."

"Ah," Jason said, his gaze going past hers. "Here's
Linus Bishop."

She turned quickly and found Linus trudging toward
them smiling. He carried a small canvas, a box of brushes
and a watercolor block. "But you see," she said hastily to
Jason, "I didn't know Linus then, either. I'd only met him
that afternoon. Am I on trial, Jason? I seem to be contin-
ually apologizing to you for having agreed, against my
better judgment, to read a few handwriting samples."

Her question wasn't answered, however. Linus Bishop, slightly out of breath, greeted them jovially. "Splendid morning. What gets you out here so early?"

"The anemones below White Head," Jason said. He began to put the empty coffee cups and leftover food back into the paper bag.

"Leave that trash with me," Linus said. "I'll dispose of it for you. You don't need any excess baggage with you. It's quite a scramble." Linus checked his watch and then gazed at the morning sun. "Should be good viewing now but you'd better move fast and watch your step. That's a contradiction in terms, but it's no picnic getting there."

"So I've heard," Jason said.

"Want to come?" Addie asked Linus.

He shook his head. "I'm not as fleet of foot as I used to be. Go along now. They're the most beautiful anemones on the island and well worth the visit."

The climb down to the water's edge was accomplished more quickly than they'd expected. And a farther climb along boulders half in and half out of the water led them to the base of White Head.

"The rocks are slippery with algae and moss, so be careful," Jason pointed out. "And when we hit the base of White Head the rocks are going to be sharper and a lot tougher to maneuver on."

"Jason, is this trip necessary?"

"So I've heard."

"And you're hauling all that camera equipment with you?"

"Not all. I'll leave some behind."

"Where, for heaven's sake?"

"I'll figure that out when I come to it."

"Jason, have you ever been in that cave before?"

He grinned at her. "No."

"Oh, great. In the land of the blind, the one-eyed is king." She looked back to the safety of Gertie's Nose. Linus was seated at the tip, legs over the side, as they had been. He waved and she waved back. "Well," she said to

Jason, "he warned us. Lead on." As they came closer to the cliff face, Addie looked up. It seemed to her that the top of White Head bumped against the sky. She remembered Steve West telling her about waves crashing up against the tops of those cliffs and she had a slightly dizzy reaction to her first sight of their immensity.

"Water looks calm enough," she said, eyeing the pools that lapped quietly at their feet.

"When the tide comes in, it's relentless," Jason said.

"And when does that happy event occur?"

"According to the best informed sources, midmorning."

"Okay," Addie said. "Let's get it over with."

Jason placed some of his camera equipment on a dry rock well above the waterline. By the time he joined her, Addie had already eased herself along the cliff face and was staring at the narrow opening to the cave.

"Well, here goes," she said, slipping quickly into the cave, giving herself no chance to change her mind. The bottom was shiny with moss, but the water had withdrawn enough to reveal small tidal pools lit by the sun still low in the east. Addie gave up all thoughts of dry sneakers. Water had crystalized in spots, leaving a silver shine that resembled snow-white rosettes. The walls were wet velvet, smooth to the touch from the water that had filled and emptied the cave twice daily for eons. Deeper in the cave, however, darkness took hold. If there was another entrance, it cast no light.

"Here they are," Jason told her. "What we've come to see." He reached for her hand and brought her to a crevice that held what seemed to be a soft, yet bizarre floral arrangement of translucent stems supporting waving crowns of petals. "Don't touch them, Addie. They'll fight back. They're part of a class of coelenterates and they sting like hell."

"Oh, Jason, sting or no sting, how remarkably beautiful." She remembered a field trip she had taken once in college to a cave in Kentucky. It had been at a time when she wasn't certain what she wanted to do with her life. That day had convinced her that spelunking wasn't for her. But now, in this place, with its pungent smell of salt and sea things, she saw it all quite differently.

The morning sun reached deep into the cave to pick out a tidal pool farther back, revealing a palette of colors: the pale pink of anemones, the green algae, black sea urchins, barnacles, snails, the miniature denizens of the tidal world of the sea cave. The reflection of sun against the pools of water bounced against the cave ceiling setting off a dancing array of light. Addie sat on her haunches, fascinated by the way barnacles opened to reveal tiny, waving fronds that picked up nutrients in the water. The sound of water gently lapping in and out of the cave had a soft echo to it.

"How extraordinary it all is," she said to Jason, who stood at her side and she was surprised to find him gazing down at her, a contemplative expression on his face.

"Mother Nature, just doing what she knows best." He gave her his hand and pulled her up. "I'm about to photograph you in color as an example of the beauties to be found in tidal caves."

"In color? I thought you were a master of chiaroscuro."

"I go with the flow. Special moments call for special measures."

"In that case, I'll pose. I think I'd like a memento of the visit. And I didn't bring a camera to the island with me, since I'm absolutely hopeless as a photographer."

He reached out, brushed his fingers slowly through her hair and then stepped back, tilting his head to one side. "I've got a feeling I'll be focusing on one beautiful brunette and forgetting my duties as a reporter of nature." For a moment Addie thought he was going to kiss her but then he said, "Stay put, I'll have to go get another roll of film."

"You mean you came in here without film?" Addie frowned. She didn't like the idea of remaining alone in the cave even for five minutes, no matter how beautiful it was.

"I've already exposed over half the film in the camera. The truth is I figured on taking a couple of pictures and letting it go at that. I'll be right back. The film's in the pack I left outside. Sit tight." He started toward the cave opening.

"I'll give you five minutes," she said, remembering the difficulty of edging along the cliff wall and then climbing up to where he had left his things. "Then I'm coming after you."

"Make it four and a half."

"Hey, leave me the flashlight," Addie called as he began to make his way over to the cave opening.

"Sun isn't about to desert you, but here it is," he said, tossing the flashlight to her. "Have a good time."

"Jason."

He was at the narrow opening with the sun at his back. She couldn't see his face. "Yes?"

"Thanks for bringing me."

"Thanks for coming along." He ducked out with a wave of his hands.

Addie continued to stare at the cave opening and at the sun's rays. She thought how much she wanted to prove that Jason wasn't Enigma, that he was exactly who he said he was, an academic with an interest in photography. After a few moments she drew herself up and looked around. The steady drip of water from the ceiling plonked down like musical notes. Limpid pools curled at her feet. She moved along the rock wall, using its smoothness to guide her. A little off to the left she discovered a large colony of anemones. She picked her way over and examined them closely under the flashlight. Without being aware of the time, she began to explore the cave, finding a little cascade of water in a crevice and farther back, under the beam of the flashlight, more tidal pools.

Once she knelt to examine a small creature that slithered across the floor of the cave but it disappeared before she had a good look. So entranced was Addie with what the flashlight beam picked out, that she was deep into the cave's interior before she realized that total darkness surrounded her and that she wasn't certain which way she had come. A quiet fear gripped her that wasn't quite outright panic.

"Jason." Her voice echoed back at her. She heard the relentless drip of water.

"Jason?"

There was no answer. She tried to retrace her steps but had no idea whether or not she was heading toward sunlight and safety. She played the flashlight around the huge cavern in which she found herself, remembering from her one previous foray into spelunking that caves are tridimensional and meander without rhyme or reason with no fixed points, no symmetry. Without guideposts, there was no way to tell east from west, north from south. Had she come from the right or the left? The gloom was unrelieved around her. She had to think and switched the beam off, knowing she must conserve the battery.

But then, suddenly, she realized time meant everything. The water lapped around her ankles. And it wasn't ebbing out, she realized with horror, it was coming in.

Chapter Seven

How much time had passed since Jason had left her? Addie had no idea. Minutes? Hours? The water level was rising rapidly. If she couldn't find her way out soon she would drown.

"Jason!" The word burst out of her, but Addie was suddenly certain he wasn't in the cave, that he had deliberately left her there alone.

The most important thing was to keep a tight grip on the flashlight; without it she'd be lost. As the beam picked out the movement of the tide, Addie set out to follow the direction of its strong ebb and flow.

She waited for the tide to pull back and then raced forward, her heart pounding in her chest. She tripped once, grabbed the slippery surface of a rock and, after taking in a deep breath, crawled forward again. Scarcely had she gone a few yards when her foot caught between two rocks, and she slid to the cave floor. Water seeped into her clothing. Her sweater, which she had carelessly thrown around her shoulders when she left her cottage, was heavy with water and she shrugged it away fearing its weight.

She remained still for a moment, then twisted her foot and carefully worked it out of the crevice. No damage was done. Even the flashlight was still working. There was only a slight twinge in her ankle as she struggled to her feet.

Jason had lied to her about the tide and left her there to die. Perhaps it was anger more than anything that kept her going when reason told her to give up. Her mind was sharp and clear. Except for her narrow beam of light, the cave was still pitch-black and smelled richly of the sea. The water gushed in with a heavy, melancholy sound, scraping, slapping, gurgling like plumbing gone crazy.

She was freezing. Her clothes were soaked through and her hair hung in damp strings around her face. She was breathing hard, a scream strangling in her throat that refused to be released.

Stepping on a stone covered thickly with something soft she hoped wasn't a colony of anemones, Addie slipped once more. This time, as she fought to keep her balance, the flashlight bounced away and the light, which marked its progress for a few feet, went out. Addie blindly searched for it but gave up after a moment knowing it had been carried off by the tide.

With fingers outstretched, she reached the cave wall and waited again to feel the tug of the tide. Slowly, without lifting her hand, she moved ahead with small, careful steps. The wall angled to the right and when she made the turn she saw a tiny change in the light, as though not far away an opening allowed something of the morning air to sift through. She moved through waist-high water not blinking but keeping her eye on the hopeful cast of light. Then the wall angled once more and the light became the opening of the cave. Addie raced toward it, her heart lifting.

Tears stung her eyes as a patch of morning sky appeared. She clambered along the slick rock siding, gripping whatever surface was available. She pulled herself toward the narrow opening and dragged her soaked body out. But she wasn't free yet. She had to maneuver along the base of the cliff for a dozen yards or more fighting against the waves that hammered the bulwark of White Head, then withdrew, only to hammer in again.

When at last she reached safety, she fell onto a large rock outcropping and buried her face in her hands. She could scarcely breathe and thought her heart would burst. Then slowly she regained her strength and with it the quiet fury that burned in her chilled body.

Jason Farrell had tried to trick her. And if he knew she'd survived, she had no doubt he'd try again. Her one thought as she struggled to her feet was to escape him, to make her way quickly into the village where she could seek help. She began to climb along the rocks, calling upon strength she never knew she possessed.

Addie suddenly came upon Jason Farrell. He was crouched over a tidal pool higher up the slope than the cave entrance, his camera poised. His bearing was calm. He was waiting out the inevitable. Instinct told her to slip by him, to make her escape, but she couldn't. Instead she confronted him straight on, spitting out the words.

"You slime."

He looked up, surprise widening his eyes. "Addie, what—"

"You left me to die." She was no longer aware of her wet clothes pasted to her body, or her dripping hair.

"What are you talking about?" He followed her gaze to the sea and saw the incoming tide. He squeezed his eyes shut for an instant, then reached toward her. "Addie, I had no idea. He lied to me, dammit, I'll kill him. Addie, you have to believe me."

"Tell it to the police." She turned and began to race along the rocks to safety. Looking right toward Gertie's Nose, she saw that Linus was no longer there.

She heard Jason moving toward her. "Hold it," he called.

She raced on without looking back. He grabbed her arm and spun her around. "Hold it, calm down."

"Calm down!" Addie shook him off and sprinted away. She was an experienced runner, but she was no match for his longer legs and greater strength—especially after her struggles in the cave. "Addie," he said, grabbing her arm, "stop and give me a chance to explain what happened."

"Oh, brother." She knew if she stopped running she could easily collapse, but in another moment she gave in and turned around to face him, her breath coming in short gasps. "I don't want you near me, just leave me alone."

"Addie, I was told the tide wasn't due to turn for another hour."

The horror of what had happened was clearly evident in his eyes and for the first time the tight fear in her chest gave way. She had no strength left. "Oh, Jason, I lost the flashlight. And my sweater. It's gone. My favorite sweater." She began to laugh knowing she was close to tears. This time he gathered her in his arms and she felt herself go limp against his heavily pounding heart.

"Hello, you two. Is that a drowned rat I see or our handwriting expert?"

They jumped apart and looked up to find Sally Draper, who billed herself as a poet, making her way down toward them.

Jason swore. "What's she doing here?"

"Rescuing me," Addie said. She hugged her arms, thankful for the sun's warmth.

"I don't recommend swimming in these parts," Sally said with a good-natured smile on her face. She wore a wide-brimmed straw hat, sneakers, and a voluminous ankle-length print dress with a touch of fur at her neck that turned out, upon closer inspection, to be a live ferret. She carried a blanket and a straw bag out of which a notebook peeked. Her mouth was a slash of crimson drawn into a smile of curiosity and surprise. "It's cold even with your clothes on," she added. "Don't tell me you fell in."

"I'm afraid I did in a way." Addie felt Jason's arm close tightly around her. "I was caught in the cave looking at anemones when the tide came in."

"What? Good Lord, what were you doing there at this time of morning? Absolutely the wrong time." She came forward with the blanket. "We're blessed with the spring tides, which means they're at their fullest right now. The absolute worst time to do some exploring. I was on my way down to the cove for a little inspiration before lunch, but here, put my blanket over you and come along at once. I can't imagine what could've possessed you to take the chance. Well, never mind, we can sort it all out later. My house is the closest thing and I've a nice dry caftan that will do you nicely. And something hot as well. Come along, come along,'' she said, clearly expecting no refusal. She turned and led the way, the ferret still draped around her shoulder.

JASON, GATHERING UP his photographic gear, allowed a little distance to separate them. His mouth formed a grim line as he remembered exactly who had told him about the cave—and the tide. Someone who should have known better; someone who knew the island from childhood, who knew its tidal timetable as surely as a sailor navigating into a well-traveled port. Steven West, and at that moment Jason knew he could kill the man bare-handed.

Of course, it all made sense. West wanted him dead. West had offered a bribe of a quarter of a million dollars just to get Jason off his back. Jason, in fact, obviously wasn't acting at all the way West expected, and that was enough to knock the man off his perch. Feeling squeezed, West's response had been to try to rid himself of Jason in the easiest way possible. Let Galbraith and nature do the job for him. Only Jason had gone out after his color film and Addie had been left to face the tidal force alone.

The way Jason figured it, Addie must have wandered deeper into the cave without realizing it. He had warned her to stay put until he came back, but then he hadn't come back, had he? He'd gotten distracted and left her to her own devices while he explored the sea creatures in a nearby tidal pool.

He packed his camera gear and took off after Addie, his heart still pounding. The front of his shirt was wet. He could still feel her limp body against his and the notion that she could have died for his mistake caused cold fear to grab his insides.

A quick glance at Gertie's Nose and Jason saw that Linus had packed his drawing gear and left. Linus's warning came

back to him. He remembered now. The artist had looked at
his watch and then said they'd better hurry. The tide was
due, Linus knew it and had assumed that Jason and Addie
knew it, too. Except they didn't and Steve West had
counted on that.

Jason realized he'd been a bit lax in believing everything
was settled about West, everything in place. Maybe it was
time to rethink the whole business even though all systems
were still go.

Tim Gruesin and Noah Roberts were both on the island,
staying at West Wind. The meeting had been set up. West
would be wired and all they had to do was spill their guts
into West's little tape recorder and the operation would be
under way.

The people Jason worked for took money laundering
very seriously. Money laundering that involved the top ex-
ecutives of three Boston banks was taken more than very
seriously.

Mob money sent offshore through those banks as though
they were legitimate funds might not be a capital offense,
but it came pretty close. And it was money made in any
number of nefarious ways. There were probably plenty of
bodies at the bottom of Boston Harbor wearing cement
shoes to attest to it. Anyone involved knew the risks as well
as the payoffs. Well, this time payoff was close at hand if
West could be kept in line a little longer.

The trouble was Jason had thought all along that West
was in his pocket, West with the extravagant wife and high
style of living, West who cried when he was pushed to the
wall and had seemed to be made of jelly.

Only now, Jason would have to see West again, put the
squeeze on, tell him things hadn't changed. This time trust
wasn't a word Jason was keeping in his vocabulary.

Yeah, it must have been refusing the quarter of a million bribe that had ticked West off. Jason, on the other
hand, hadn't even taken it seriously. Now, as he made no
effort to catch up with Addie and Sally Draper, he wondered why he'd been so quick to shuck it off. Two hundred

fifty thousand dollars could buy him a little house somewhere and the rest of his life to admire the scenery. He
could leave the States, change his identity. They probably
wouldn't even come looking for him. Some remote Italian
fishing village where the beach and the sea and the sun
swept you up and held you tight in its hot little grip. He
could concentrate on playing. No work. Just him and the
blue sky and the seabirds floating on the air currents. He
knew just which camera he'd get and the pictures he'd take
with it. He wondered what it would be like having Addie
Cordero laughing beside him on the warm sand. No wor-
ries, no suspicions, no rising tides.... He shook the idea
away. *We are such stuff as dreams are made on; and our
little life is rounded with a sleep.*

Sally Draper's cottage was a squat comfortable-looking
building of gray shingles with blue shutters. It was set well
back from White Head in a small copse that opened out to
the west side of the island with a view of the southern edge
of the Cathedral Woods and the village through a large bay
window. The day was bright and clear, the sun nearly
overhead. It seemed to Jason that every leaf, every bird
feather could be seen and counted a mile away.

The door was open and when Jason knocked Sally called
out, "Come on in."

He stepped through the door directly into a large, airy
living room. "Addie okay?" he called.

"She's fine, Jason. I insisted she take a nice warm shower
to wash away all that salt. Meanwhile make yourself at
home. Be with you in a minute."

The living room was filled with white rattan furniture and
colorful throw pillows. From the look of things, Sally
Draper was obviously a poet with a respectable income. A
watercolor painting above the couch depicted a carefully
rendered seascape with rocks in the foreground and birds
against a lowering gray sky. Jason studied it, admiring its
portrayal of nature and of solitude. He realized that it had
been painted from the vantage point of Gull Rock and,

from the neatly printed signature in the lower right-hand corner, that the artist was Linus Bishop.

"Ah, you're admiring my Bishop," Sally Draper said coming into the room. "He's done dozens of pictures from that spot." The small ferret scooted into the room and made for the narrow space under the couch. Jason had read somewhere that ferrets were mild, sweet-tempered pets. He didn't believe it for a moment. The animal had a nasty gleam in its eye and Jason hoped it wouldn't poke his head out from under the couch.

Sally stood in front of the painting, her arms crossed, her head tilted in admiration. "One of Linus's best. The untamed and solitary spirit of the Galbraith we all know and love."

"He's there every day, is he? On Gull Rock?"

"More or less, the weather and everything else permitting."

"Too bad he wasn't around when the stranger fell to his death."

Sally turned to him sharply. "Good heavens, man, he's only there at certain hours of the day, depending on what light he's painting. Early morning, noon, midafternoon, dusk. He's not the guardian of Gull Rock, merely its interpreter."

Jason was surprised at the way she'd taken him on. He courteously backed away. "What I like about his work," Jason said, "is his mastery of detail."

"Patience rewarded." Sally gave him a forgiving smile and then headed for the kitchen. "While Addie's drying out, I'll get the tea things ready. Unless you'd like something a little stronger."

He would have but at that hour of the morning he decided it would be wiser to refuse. He thought, with an inward smile, that he could use a little drying out of a different kind.

"Have a seat, be with you in a minute," Sally added.

Addie came into the living room wearing a Persian print caftan that was several sizes too large but flattered her anyway. Her hair had been roughly dried and formed a shiny cap around her face. She was holding her wet clothes. "I'll just put these outside to dry," she said. "Oh, you're wet, too." She frowned and then, as though nervous at remembering the way he'd held her, went past him quickly.

He couldn't quite make out whether she was still angry or not. He followed her outside to the back of the house where a clothesline was strung. The silence between them was heavy. As she secured her shirt with a wooden clothespin, she said, "I'm still not sure whether to trust you or not."

"Maybe you'd better hang me up to dry, too. I'm still wearing a lot of the water you brought out with you."

She turned, her face lit with a brief smile, the first she had managed between them since leaving the cave. "I don't feel sorry for you in the least. But perhaps Sally has a second caftan that would fit. You don't mind if I voice some doubts about why you left me alone in the cave."

"Addie, I was just about to come back, believe me. I had no idea the tide was due to turn. Somebody—" He stopped, knowing she'd question him and that would be opening up another can of worms. "Look, if anything happened to you after both of us discovered that body yesterday, I'd have a lot to answer for."

"Ah, worried about your skin as usual. Well, at least you're running true to form. And didn't you just say both of us discovered the body? Now that no one's around to hear you, you're singing a different tune. I seem to remember you telling the sheriff yesterday that I was undoubtedly guilty of pushing the man off the cliff. And who's the somebody who told you about the tide?"

"I can't remember," he told her quietly. "It came up in conversation."

"Just like that. And how amazing that you were so conveniently out of the cave when the tide roared in. Remind me to count on you the next time I'm in trouble."

"Addie." He almost reached for her but Sally's high, faintly eccentric voice interrupted them.

"Yoo hoo. Tea's just about ready."

When they came back into the living room, Sally brought in a tray with a teapot, under a thick cozy, and three delicate glass teacups. There was a plate of tea biscuits as well. "I get specially imported tea from a remote province in China," she remarked. "Takes a half hour to brew. It's ready because I put it up before I went on my little jaunt."

"I'm glad you went on your little jaunt," Addie said, sitting down on the couch. "Walking back to my cottage soaking wet wasn't something I wanted to think about."

Jason took a straight-back wicker chair on the opposite side of the cocktail table. Sally put the tea tray down and with great ceremony lifted the cozy to reveal a glass teapot filled with a dark, almost opaque liquid.

"Sugar?" she asked Addie and Jason in turn.

Addie refused sugar but Jason asked for three teaspoons, which Sally Draper heaped into his cup with a disapproving air.

Jason dutifully took a sip. It was as strong and bitter as it looked. The sugar didn't help and might possibly have made it worse. He carefully put the cup down on the cocktail table. "All the way from China," he said.

"It's great," Addie said.

He thought, admiringly, that Addie was either the most polite individual he had ever met or she had lost all sense in the cave below White Head.

"Of course it's a cultivated taste," Sally said. Then she added, without noting that Jason had not taken another sip, "Addie, I must confess a delicious little lie."

Addie looked at her with surprise. "Not about Chaucer, surely."

"I have to confess," the woman went on, "that I wanted to give you a particularly apt piece I'd written but I was afraid of being found out."

"Apt?"

"Oh, yes, something I'd done a couple of years ago. You know, about how we reveal ourselves in unexpected ways.

It's called 'Written on the Wind.'" She smiled and before anyone could stop her, began reciting:

"All else was gone
Fact, place, who, what, when and how
Four lines remained
And sketched a soul forever."

For a moment Jason had a sickening feeling that she would begin quoting her collected works. He caught Addie's glance but she shook her head almost imperceptibly as though she understood Jason's reaction and was begging him to behave himself.

"You know," Sally went on, "we all harbor secret feelings that one day the world will see us as we really are, that we'll give ourselves away. And then along you come with your graphological talents and you can see right through us. You make words nothing more than vehicles for our emotions. I settled for Chaucer."

Pretty nice setting, Jason thought. She was being very clear about revealing which handwriting was hers. Addie, to his surprise, however, didn't show the slightest interest in discussing handwritings.

"That was a beautiful poem. I collect books of poetry," she told Sally. "Contemporary stuff."

"Really? How wonderful. You don't happen to be a poet, too. I mean, the average layman, lay*person* doesn't go around collecting books of poetry." She took the seat next to Addie on the couch. "You know, we may be gone a thousand years but we linger on in a few desultory words, and our handwritings. Funny, isn't it? I've spent a lifetime trying to explain myself in my poetry and you did it in a few seconds."

"But poetry is explaining the world to the world," Jason said.

"Yes, yes, of course."

"I'd love to see some more," Addie said.

The woman flashed her a smile. "Why, how incredibly sweet."

"It's an odd thing," Addie went on. "What I like best is ultra contemporary poetry. If it were written yesterday, *today*, I like it best."

"You continue to amaze me," Sally said. "Most people go for the old tried-and-true."

Jason fidgeted. He wasn't about to sit through another reading of Sally's poetry. "Addie, I ought to get you home. You've had a rough time," he said.

She turned to him with a cold smile. "You should certainly know, shouldn't you?" Then she smiled at Sally. "One more, your latest."

Sally regarded her for a long moment. Then she went over to her desk and took up a notebook. She turned the pages and proceeded to read a short, respectable poem on the discovery that so feral a creature as ferrets could be domesticated. As if on cue, the animal came out from under the couch and darted over to her.

"Lovely," Addie said when the poem ended. "May I take a look at it? I always sort of like to look at a poem, even when it's read so beautifully."

"Of course," Sally said, her pale face reddening with pleasure.

There was something about the way Addie took possession of the book and the way that she bent over it, that drew Jason's attention. From where he sat he could see the short poem written in pen in an even, smooth line. Damn, he thought, she's after something and it has nothing to do with poetry and everything to do with handwriting. She was probably no more interested in Sally's poetry than he.

The thought struck him then with some force. Addie wasn't playing games, not by a long shot. He had no idea what she was up to, but he had no doubt she had wanted to see the woman's handwriting and had used a simple ruse to do so.

Addie handed the notebook back to Sally and said with a sweet smile that Jason interpreted as vaguely triumphant, "I'd like to come back if I may, see more, talk more. You're my first poet."

"Anytime, my dear, anytime."

"I'll return the caftan tomorrow," she said. "Oh, incidentally, you have very beautiful handwriting."

The woman beamed. "Well, on Saturday you told me I was levelheaded but inclined to be bossy. True, I thought, but I was a little unhappy over not being thought more *creative*."

"But you are," Addie said. "Creative but at the same time you know the pitfalls of being a poet. Lack of financial reward or even excessive fame. You know you'll never do the talk shows on television, but your inner soul means everything to you. You're determined, you let nothing stand in your way, and if you had to starve for your art, you would."

"My dear," Sally said, giving Addie a spontaneous hug, "you're an absolute, certifiable genius yourself."

Outside Addie picked her still-wet things off the line. "I'll finish drying these back home," she told Jason.

It was only when they were well away from the cottage that Jason turned to Addie and, in a voice that was carefully noncommittal, he said "Get what you came for, you certifiable genius, you?"

"You mean about drying off?" She touched her hair. He suspected it was still damp. "Yes, I most certainly did."

"Admirable, your taste in poetry. Nothing like a poem hot off the creative fires and especially poems about beady-eyed animals."

"Ferrets are cute animals."

"They like to dig things out."

"Why so they do, Jason. Maybe that's why I like them. I turn here to get back to my cottage." She stopped and said, smiling sweetly at him, "You don't have to walk me back, if that's what your plans are."

"I'd like to see you safely home."

"Really? Safely?" She shook her head and then began to walk rapidly away from him, the words tossed out with a particularly careless ring. "Odd you should think of that now."

Chapter Eight

Someone had told Jason the tide would flood in an hour later than it actually did. Someone who? Jason had coolly pretended he'd forgotten. So he was protecting someone. Addie was certain of it, but she couldn't afford to be wrong.

Unless Jason was a consummate actor his shock had been genuine when he realized the tide was coming in a lot earlier than he'd been told. But then again he could have just been surprised to find her still alive.

But that didn't make sense. Linus had seen them, talked to them. Even, she remembered, warned them in an oblique way that the tide was coming in. Jason would have had a lot of explaining to do if she had been killed in the cave. If Jason *were* Enigma, however, he'd undoubtedly have been able to handle it.

Addie wanted to believe in Jason's innocence in that little matter of a tidal hour. But she'd be a fool if she did so without proof. She was a fool anyway, sitting there in a remote cottage on a dangerous little island with hazards built into every turn.

And then there was the odd notion she'd gotten that the denizens of the summer colony were too protective of one another—and by extension, perhaps of Enigma if he were one of them. Was Jason part of it? Or was he, like Addie, on the periphery, allowed in for a while yet given nothing but smiles and the charm that was laid on like a groaning buffet.

Jason had suspected something was up when she'd gone after Sally Draper's handwriting so aggressively. It was possible he had found the samples from the party in the art book on her cocktail table and was still trying to work out why she'd kept them, and kept them hidden.

Sally Draper was clearly off her list, along with Meg St. John and Vladimir and Ivy Tatlin. Also either Veronica West or Noah Roberts possessed a European handwriting, meaning one of them was also off the hook, although she couldn't guess who. Four or five down and seven or eight to go. Maybe... Perhaps...

Furthermore, Addie hadn't cleared up the question of whether Enigma was on the island for a reason. The only viable clue the Boston police had to Enigma was a sample of handwriting. However, the deaths of four women in the Boston area had revealed enough similarities for the police to consider it likely that they had all been murdered by the same hand. They had all been of a certain age and living alone on respectable incomes. They were loners who had no relatives living close by nor friends who took a personal interest in them. They were, in other words, all women vulnerable to the charms of someone who would make them feel good about themselves.

Sally Draper fit the bill neatly.

Addie's head was swimming. It wasn't worth it, she thought with a sigh. She simply wasn't being paid enough to stick around and fall into danger everywhere she turned.

The sheriff would undoubtedly lift travel restrictions in a day or two and then perhaps she would take the ferry back to Port Clyde where her safe little car was parked. She decided to go down to the Island Inn and place a telephone call to Pam. One traveler with a missing briefcase, who showed up dead in the wrong place, and one tide coming in at the wrong time were two too many frightening incidents in her life.

She removed the handwriting samples from the art book on the living-room cocktail table. There was an old black-and-white lithograph on the fireplace wall. The scene was of the sea and the artist, in fact, was David Larimee, the one whose art book sat on the cocktail table. The frame was antique. Addie lifted it from the wall and examined the backing, which turned out to be of wood held in place by little flat movable hinges.

"Wonderful, the way they made things in the good old days," she told the cat who had just sauntered into the room. She removed the backing and slipped the handwriting samples under the cardboard mount that held the lithograph in place.

She refitted the wood and then, as an added precaution, covered the entire back with brown paper carefully cut from a paper bag, and glued the corners.

"There," she told Fitzgibbon, who had curled up on the couch. "Nobody will have a clue."

She rehung the frame and stood back to admire her work. Perhaps a sprinkling of dust on the top or a hair strategically placed to show if it were tampered with. No. She wasn't playing detective, just protecting her investment.

She suddenly felt energized. When she called Pam, she'd give her a list of all the people who had attended the West party and ask her to run them down. And perhaps Pam would have more information on Enigma. Meanwhile Addie would go aggressively to work with her graphological talents. One step at a time, however. She knew quite well how to spell the word danger.

"WHAT DO YOU mean the line is down?"

Pam Hellman screamed the words into the telephone receiver. Her secretary at the other end drew in an audible breath and went on to explain once more that the telephone lines between Galbraith and the mainland were down.

"Some kind of power outage during the night. It happens from time to time, Pam. The island *is* ten miles off the coast. The cable runs along the ocean floor. You know, continental shift, storms, some little underwater rat comes along and bites through it, that sort of thing."

"Continental shift," Pam exploded. "I don't want to hear about continental shift. I don't want to hear about underwater rats. Just keep trying." Pam placed the receiver back in its cradle and stared straight ahead unseeing.

It was the silence from Galbraith that bothered her. Addie hadn't called, which either meant she'd made no progress or entirely too much.

Pam was worried she might have been a bit too cavalier about sending Addie out alone. At the time the plan had seemed perfect. All Addie had to do was check the handwriting of everyone on the island who could conceivably have murdered four human beings. Small order. Very cut-and-dried. She should have known better. Addie never did anything in half measures.

Pam took up the small article culled from the *Port Clyde Examiner* sent to her by a friend living in a nearby town. The newspaper covered the social doings on Galbraith and Pam had decided early on to keep abreast in every way she knew how. The article said an unidentified middle-aged male had been found dead in a tidal pool on Galbraith Island. Cause of death as yet unknown. The body had been discovered below Gull Rock. She remembered Gull Rock and the treacherous jam-up of boulders and rocks and slippery algae leading down to the water's edge there. And why the devil hadn't Addie called before the lines went down? She had half a mind to ring the Port Clyde sheriff's office.

She read the article again and then again. There was nothing in it that told of foul play. The shoals were treacherous, the victim could have slipped and the seemingly innocent tidal pool would have taken him into its wet bosom.

Instinct told her to keep worrying. She picked up the receiver. Perhaps two or three minutes had passed since her last call. Her secretary answered curtly as if scarcely containing her anger. "Yes?"

"Try again."

"Right. I was just about to."

Pam hung up. It wasn't merely the article that had set her on edge, it was also learning something new about Barney Barnstable, husband of Enigma's last victim, Eda Barnstable. Until his sudden death the previous year, he'd been a senior partner in a law firm representing Boston National Bank. Steven West was president of Boston Bank. Steven West, grandson of Cyrus West who had invented a better mop pail, and who summered at West Wind on Galbraith Island. And so had the Barnstables, as a matter of fact. It turned out there was even a Barnstable relative who had inherited the house on Galbraith and was there now. Eda's grandchild, Ivy.

It might be nothing more than the usual hair-raising coincidence but to Pam the silence from Galbraith seemed ominous. She had to speak to Addie.

Pam's intercom went off. She grabbed the receiver. "Yes?"

"Sorry, nothing."

"Keep trying."

She put the receiver down again, but not before another shiver of fear moved along her spine.

"TILLY, how long has the phone been down?"

The telephone operator at the Island Inn continued to buff her nails, not looking at Addie. "Overnight, all day."

"What happened?"

She shrugged. "Your guess is as good as mine. Happens from time to time."

Addie leaned her elbows across the counter separating them. "Gives you a sort of vacation, doesn't it?"

"Not when people keep pestering me all day."

Addie straightened. "You mean I'm not the only one. Everyone wants to call offshore."

"Some are lucky. Mrs. West was the last one to get through. Five o'clock last night and the line went dead right after that. And I'll tell you why." Tilly suddenly looked up and gave Addie a vaguely conspiratorial smile. "Line exploded out of sheer embarrassment." It was clearly a bit of gossip she had repeated before and couldn't keep to herself.

Addie didn't move an inch, although she gave the operator her full attention.

"Her tone was sexy, let me tell you. Mmm mmm *mmmh.*"

"She's an actress," Addie said.

"Better believe it. I don't know who was at the other end, but he had an earful. She hangs up. Mr. Farrell comes down right after and no dial tone, nothing. Fit to be tied. He's fit to be tied right now." Her smile showed that she had enjoyed the handsome Mr. Farrell's fits and was looking forward to more.

Addie resisted the temptation to ask whom Mr. Farrell might be calling. Perhaps a woman, perhaps his mother. She realized she knew less than nothing about the man, not even trusting his putative professorship.

"Anybody have a cellular phone on the island?" she asked.

Tilly shook her head. "No. There's no cellular network on shore close enough, far as I know. Believe me, if there were, I've a suspicion Mrs. West would be the first to have one."

"No other phones on the island?"

"No. It's been traditional on the island not to have electricity or phones. Of course some people are beginning to break down and talk about putting in transformers. Too bad," she added before returning to her nails. "Progress."

For the first time Addie realized that the guest book lay on the counter at the far end, open and waiting for anyone to see. A quick rundown of the signatures in the book wouldn't be a bad idea, Jason's included.

"Do you know when the phone might be working again?" she asked.

"Your guess is as good as mine."

"Right." Addie gave a little tap on the desk with her fingernails and moved along the counter to the guest book but before she had a chance to check it over the manager materialized.

"Wanted to make a phone call," she murmured and turned away, frustrated. She'd never felt more isolated in her life. No phone, no progress, nothing. She left the hotel after glancing around the lobby. No Jason in sight. It was nearly six and she contemplated having dinner at the hotel where she might bump into him. Maybe she could catch him signing the check or ask him for his autograph, something subtle like that.

"My dear Addie." Linus Bishop came hurrying along the road. "Just the very person I was looking for." He bent to place a kiss on her cheek as though they were old friends. "What the devil happened to you today? You're a regular traveling disaster area. I heard you nearly drowned."

"Well, news travels fast."

"What possessed you to stay so long in the cave? You knew the tide was due. Time and tide wait for no man, need I tell you?"

"Linus," Addie said, pausing uneasily. "How come you didn't tell us how dangerous the tide was? How come you didn't tell us it was really too late to go anemone hunting?"

He hesitated for only a moment, leveling a gaze at her that revealed a mild hurt. "I took it for granted you knew. There was time to get down there, take a fast look around and get out. I believe I said something."

"You did," she admitted. "You said something about our getting a move on. Only we thought, or rather I thought you were talking about the sunlight."

"Well, you're safe now," he said, patting her hand. "Come to dinner tonight. Spontaneous thing. I'm having some people over. Don't say no, I won't allow it."

"I'm free, but no handwriting games."

"Scout's honor. Besides, if you continue to tell people what they think they want to hear, you'll make a pariah of yourself in short order. Anyway, you should know everyone."

Everyone. Splendid. Perhaps she could make some progress after all. She kept her expression quiet in an attempt to hide her excitement. "What time?"

"Seven."

"Great. See you then."

COVE HOUSE, a rambling sea-buffed cottage of brown shingles, sat on the southwestern end of the island where the rocks sloped gently to the water's edge. Beyond it was a small converted lobster shack that served as Linus's studio.

The front door to the house was open. All the rooms on the first floor were lit with gas lamps that cast a warm glow into the mauve dusk. Addie went directly into the living room, a comfortable old piece filled with art and books and papers, a bachelor pad of sagging slipcovered couches and dowdy chairs. Linus, who was by the kitchen door, blew her a kiss and mouthed a welcome.

They were all there, the Wests, the Tatlins, Kevin Morgan, Sally Draper, George Evans, Meg St. John, even Gruesin and Roberts and there were also a couple of other people she had never seen before. As for Jason Farrell, he stood at the window talking with Ivy Tatlin and did not turn at her entrance.

It was George Evans, of course, who boomed her name out at once. "Adele Cordero, cat-sitter supreme," he cried, flailing his arms and almost spilling his drink. He was part of a circle sitting around the stone fireplace that included Veronica West, Meg St. John and Kevin Morgan. "Had the ritual dunking, I heard," he went on with a harsh roar that was meant to pass for a laugh. "First you find a body and then you almost become one. Man, we're going to have to send you around with a bodyguard. And," he added with a sly glance at Meg St. John, "I'm volunteering for the job."

Addie pulled up a chair. "I guess when I write that essay on what I did for my summer vacation, it'll be a doozy."

"Oh, you'll pass with flying colors," Meg said. "Maybe you'd better go into hiding for the rest of the vacation."

"I was considering it, but the lure of your company persuaded me otherwise."

At the sound of George Evans's voice, Jason had turned around and nodded at her, not breaking his conversation with the young musician. Addie pointedly ignored him. She turned to Kevin Morgan. "Tell me, doctor, what's your specialty?"

Veronica interrupted with a high, little laugh before he could answer. "Poetic license."

Kevin smiled patiently. Addie thought he was really rather good-natured, considering the digs both Veronica and her husband seemed to level at him about his poetry. She glanced up to find Jason watching her from across the room. Serve him right, she thought, if she entered into a flirtation with Kevin, even had a date or two with him. Then Addie wondered why she wanted to make Jason jealous when she knew nothing about the man and didn't dare trust him. She was diverted by the doctor's thoughtful answer.

"I'm a general practitioner."

"A dying breed," George Evans said. "Or is the breed dying because you're attending them?"

Kevin was the first to laugh. "Oh, we're coming back," he said in his soft, inviting voice. "The specialists have specialized themselves into a corner. What the average citizen wants is to be able to go to the same doctor whether it's warts or—"

"Acid indigestion," George finished for him.

"I may have to come to you for help," Addie said. "Sometimes I get an awful allergy to cats and I left my pills at home. And," she said with a glance at George Evans, "with Fitzgibbon hanging around Winehart, I may have a problem."

"Any antihistamine will do," the doctor told her with an earnest smile.

"The over-the-counter pills make me fall asleep," Addie said.

"Go on, Kevin," Veronica urged. "Write the lady a prescription."

She suddenly realized that all Kevin had to do was write her a prescription and she'd have a sample of his handwriting. She had to repress a smile at how easy it was going to be. And if he *were* Enigma...she shuddered slightly and left the thought unfinished.

To Addie's annoyance, Linus broke up the conversation before Kevin could follow through on Veronica's suggestion. He handed Addie a wineglass. "Seems to me you were drinking white wine at the Wests," he said.

She supposed she'd have to fake an allergy attack later to get the prescription. She smiled at Linus, saying "Well, thank you, how good of you to remember." Taking a sip of the dry, mellow wine, Addie understood just how successful an artist Linus was: it was all there in the expensive wine in its crystal glass, the Persian carpet underfoot, and in his collection of paintings and sculptures, many clearly by other talented and well-known artists, as though he had no need to sell himself or even his work.

"I'm dying to see your paintings," she said to him.

"In time, all in due time. First things first, however," he said. "Meg has kindly offered us a first reading of her new play, 'Island Sacrifice.'"

"Inspired by those odd sacrifices that go down at Gull Rock," George threw in.

"Ignore him," Meg said, reaching for the copious bag at her side and pulling out a pile of manuscripts. "Had to

send to Port Clyde to make copies but I don't think I have
enough anyway. You'll have to pair up, folks.''

Addie looked across the room and caught Jason's eye
and crooked grin. She smiled back. Egos, his expression
stated clearly, the island could sink under the weight of all
the egos on it.

Kevin took a copy of the play from Meg and came over
to Addie and sat on the arm of her chair. "We'll share," he
said, bending over her. Addie, knowing that Jason's eye
was still on her, felt her face grow warm. She reached for
the play and held it up so that they both could see it. There
were some scribbled notes on the margin.

"Are these your notations?" she asked Meg.

"Right. I can't put down two words without changing
them. A thousand apologies. I didn't have time to retype
the play and send for fresh copies."

As Addie had expected, the handwriting was not Enigma's. She looked around the living room and took in Linus's guests, each in turn, as Meg began to read her play.
George and Veronica were standing together at the fireplace bent over a script, Veronica's expression one of deep
concentration. Gruesin and Roberts, together as usual,
seemed to be having a hard time paying attention. Steve
West, alone in a corner, stared moodily into a drink. His
copy of the manuscript rested on his lap unopened.

Meg read on, smiling at her audience every now and then
and gesturing to make a point. Sally Draper, sitting on the
couch, shared her manuscript with the two young men who
sat on either side of her. Vladimir Tatlin walked restlessly
around the room, gazing at paintings while his wife and
Jason shared a script.

Enigma was still among them and Addie was scarcely
closer to him now than when she had stepped off the boat
from Port Clyde.

Kevin Morgan took the manuscript out of her hand,
turned the page and was about to hand it back to her when
Linus came over and whispered in her ear. "Come on, no
one will miss us. I promised to show you my pictures and I

guarantee they're much more interesting than 'Island Sacrifice.'"

Addie threw an apologetic glance at Kevin and he gave her a little disappointed shrug in return. She slid from her seat and followed Linus through the kitchen and out the back. It wasn't quite dark yet, just that short breath of space when the night seems suspended and anything could happen.

Linus's studio was lit by gas lamps, which he turned on one by one. In a few moments the interior shone with a genteel glow that seemed to come from another century. There were canvases and framed paintings all over the sizable space, huddled against the walls, piled on tables, and stuffed into racks. An unfinished work stood on a sturdy easel.

"Can't paint here at night," he explained. "The light's off, but for showing my works, it's just about perfect." With a self-deprecating little laugh that Addie knew he didn't believe for a minute, he added, "Sell most of my works at night."

Addie looked around the studio in awe. "I don't know where to begin, Linus."

"Start with my Gull Rock, Mornings, series. I'm about to ship them to my New York gallery." He held up a small canvas of the familiar scene and the very tidal pool that had, two days before, thrown up a corpse.

"I'd better get back to my guests," he told her putting the painting back. "I might even be able to cut Meg off at the pass by handing around some food. Take your time looking. When you're finished, snuff out the lights and close the door. I'll lock up later." He handed her the flashlight. "You keep it. I know the path back well enough."

Addie waited for him to leave, then did what she'd been aching to do from the moment she'd entered the studio: examine his handwriting. But she was in for a disappointment. He signed his name in clear, printed, upright letters, and always with delicately handled brush strokes.

She would find a note in his handwriting, she had to. She went slowly around the studio. There was a sudden gust of wind and Addie felt rather than saw the studio door slam shut. When she grabbed the ancient knob, she saw almost at once that it was a useless appendage. She remembered now; the door locked with a simple combination lock on the outside of the door. When she tried to pry the door open, it wouldn't budge.

The only windows were a bubble skylight cut into the roof and a high, circular window over the door that looked like it was nailed shut. Addie tried to still the quickened beating of her heart. She could hear laughter from the house and knew that if she called out someone was bound to hear her. Maybe. She heard the screen door slam.

Someone was outside. She could hear muted footsteps on the gravel. In the silence that followed, the only sound was the chirp of insects. Then she heard a small noise but to Addie in the still space, it seemed to explode like a bomb. Someone was trying to push the door open.

"Linus?" She asked the question softly, wondering why fear pounded at her heart.

The door slid open and Kevin Morgan stood there. "Linus managed to stop Meg halfway through the first act by handing around food. She's in retreat and not a minute too soon," he said. "I was sent to fetch you."

"Great." She was just about to follow him when she realized there was a note tacked to the door. She had been so blinded by irrational fear, she hadn't noticed it before. Pretending interest in a group of paintings nearby, she began going through them one by one to cover her interest in the note.

"I just love Linus's work, don't you?" she said enthusiastically.

Kevin came over to her and slid his hand around her waist. "Mmm, especially when they smell like Chanel No. 5."

"I'm not wearing Chanel No. 5," Addie said as she moved away from Kevin and over to the door. The note, in a careful, upright hand and signed by Linus Bishop, contained a short message and some names and addresses. Bless you, Linus, she thought, you're decidedly not Enigma.

Kevin came up behind her and put his arms around her, resting his chin on her shoulder. "'In the event of an emergency,'" he read, "'contact any of the following.' I like the contact part the best."

"Kevin," she said exasperated, "what are you doing?"

He smiled and his grip tightened. "I knew the minute I saw you that you'd add a bit of interest to an otherwise dull summer." He bent his head toward her and Addie knew that if she didn't move swiftly, he'd try to kiss her. She pushed at his chest but he didn't loosen his grip. She noted the scent of liquor on his breath.

"The answer is no, Kevin, to whatever you have in mind."

He moved back as if stung. "Hcy, no offense," he held up his hands. "I just thought . . ."

"Let's forget it. Just a small misunderstanding." She went sweeping past him out the door. She had asked for it but if she wanted a sample of the man's handwriting, she'd have to keep communications open between them. "I'm starved," she said, "aren't you?"

"So I am," he said, tossing her a charming smile that did not seem at all forced.

"Oh, come on then," she said heading back along the path.

He came up behind her and, in a quick gesture, drew his fingers along her neck. "Hungry," he murmured, "but not for food."

Chapter Nine

Addie moved quickly away from Kevin's touch and achieved the back door of Linus's house at a near run. Still, when she reached for the doorknob, Kevin beat her to it, placing his hand over hers for a moment. She pulled away and he laughed lightly. She realized then that he had probably been drinking a little too much.

He pushed the door open and stood aside, bowing her in. "Mademoiselle, entrez."

"Thank you, kind sir." She whisked past him, relieved that he wasn't going to hold any grudges. It would make going to him for a prescription later much easier. Another day or two should do the trick. She would have to practice the art of the big sneeze. His handwriting would undoubtedly be in a doctor's cramped, busy hand, readable only by pharmacologists. There were at least three samples in her possession that would fit that bill.

When they came into the living room, Meg was holding forth in an animated conversation with Veronica West. She never missed a beat although Veronica turned to gaze at both Addie and Kevin in a distracted manner.

Jason, too, caught their entrance, his eye sliding quickly to Kevin and then back to Addie.

She found herself wanting to smile with something that might resemble triumph, but didn't dare. Jason was exhibiting all the signs of jealousy she could have hoped for. The idea unsettled her yet filled her with a heady excitement that drew a flush to her cheeks. Her instincts, as always, whispered that Jason wasn't Enigma. He couldn't be. He was too smart, too attractive, too relaxed, too masculine.

Foolish girl, she told herself, throwing him the merest glance. She deliberately went over to Linus, who was standing at the serving board, dispensing wedges of the local cheddar cheese with crackers. "Your paintings are so beautiful," she said. "I'm overwhelmed."

Linus leaned over the cheese board and cut a slice for her, which he popped into her mouth. "Thank you, my dear, I've been waiting for just such a compliment all evening."

She threw him a genuinely happy smile. He wasn't Enigma, and that was cause for a celebration. In another moment, however, the shattering thought struck her that Linus also fit the bill as a possible target for Enigma since the police weren't certain that Enigma never victimized men.

"Cooking snails in a little while over the fire," he told her, pointing to the brick fireplace in which logs were burning merrily.

She wanted to say something, but of course she couldn't. She was chasing ephemera with a butterfly net made of cobwebs. And she had no desire to taste snails, roasted or otherwise even if they were the only dinner she would get. She took another wedge of cheese, some crackers and a glass of wine and stood surveying the crowd.

Sally Draper, off the hook. Meg St. John, off the hook. Vladimir and Ivy Tatlin, off the hook. Dear Linus, off the hook. The owner of the foreign handwriting, possibly Veronica or Noah Roberts, off the hook. Leaving Addie with a neat half dozen or maybe a baker's half dozen suspects. Jason, Kevin, Tim Gruesin, Steven West and George Evans. Maybe Veronica. Maybe Noah Roberts.

Jason came over to her. "What do you think of Linus's work?"

"What I think of Linus. Splendid just about describes both the artist and his paintings. I didn't dare ask the price of even the smallest."

"Addie," Jason said suddenly, reaching for her glass of wine, which he put down on the table, "I hate small talk. Let's get out of here."

She thought of the snails. She thought of Enigma. She thought of Jason's handwriting. It seemed worth the risk—after all there were too many witnesses to their leaving together for Enigma to risk anything. She made her apologies to Linus, giving him a kiss on the cheek. "Long day, Linus. That adventure in the water has exhausted me. You won't mind if I leave."

"Snails can't tempt you, is that it?"

She put her hand on the artist's arm. "I am tired, Linus."

His smile took in Jason. "Right, better hurry. Fog's starting to roll in."

Outside a half moon shared space in the sky with high skittering clouds. The water seemed extraordinarily still, a silver path sprinkled along its surface by the moon. The developing fog, which seemed to hover over the hilltop, lent a whitish haze to the night.

"Hungry?" Jason asked.

"Starved."

"Come on, then, so am I. We'll get something at the inn."

"Served without small talk."

"Promise."

WHEN THEY ASKED for the dinner menu the night manager apologized profusely and explained that the kitchen at the Island Inn closed at eight-thirty.

"Maybe you could scrounge up a couple of sandwiches for us," Jason suggested.

The manager gave them an obliging smile. "If you're not particular."

"Do we look particular?" Jason said.

"You planned this, didn't you?" Addie asked when they were seated in a small bay window that doubled for a sun porch in Jason's room on the second floor. On the table between them were a plate of sandwiches, a bowl of potato chips and a small jar of pickles. She glanced around the bright and airy room. It was of a medium size with rose-patterned wallpaper, and furnished with old oak pieces. The floor was of wide pine boards stained a honey color and there were two needlepoint rugs. There was a bed and a white wicker couch as well. Bedspread and window curtains were of a starched white muslin. A variety of well-framed paintings were hung on the walls and above the fireplace.

A large bouquet of fresh flowers stood on a table below the window and the room held a respectful air of scarcely being lived in. Jason Farrell, she decided, was very neat in his habits. Not a piece of paper in sight. She'd have to dig a little.

"Planned all this? Right," Jason said with a grin. "I bribed Linus to throw a party, make certain you came and even brought the snails as I had a sneaking suspicion you'd starve rather than eat them."

"I don't even know why I bothered asking."

"I think a more important question is, why did you agree to leave with me? I thought I was on your list of disagreeable things, well below snails."

She hesitated before answering. Why had she come? Because she was stupidly attracted to him, because once again she wasn't paying attention to what her brain told her.

Because, she thought with a sigh, she still needed a sample of his damn handwriting. Hopefully it would prove, once and for all, that he wasn't Enigma and really hadn't been trying to kill her at the cave. "I wanted to see your photographs," she said with an uneasy laugh.

He studied her for a moment. "That assumes I carry around a portfolio for the specific purpose of luring beautiful women to my room on the pretext of showing them my photographs and with every intention of seducing them."

"Oh, I figured you'd have something for all emergencies," she told him. "First-aid kit for scratches and other minor disasters, photographs for showing that you're not all starched and professorial.''

"Clever, Addie, you caught me out and not a minute too soon. As a matter of fact, I do have some photographs with me. A gallery in Boston expressed an interest in seeing some of my work.''

"Ah, Boston. The name of the gallery, please. I'm a regular gallery goer.''

"Boston, hub of the intellectual universe, so they tell me.''

"Name of the gallery, please, Jason. I'll bet I know it.''

"Boston Arts," he said with some hesitation. "They have a new photography department.''

She'd get Pam to check it out. "I'm impressed," she said. "Have you exhibited before?''

He shrugged. "Group shows, mostly at the university. I might add that the Boston gallery owner and I went to school together.''

Addie shook her head. "That's right, soften the blow before I see them and form my own opinion.''

Jason grinned and abruptly went over to the closet. He pulled out a suitcase and extracted from it a small portfolio, held together with strings, which he undid with great care. He removed several black-and-white photographs framed in white mattes and placed them on the bed side by side.

"Not the best way to view them," he said, standing back and eyeing his work critically.

"Oh," Addie said, easily expressing her surprise. "Somehow I thought they'd be of Galbraith, but of course they wouldn't be.''

His subject matter was instantly recognizable, each picture taken straight on in a pure, clear light as though Jason Farrell weren't a man for subterfuge.

There was one of the Washington Monument, a powerful white monolith taken at a very dramatic moment, as though it were a shaft of light caught against a darkening sky roiling with heavy clouds. She glanced at Jason and was surprised to find him frowning down at the photograph as though he were seeing it for the first time.

Next she picked up a vivid photograph of a rundown area filled with a jungle of signs, garish store windows, lampposts, wire strung overhead and indigents lounging lazily about. It could be Washington or it could be Anywhere, U.S.A.

Then there was a photograph of children playing on a sidewalk in front of a long wooden fence covered with graffiti; their figures had been caught in a moment of exhilaration.

"Some children have trees and grass and some have graffiti," she observed.

Jason silently picked up and handed her a view of the Lincoln Memorial, the great man sitting stolidly in his chair, his strong face in deep, thoughtful shadows. Below him stood half a dozen tourists looking not at Lincoln, but at Lincoln in the viewfinders of their cameras. Addie didn't profess to any knowledge about photography. She understood enough to be deeply impressed with the sharpened contrasts of black, gray and white, the composition, the clarity of the scene and its irony. Pretty good work for a history professor, she admitted to herself.

"Jason, where are you from?"

"Washington."

"Teach at the university there?"

"You got it."

"No wife, no kids tucked away?"

"Would it matter, Addie?"

"Yes, of course it would."

"Mind if I mull over the implications of that remark?"

She laughed. "Better not. I'm not even certain what I meant. It's just that I'm here alone with you in your hotel room. If you had a wife...."

"Which I don't, not now and not in the past."

"If you had a wife and she called."

"She won't, as she hasn't been invented yet."

"Well, I'm glad you haven't invented her on my account." Addie reached over and picked up another photograph. It was of a diner on a highway. Stark, dramatic, lonely, the sky awash in cirrus clouds. "Why are you on Galbraith? I don't see any nature photographs here. From the look of these, you're interested in the human condition and its icons."

"So am I. I've always liked to photograph what man hath wrought, but it's about time I moved on to the natural world to capture what he hasn't destroyed yet."

"And that's why you're here, of all the places in all the world."

"That just about describes it," he said.

She turned the photographs over one by one. No handwriting, just labels with typewritten descriptions of the scene, his name and a date. She turned the photographs face up. "No signature. The gallery will want a signature."

"They'll get it by and by."

She handed them back. "Angry skies, bleak downtown areas, tourists who sightsee through their viewfinders. Are you the last angry man?"

"I point the camera and go click."

"You're awfully talented, you know."

"Just a hobby," he said quickly and began to gather up the photographs.

"No don't," Addie said. "They're wonderful, creative and sensitive. I'm impressed, Jason. Why aren't they sitting around the room so you could see them?"

"Gathering dust?" He seemed embarrassed by her enthusiasm and quickly put the photographs back into the portfolio. "Anyone in possession of a good camera could take the same thing."

"You don't believe that any more than I do."

He looked over at her. "Don't I?"

"No."

"An unequivocal no. Obviously you understand more about me than I do about myself."

"On the contrary, I know absolutely nothing about you. I'm judging the message, not the messenger. Why do you do that, denigrate your talent? If you think so little of your work, why did you show the photographs to me in the first place? Then, when I complimented you, you stepped back. Why are you carrying them around with you and offering them for exhibit in Boston?"

He sucked in a breath and stared at her in apparent surprise. "Lady, you ask a lot of whys."

They stood facing each other, a couple of feet apart, hands clenched at their sides. "Yes, I suppose I do," Addie responded thoughtfully.

"Keep asking them," he said in a quiet voice. "I think I like your questions, tough as they may be."

She knew she should turn and run away, not face the anticipation that all but heated up the air around them. This wasn't the right time. "Funny, but I think I've just about finished with questions for the time being." Even so, his willingness to face her questions pleased her. It was quite a change from Rafe. Jason seemed a man she could trust.

And then the whole world began to fade into some gray, floating mist. They were two people alone in a hotel room on a remote island in the midst of the endless, punishing ocean. The danger snarling and yipping around them was suddenly forgotten.

Jason's look spoke of too many lonely nights, too few people to care about. Addie had seen that look before; she recognized it in herself, but still, aimed at her that way, it broke through her defenses.

Whoever he was, this Jason Farrell walked a strange line and Addie wasn't afraid of him. In fact, for reasons she didn't understand, she hadn't been since they had stood clutched in each other's arms out at White Head. She had been soaking wet, shivering, in shock. Yet it was the hammering of his heart in unison with her own rattled beat that had calmed her, warmed her, made her want to trust him.

Now, standing here under his gaze, Addie knew he would reach out to her. And with every pulsing nerve ending she wanted him to.

Jason hadn't moved and yet everything had changed. Without a word he reached for her and pulled her into his arms. There were no preliminaries, no hesitations and Addie made no attempt to resist the kiss he bent to give her. He held her close, his mouth joined to hers, the beat of his heart matching the wild rhythms of her own. But his tender caress was new, different, in a way that stunned her. She drew her arms around his neck and it was her own sudden aggressive movement that stayed her, made her pull back. What was she doing?

The smile he gave her was unexpectedly open. "And just when we were beginning to get along so well," he said, relinquishing his hold on her.

"We were talking about photography, I think." The words came out in a breathless little stutter.

"No, we weren't. We were talking about everything but photography, Addie." He reached for her again.

"Oh, that's right. We were talking about how anyone can point a camera and come up with the same photo." She disengaged herself from his embrace and moved on rubbery legs to the other side of the room. "How about letting me see more of your work?" She snapped her fingers together and groaned. "I mean more photographs."

"You've seen the entire Farrell collection. For more you'll have to come down to Washington. I'll gladly give you a private viewing."

"Thanks. I'll wait for the Boston opening."

"You may have to wait a year."

"It'll be worth it," she told him with a smile.

He gazed at her for a long moment then seemed to resign himself to the change in topic. "I'm fascinated with photography, fascinated with its possibilities," he told her in an unexpected burst of enthusiasm. "Maybe I don't think it's art. Maybe anyone with a good eye and good timing can do the same thing. I can't explain why I walk around with a camera as an appendage."

He continued. "Look, tell you what, I can explain myself better if you can see the direction I'm headed. Photographywise, that is," he added with a grin. "There's a magazine downstairs in the lobby that shows a group of photographs similar to what I've been trying to get at." He pointed to the uneaten food on the table. "Help yourself. I'll be right back."

She put her hand out. "Jason." But he was already gone, closing the door quietly behind him. Addie waited a pulse beat or two. She heard his footsteps move off down the corridor. He seemed to be taking the stairs two at a time.

She couldn't afford to forget for a moment why she was on Galbraith. He had calmly left her alone in his room, giving her carte blanche to spy. She couldn't let this opportunity pass by and she hadn't a minute to waste.

She began a systematic search of the room. There had to be something with his handwriting on it. She went through two suit jackets hanging in the closet. She opened drawers and rummaged through them. She examined the notepad on the night table and came up empty.

She pulled at the small drawer in the night table. It opened easily, silently.

"Ah, pay dirt."

His black leather wallet lay under a striped handkerchief. She stared at it for a moment or two, still tasting his lips, still feeling the warmth of his arms around her. Perhaps she didn't want to learn more about Jason Farrell than she already knew.

"He's not Enigma." The words were ground out. Addie couldn't be that much of a fool. Like those others, those sad women who had died trusting.

She reached gingerly for the wallet. Against her better judgment she must see Jason Farrell in every possible light, including the message revealed by his handwriting.

She held the wallet in her hand an instant longer, putting off the moment of truth. She flipped it open. Stamps, some cash and two or three credit cards. She ran her finger along the soft edge of a much-worn license. His signature might have to do. As she reached for a credit card, she heard the door open and snapped the wallet shut. She didn't even try to put the wallet back as Jason stepped into the room, closing the door behind him. Addie felt an icy shiver of fear.

"It's not what you think," she began.

"Maybe I've got it all wrong," he said in a low, tight voice, "maybe you're nothing more than a common thief." He came toward her slowly, watching her out of veiled eyes. "Maybe you're not even a psychologist. I've already written off your graphological abilities. Maybe you've got a record as long as my arm. Anything is possible."

Addie swallowed hard, knowing there was nothing she could say. She could feel the soft, leathery surface of the wallet between her fingertips. It felt as heavy as if it were stuffed with gold bars.

"Look, I'm sorry," she began lamely. "You don't think I'm interested in your money."

He looked down at the wallet but made no move to retrieve it.

"All right," she said as forcefully as she could, "I'm a little compulsive about handwriting."

"That so?"

She shoved the wallet at him. "Here. I did something stupid and I'd like to apologize."

"Go ahead." He put the wallet into his back pocket without looking at it.

"I'm sorry." The words sounded empty enough. He had caught her in an act of thievery and any apology she might make would sound equally hollow. "Look, I *am* a psychologist, Jason."

"Patients know you're given to thievery?"

She decided to ignore his remark and plowed on. "I'm a little compulsive about graphology. It's fast, accurate and—"

"Accurate?" His look was unbelieving. "I believe it can be a great scientific tool, Addie, but not in unskilled hands."

"Jason, just listen to me, please. We're talking about one thing only. You caught me with my hand in the cookie jar. I wasn't after cookies, I was after *you*. Oh, dammit, you know what I mean. I'm stumbling over myself," she said when he gave her an involuntary smile. "I've discovered that reading handwritings gives me an edge in profiling the problems of my patients. Wading through their subterfuge and defenses takes up too much time. I rely on a cleaner, simpler, more direct route to the truth."

"Simpler, more direct route to the truth? Methinks the lady protests too much. I don't believe a word you're saying."

"I'm sorry, then. I was curious about you and I did a very stupid thing."

He laughed out loud, a good, tension-releasing bellow. "Well I'll be. Know what, Addie, I believe you. Just think, you needn't bother with a visceral reaction to a man at all. You could send for a husband through the mail. Attraction has nothing to do with it."

"You're afraid to let me see your handwriting."

"I'm not afraid. You already read my handwriting. It was like reading tea leaves, some truths you stumbled on to, but as for discerning the real Jason Farrell and what makes him tick, better consult the expert, namely me. You were off a hundred and ninety degrees. But that's not what's stopping me. I believe in eye, body and mind contact, not scribbles on a piece of paper. You take me as you see me. The guy who thinks you're bright, charming, a pretty sexy number and a good kisser as we used to say at George Washington High. What you just pulled indicates an aberration of some kind I'm perfectly willing to forgive. But Addie, I never did like tests. You make what happened between us sound like a job application. Not complete because I didn't sign my name on the dotted line. Why don't

I give you another sample of the work I do and we can dump the other nonsense?''

He didn't wait for her to respond and she wasn't quick enough to fend him off. In an instant his arms locked around her and this time when his lips came down on hers, they were hard and insistent.

A flash of fear flooded through her blocking out any other sensation. Who was he, this man who crushed her so tightly she could feel his heartbeat, could feel his body responding to hers? She tried desperately to resist, to hold herself rigid, but as his kiss deepened, it changed, softened, asked for a response. A glowing heat melted all resistance.

And in spite of logic, she did respond. She opened her mouth to him, felt his body mold itself to hers. She raised her arms to hold him, aware of a dizzying sensation of falling and soaring at the same time.

Perhaps his mistake was to pull back, to smile at her as though it were a game he might be winning.

A window opened in her mind, letting in a prudent gust of reality. Four people were dead. She had come to find a madman who, incidentally, was possessed of a high degree of sexuality. She'd known that before coming to Galbraith, and she'd still allowed herself to be lured into a stranger's hotel room. Locked in an embrace, possibly with the very man she'd been sent to find was one of the stupider moves of her life. Somewhere devils were laughing.

Without saying a word Addie pulled herself out of his arms, grabbed her bag and went straight to the door. She reached for the handle, then paused. She might be walking out on the most important moment of her life but if she was wrong about Jason she couldn't afford to stay and find out. The room was dead silent. He was waiting, not believing for a moment that she would walk out on him. She turned the knob, heard the discreet sound of the lock disengaging and pulled the door open. Another second and she'd slipped through and closed the door behind her.

Chapter Ten

The Lincoln Memorial. The Washington Monument. Children playing in the dust against a background of graffiti. A sleazy downtown view of what was possibly the nation's capital.

"Where are you from, Jason?"

"Washington."

"You teach at the University."

"Yes." Or words to that effect. And Addie, coming slowly down the stairs of the Island Inn, knew there was something else she'd never forget about Jason Farrell, besides a near drowning because of a miscalculated tidal hour. He was protecting someone on the island, and Washington was a long way from Galbraith.

The trouble was, she could still feel the warm pressure of his kiss and the tender way he had held her. She had liked it a little too much; wanted the feeling to go on forever. Damn, she was letting her emotions run away with her. She wasn't on vacation. Galbraith wasn't Club Med and she knew Jason Farrell wasn't on the island just to pass the time of day. She couldn't afford any mistakes.

But Jason wasn't Enigma, Addie would stake her life on it. She wanted to believe it. Anyway she was certain Enigma would have pressed his advantage, and worse, wouldn't have let her go so easily.

However, reason told her it was time to call Pam, time to ask for a background check on Professor Farrell to find out just who he was. The night manager was sitting behind the reception desk reading a newspaper; there was no one at the switchboard.

"Is the phone working?" Addie asked, already knowing the answer.

He gave her an apologetic smile. "By tomorrow morning, that's what they tell me."

"Thanks. By the way, would you know when ferry service will be restored?"

"Tomorrow, too. Everybody's been asking the same question."

Addie noted the time, ten-thirty. Several people were still lounging around the lobby. Someone was bent over the record player, listening to a recording of birdcalls. A chess game was in progress near the window. One of the players, she saw with surprise, was Tim Gruesin. A quick check failed to reveal the presence of Noah Roberts. Odd. She had begun to think of them as a team. She stared at Gruesin. Hadn't he questioned Jason about seeing him in Boston? Jason's answer at the time had been appropriately vague. She wanted a sample of Gruesin's handwriting and wondered how to find an unobtrusive way of approaching him.

Gruesin's air of concentration, however, was forbidding and Addie had already had a long day. She decided to tackle him in the morning. At the front door she cast a last lingering glance around the lobby. She wasn't in the least sleepy and didn't look forward to the long lonely walk up the hill to her cottage. And, as she discovered the moment she stepped outside, it promised to be tough going. A dense fog had settled heavily over the island, accompanied by the lugubrious blast of the foghorn.

To make matters worse, she had left her flashlight in Jason's room. She stood on the porch steps wondering how she could go back and retrieve it with dignity. Two figures emerged from the fog and came up the steps.

"Flashlight won't help you," one of them said to Addie, echoing her thought uncannily. "Bounces the light right back at you. Best thing is one step at a time. And stick to the town road, macadam underfoot.''

"Damn foghorn,'' his companion said. "Could make you crazy bleating like that every few seconds.''

"Well, good night,'' Addie said. "Wish me luck.''

"Just take it easy.'' They pushed the door open and stepped into the brightly lit lobby. Once again Addie heard the record player and the sound of birdcalls and the murmur of voices. Then she stepped out into the thick and murky soup. The foghorn sounded. There was an odd, fragrant breeze that carried the scent of night sea air mixed with the heavy odor of ripe flower petals. In the sudden, intense silence between the warning notes of the foghorn the world seemed to stop, then the foghorn intervened again, nagging and insistent.

It was easy enough making her way along the macadam road, knowing that buildings lined either side, the post office, the general store, a small restaurant that was a popular hangout. Once the road began to swing up into the hills, however, the fog thickened considerably; it was a gauzy curtain that distorted images. At the turnoff toward Winehart, the road was no longer paved. Trees took on the shapes of discus throwers or boxers, crouched into exotic positions through decades of fighting the strong sea winds. Dark unidentifiable shapes loomed up suddenly like creatures out of the ocean covered with sea weeds.

Addie experienced a sense of impending disaster, of someone nearby quietly waiting. It had nothing to do with the fog. Once a creature skittered across her path and disappeared on the other side of the road and she barely held back a scream. It was bigger than a cat, a raccoon probably. She heard it rustling in the grass, the small sound obliterated almost at once by the foghorn. She thought of turning back to the Inn but had passed the point of no return.

The foghorn ceased its cry and time seemed to stretch as though the foghorn was gathering its breath. In the time between blasts Addie heard the clear scrape of a footstep.

She stopped. The scraping continued, slowly and inexorably, but she couldn't be certain of its direction. She turned and saw nothing but masses of pale, shifting fog. The foghorn sounded once again. She hurried on, looking for known rocks or trees and not finding them. It was as though they had moved or turned around or even cast themselves into unfamiliar shapes.

She cursed herself for ignoring the very real danger signs that were already there and had nothing to do with rocks or trees. At West Wind Linus had seen her slipping the handwriting samples into her bag. If he had, then others could have as well, principally Enigma. She had dismissed the intruder at the Winehart Cottage as a village kid bent on mischief, merely because of a gum wrapper and a piece of silver foil. But it could have been Enigma looking for those samples.

And then there was the matter of the high tide. Someone had told Jason a lie, or else Jason himself had lied to her. Addie's heart began to beat preternaturally fast.

The foghorn stopped again, or perhaps it was the dead silence that intervened. There was another scrape along the road. A dark shadow planted itself in the middle of the road ahead of her.

Addie glanced quickly around. It seemed to her that the shrubbery had assumed human form and that she was surrounded with no way out. The shadow on the road moved toward her, materializing slowly, like a negative in a photographic solution. Suddenly a man stood before her blocking her path and smiling.

"It's you," Noah Roberts said in a conversational tone. "I heard your footsteps and wondered who else would be fool enough to come out on a night like this."

Her heart rocketed in her chest. It was a moment before she could speak. "Linus warned me about the fog, but I had no idea it could be like this," she said in a shaky voice.

"I'm trying to get back to West Wind," he told her.

"You're a long way off, aren't you?"

He laughed in an embarrassed way. "I figured on a shortcut but there's a forest in between. I haven't been out alone since I got here. And the wife says I don't have much of a sense of direction to begin with."

A wife, a genuine wife who berated him about his sense of direction. Addie's relief was a palpable, visible thing. Somewhere there was a wife. "Are you sure you're going in the right direction now?" she asked.

"I'm headed back to the Island Inn. If I have to sleep in the lobby all night, I will."

"Do you think the fog will linger through the night?" Addie was talking rapidly now, not really listening carefully to his answers.

He shrugged. "Your guess is as good as mine. Which way are you headed?"

Her mind raced. Wife or no she had to calculate the weight of his question. "My place is just along the road a bit," she admitted. "No problem. I could walk it blindfolded." She started down the road. "Well, good night."

"I'd better tail along, see you arrive where you're going," he said.

"No, thanks, that's very kind of you but I'm perfectly all right."

He took her arm insistently. "Wouldn't want you missing your turn. You could hit the edge of a cliff and before you knew what happened to you..." He left the sentence unfinished. "I'd hate to be responsible. Hey," he added, looking curiously at her, "you're the one who found that body, aren't you? What was that place called? A bird something."

"Gull Rock."

"Ever learn who he was?"

"Nobody's confided in me, Mr. Roberts."

"Noah, to you."

She saw the small sign that indicated the turnoff to the Winehart Cottage. "Okay, thanks, Noah, I'm fine now." She extricated herself from his grasp, then stuck her hand out.

"Come on, I'll see you to your front porch. It's my duty as an American citizen." The last was said with a broad smile.

"I really can make it on my own. In fact, I'll wait right here and make certain you turn back in the right direction," she said, "You've done enough, American citizen or not. Incidentally, I can't make out your accent. Where are you from?"

"The state of Oregon."

"I mean originally."

"I'm American born, bred and schooled. My parents were from Norway, however," he said with the air of having told the story more often than he liked. "I spoke Norwegian until I was a teenager. But, believe me, I'm as American as you are." He took her hand and squeezed it. "Come along, let's see you tucked safely inside."

Addie felt a panic so intense it took concentration and willpower to keep her outwardly calm. She looked helplessly around, wondering if she could cut and run. Run past the cottage into the tangle of bushes behind the house. Hide until he was gone, or crash through down the hillside until she hit the safety of the village. Or she could head for George Evans's house or Sally's a little farther on.

A second dark shape appeared out of the fog and moved toward them silently. The foghorn sounded again. Addie waited, tense, indecisive, aware of Noah stiffening beside her. Then the tension rolled away. It was Jason, taking in Noah's presence with a slight frown.

"I didn't think you could make it this far," he told her. "Why didn't you turn back?"

"I wasn't worried," Addie said. "I'm surprised you were."

"You're a long way from West Wind," Jason said to Noah.

"Man, I'm a long way from everywhere," Noah said. "I was just saying the best thing for me would be to head down to the Island Inn and wait out the fog."

"Thanks for escorting me," Addie said. "I'll be okay now."

Noah saluted her and nodded to Jason. "That blasted foghorn," he muttered to himself, then he turned and in another moment was swallowed up by the fog.

Born and bred and schooled in the United States... If she could believe him, then the small, upright hand with its English correctness couldn't be his. It would be Veronica's.

A tight curl of fear wound its way through her body. There was a very real possibly that Jason had just rescued her from Enigma.

Jason was eying her with curiosity. "Where'd you meet him?"

"He came out of the fog. Nearly scared me to death."

"Come on," he said. "I'll see you to your door."

Addie nodded gratefully, glad that he didn't seem angry about the way she'd left him. She led the way along the path to her cottage. "What made you come after me, anyway?"

"Thought I couldn't let a kiss linger in the air like that."

She wanted to laugh out of sheer relief but didn't dare.

"The truth is," he went on, "I looked out the window, saw the fog, then discovered you'd forgotten your flashlight. I figured that was a clever move on your part."

"Clever? Leaving my flashlight behind after dark?"

"The guest who forgets her umbrella—or flashlight—so she can come back for it, that's what I thought. But you didn't. Stubborn woman, I told myself after a while and came out after you."

"The flashlight wouldn't have done me any good," she told him, "in this pea soup."

"I should have realized someone would come along to rescue you."

"Noah Roberts? He was lost, too."

"But he figured on escorting you home while he was at it."

"Believe me," Addie said. "I wasn't about to let him escort me back to the cottage. Ah," she said, "there's the light in the window."

Before leaving for Linus's party, Addie had lit her kerosene lamp, turning the wick down as far as it could reasonably go. It was still burning, casting a soft reassuring light in the window. As they came up the porch steps, she realized that Fitzgibbon wasn't waiting for her, and assumed he was curled up and warm at George's place.

Addie had learned early that most people on the island left their doors unlocked. However, since her intruder, she had kept the door locked and carried the key with her. When she opened the door, the little foyer was wrapped in deep shadow, broken only by the flickering light from the kerosene lamp. Beyond all was blackness.

The fog seemed to have come into the house with them and, like spirits loose in the night, floated in midair. She turned the wick up on the kerosene lamp and then carried the lamp into the living room. She heard Jason close the door and come in behind her. She remained stock-still on the threshold, holding the lantern up, her mouth open in surprise.

"Trashed," she said to Jason in a breathless voice. "Someone's been here and trashed everything." Then, in another moment, Addie understood why. She ran over to the wall where the David Larimee lithograph should have been, where she had concealed the handwriting samples. She needn't have been so clever. Enigma had been there and had found her hiding place. The picture frame was on the floor. The glass was smashed and her cache of handwriting samples was gone.

Chapter Eleven

"What the devil was he looking for?"

"And I thought he was a Peeping Tom, a little gum-chewing brat who liked opening dresser drawers and casting his eyes on ladies' underthings."

"Addie, make a little sense. What are you talking about?"

She shook her head at the mess, feeling thoroughly numb. She had a sour taste in her mouth and each breath she drew caused a dull, throbbing pain in her chest. Enigma had seen her spirit away the samples and he'd put two and two together. He must have realized she was the link to his identity.

"Oh, God, he's on to me," she said at last. She heard a quiet hysteria building in her voice. She knew the feeling and thought she had conquered it a long time ago. Events were controlling her life and playing havoc with her well-ordered sense of competence.

Jason gripped her shoulders. "Who, Addie, who's on to you?"

"I don't know."

"Somebody's on to you, but you don't know who he is. What was he looking for? Did he find it?"

She nodded dumbly. Nothing was clicking in but the certain knowledge that Jason wasn't responsible for the damage. She had been with him almost all evening. He couldn't have raced up from the Inn, destroyed her place in record time, found the evidence and then circled back to meet her. It made no sense.

"Addie." He said her name gently.

She looked directly into his eyes and found concern and tenderness there. His gaze was direct, his grip on her arms steady and reassuring. *Trust him, you have to. Trust him.* It was visceral, a humming sensation blocking out all other thought. She was functioning as if her clinical training was just so much smoke.

"Where's Fitzgibbon?" she asked. "If he so much as touched a hair on Fitzgibbon's head . . ." She went quickly around the room, kicking lightly at fallen objects with her toe, looking under the couch and chairs. There was a light scratch at the closet door. Addie pulled it open and the cat came scooting out, snarling his anger. When Addie tried to pick him up, he backed away hissing, then went running into the kitchen. She followed him but discovered the porch door open and the cat gone.

She might have to count George Evans out as Enigma, after all. Fitzgibbon wouldn't have gone running into a closet to escape him. Chances were he'd have sat on his haunches and watched the goings-on.

When she came back into the living room, Jason was waiting for her. "You're not plain Addie Cordero," he said without preliminaries, "hardworking psychologist on a much-needed vacation."

It wasn't a question, it was a statement. "Any more than you're plain Jason Farrell, professor of medieval history, address Washington, D.C.," she responded, meeting his glance straight on. It was a gamble, all right, but the mote of light in his eyes, and the admiring smile he flashed at her, told her she was right.

"Who trashed this place and why?"

"I said I don't know. That's an honest answer. You haven't bothered to answer my question. Add an 's' to that. You haven't bothered to answer any of my questions. For instance that business of the tides. You're protecting someone, aren't you?"

"Not protecting him, Addie. I'll deal with him in my own good time. Let's concentrate on you and what happened here tonight. You're hurting, you're into something up to your eyeballs and you need a friend you can trust."

"This character you're protecting tried to kill me, and almost succeeded."

"No, not you. You never figured into his plans at all. I'm the one he was out to get."

Addie stood her ground. Her eyes slipped past him once again to assess the damage in the cottage. Not only had Enigma come there to find the sample of his handwriting that she possessed, but he was in a fury, his anger sudden and unchecked. The first time he had been in her cottage, she had interrupted him by her unexpected arrival. She pulled away from Jason and began methodically to straighten things up.

"I wouldn't if I were you," Jason said.

She spun around. "I don't think the Wineharts would appreciate my housekeeping."

"The sheriff is going to have to be called in, Addie."

"No." She spoke more sharply than she meant to. "And I wish you wouldn't interfere."

Jason reached into his back pocket and extracted a thin leather folder. "The one thing you missed when you ransacked my room," he said, opening it and showing it to her.

"I thought I told you why I was—" She stopped in midsentence. Jason's picture was on a small laminated card that identified him as an employee of the Federal Bureau of Investigation.

She felt a little lift of her heart. The FBI, it was as simple as that. Or was it? Addie realized Jason was watching her closely for a reaction and she had to remind herself how clever Enigma was. She still couldn't afford to trust Jason completely. "I suppose your signature is on the back of the card," she said.

"Probably. Haven't checked it lately."

"I guess we've a lot to tell each other," she said, choosing her words carefully. "Would you like to begin?"

He bent his head in acknowledgement, a small smile playing around his lips. He put the folder back into his pocket with an exaggerated motion. "I see a certain amount of suspicion in your eyes," he said.

"It might go away if you showed me your handwriting."

"It might help more if you'd put a little trust in me."

"Why?" she asked. "Because of your pretty smile?"

"Maybe that's as good a reason as any. I'm taking you on faith, even though I have irrefutable proof that you'd pick my pocket, given the chance. In fact, you had the chance and you did."

"You really like to rub it in."

He shook his head. "That's just what I'm not doing, Addie. I've decided to trust you and I'm asking the same courtesy from you." He waited a long moment then said, "I'm here on business that isn't quite medieval, although trying to trick governments out of money goes back a long way."

"Somebody on the island . . . ?"

He nodded.

"And if I asked who, you'd tell me it's none of my business."

"For the moment. Your turn, Addie. It's confession time."

"I guess I ought to tell you that I'm here at the request of the Boston District Attorney's office."

He smiled. "A lady cop."

"No. I'm a psychologist, as advertised."

"But not a graphologist." He used the words with a certain amount of satisfaction, as though her admission confirmed what he'd known all along.

"On the contrary. I'm a board certified graphologist. That's the reason I'm on Galbraith. And the reason I want to see your handwriting."

He looked at her in astonishment. "Then that little game at West Wind the other night—"

"It wasn't a game," she told him evenly. "But I couldn't afford to reveal anything I knew."

"You mean the Wests invited you for the specific purpose of reading handwritings."

"No. They knew ... know nothing about my reasons for being on Galbraith."

She hesitated. Jason came over to her and placed his hands on her arms. "Addie. Trust me."

She felt the warmth of his hands. She wanted to let everything go, to lean into him, to feel his arms around her. Then she remembered what Pam had said just before Addie left for Galbraith. *Enigma's a lot smarter crook than you are detective.* He would have to be, she thought. He had a lot more experience and much more to lose.

Jason spoke once again, his voice little more than a whisper. "Trust."

The breath she took was deep and seemed to hold all her uncertainty. She glanced past him, taking in the room. Enigma had been there. Enigma had stolen the handwriting samples. Jason had rescued her from Noah Roberts, from the fog; he couldn't possibly have made it to Winehart sooner than she had, in time to wreak all that devastation.

"Jason," she said at last, "I'm here because a certain Mrs. Barnstable was murdered, possibly by a serial killer." She went into a brief description of Enigma's m.o. and how the Boston investigative squad had discovered what they believed to be a sample of the criminal's script at the scene of the Barnstable murder. "We call the killer Enigma," she explained, "because the only clues we have are a single handwriting sample and the similarities in the murders of four women in the Boston area over the past year. If it even is Enigma's handwriting, that is. At any rate, the character traits his script revealed were enough to send us, me, to this island to see if I could find the person who wrote our sample."

She saw Jason's eyes narrow and then darken. He turned his head slightly, as if to view her from another angle. "And is Enigma on the island?"

She had committed herself to telling Jason the truth. If she were wrong, and he was Enigma, the time for being prudent was long past. She was about to take him on as her confidant. She had told Pam finding Enigma was a game she could best play alone, but it hadn't worked out that way. She was scared and she admitted it.

"Addie," Jason said gently, "we're talking about a mysterious character called Enigma. A serial killer. Is Enigma on the island?"

In for a penny, in for a pound, wasn't that the old saying? "Yes," she told Jason. "Someone who possesses that handwriting is. You may know him, too. He was one of the people at the party at West Wind."

Jason whistled. "Do you mean to tell me you discovered a serial killer was present at West Wind and you didn't say a word? You're a pretty cool number."

"Not so cool," she reminded him. "In fact, I was pretty scared and frustrated. The game was played with full anonymity. Which stuck me with a batch of handwriting samples and no names attached."

"And that's why you took the samples with you when you left the party."

Addie groaned. "You saw that, too? I'm really great at detection. I slip a few pieces of paper into my bag and half the world catches me in the act."

"Including the killer," Jason said.

"Including the killer."

"West Wind," Jason said more to himself than Addie. "But he wouldn't have known I was taking you out to see the anemones."

"Who, Jason. Who wouldn't have known?"

"Steven West."

"Is he the one you're protecting?" She saw by the expression on his face that she was right. "And he was there tonight at Linus's," she added. Linus Bishop's party: it seemed eons back in time. "I do believe I smiled at him. I wish I'd known."

"No you don't."

"I've managed to clear a few people, but not West," she mused.

"Steve, a serial murderer? Forget it, Addie. He's too busy enriching himself at the public's expense."

"But you said he tried to kill you."

"Ah, but that was just being expedient, Addie; it had nothing to do with serial murders. I was a fool to have trusted him, that's all."

"Why did you?"

He shrugged. "Maybe I think I'm indestructible."

"Oh, you are. I'm the one who was almost destroyed."

He gave her a sheepish smile and Addie had the distinct impression that he had to stop himself from reaching for her. "Whom have you cleared so far, besides me, that is?" His voice was rough as he asked the question, as though he was making an effort to keep himself in check.

"Ivy and Vladimir Tatlin."

"The violinist and the flutist."

"Um, Sally Draper and Meg St. John. Oh, and tonight, Linus Bishop. Possibly Veronica because I think hers is an English hand, unless of course that handwriting belongs to someone else, in which case Veronica must have learned to write in the United States."

"Spare me the details," Jason said. "Who else?"

"Unless you tell me Steve West has a tiny, upright hand that is light of touch and without any blotches on it, I'd say, that's it."

"I believe his script is small and rather tight, but I wouldn't bet the rent money on it."

"Well, then, we're left with Steve West, Tim Gruesin, Noah Roberts, Kevin Morgan and George Evans. Five or six people, according to whether or not Veronica is included."

"Look," Jason said, "I don't want to go into details, but three of the people on your list are bankers. The FBI has had them under surveillance for a long time. I can't see any of them moonlighting as serial killers without our noticing it."

"Don't be so sure," Addie said. "Enigma is very wily and convincing, I'm certain of it."

Jason creased his brow. "Anything else about that list that strikes you as funny?"

"All men?" she asked after a moment's thought. "No, we can't count Veronica out. We don't know if Enigma's a man. We're just using the all-purpose 'him.'"

"Something else, Addie. With the exception of George Evans, all of them are staying at West Wind."

"You're right. Maybe Enigma has some kind of hold over West. We don't know who he is or why he's here."

"Come on," Jason said with a sudden spurt of energy, "pack a bag with some overnight things. I don't want you hanging around here tonight. Now that he has the writing samples, Enigma might come back to tie up loose ends. Namely you. Know anyone you can trust on the island who might offer you overnight accommodations?"

She shook her head.

"Then you're coming back with me to the Island Inn. They're usually booked solid, but with the recent drowning, maybe a few vacationers with their own transportation have had second thoughts about sticking around."

Addie regarded him solemnly. If he were Enigma, he wouldn't be offering to take her back to the busiest spot on the island. The trek through the fog was along the town road. There were no cliffs to throw her from. And they'd been seen together. If anything happened to her, Jason would have a lot of explaining to do.

"Addie," he said in a gentle tone, "don't even think of staying here alone tonight." Then he said, "If you're worried about trusting me, come out with it."

She flushed. It was Noah Roberts she had to worry about, Noah the born American Jason had rescued her from. Without a word Addie turned and went into her bedroom to pack. There again Pam had been right. Addie liked being in control of her life, but if she locked trust out completely because of her bad experience with Rafe, it would be no kind of life. She knew she was experiencing feelings for this man that she should examine. Wanting to be in his arms was one of them. It was a foolish, dangerous thought. Still, she felt she had no real choice but to leave the cottage, go with him as he asked and if her judgment was right and luck was with her she'd end up safe and sound at the Island Inn.

"JASON, everyone on Galbraith, including Enigma, will hear I've spent the night with you."

"Good," Jason said. "Should keep him at a distance, seeing the bodyguard you have."

Addie planted herself in the center of Jason's room, critically surveying it. One bed and one wicker couch. Her alternative had been to spend the night in the lobby as Noah Roberts and Tim Gruesin had seemed intent upon doing.

"I could have sneaked you in," Jason reminded her with a grin, "but you had to march right up to the reception desk and ask for a room. I told you the hotel was usually filled up."

"You also told me that maybe some of the vacationers had deserted the island like a sinking ship. Anyway, I wanted simple confirmation that you weren't playing your own little game at my expense."

He came over to her and trailed his fingers lightly along her cheek. "I'm as good as the next fellow when it comes to playing games. If ever I needed proof that you're in big trouble, Addie, I've only to think of the Winehart cottage. You're staying with me until the ferry to Port Clyde sails tomorrow afternoon with you on it."

"Jason, I squared with you about who I am and what I'm doing on Galbraith. But I haven't asked you to take charge and I'm not running away," she said stubbornly. "The odds are down to one in five and that *one* can happen any time now."

"Listen," he said earnestly, "you're not a professional cop and you're not thinking straight. We'll assume Enigma came here for a purpose. It may not have suited that purpose to kill you, quite yet. I doubt he wants the sheriff crawling all over the island asking more questions than he already is. You don't know Enigma's time schedule but you do know the time schedule for the Port Clyde ferry. Use your head, dammit.''

"I asked the night manager when the telephone will be working again. He said tomorrow morning. I'm going to call Pam then and discuss my next move with her. That's final, Jason. I appreciate what you're saying but I'm not walking out on a serial murderer who's running around with . . . with his handwriting *loose*.''

Jason burst out laughing at that image. "Finished on exactly the right note, Addie. Okay, let's forget it for tonight and relax,'' he said at last. "We'll sort it out tomorrow.''

"Relax?''

Jason smiled. "Don't knock a farsighted man. It just so happens I have a bottle of something I picked up at the general store. It's not going to win any prizes, but it'll chase the blues away.''

Addie reached for her suitcase. "Thanks, Jason, but I have a very orderly sense of priorities and a party in your room at a time like this doesn't get my vote.''

"Lighten up, Cordero.'' Jason took her suitcase away from her and set it firmly down on the bed. "If I let every hair-raising situation I was ever in sour me on life's pleasures, I'd have thrown in the towel a long time ago.''

"But I'm not you,'' she told him firmly. "Considering what happened to me tonight, I don't have a laugh left in me.''

"I take it you're staking a claim on the bed,'' Jason said.

"If I'm staying here, I'm afraid you'll have to be the gracious host.'' She glanced pointedly at the wicker sofa on the opposite side of the room. It had twin paisley cushions that had obviously seen better days.

"That's a killer,'' Jason said. "Spend a night on that and my spine will never be the same.''

"I'll pay for a professional massage when all this is over," Addie said sweetly. "Someone who'll walk barefoot on your back—"

He grinned. "She'll need a map for all the more interesting parts. You wouldn't care to draw one up now."

She hesitated before answering, allowing forbidden thoughts and feelings to intrude. He was handsome, he was sexy and he cared about her. Under almost any other circumstances her willpower wouldn't be quite so strong. But just now it was strictly business and anything else would be pure folly. "I don't even want to draw you a bath right now, Jason," she said at last. "And forget about telling me that I don't know what I'm missing." She let a teasing note slip into her voice to soften her decision.

Jason slowly and deliberately removed his sweater. Under it he wore a blue shirt that was open at the neck. His shoulders were broad, his hips slim. Once again forbidden thoughts tugged at her and once again she suppressed them.

He went over to the closet and pulled the door open. "Enough hangers, I believe." He pushed his clothes to one side. Addie blinked as a small piece of paper was dislodged from some piece of clothing in the closet and drifted to the floor.

"I just grabbed enough for tomorrow," she told him carefully, unable to keep her eyes from the piece of paper. From where she sat she thought she could discern a few lines of script. She sat down on the bed, suddenly fagged out. "I can't even move a muscle. Why don't you take a shower and let me get my bearings."

"A nice hot shower might just help," he said. "Alone or together as the case may be."

"Please," she said politely, "be my guest."

"But you're *my* guest," he returned with a grin. "Never mind, we could stay up all night figuring that one out and I'm not one to argue with a very tired lady about shower rights. I suspect there's enough hot water to go around." He apparently hadn't seen the slip of paper drift to the closet floor. He went over to the dresser and picked up a small leather toiletries kit. "Incidentally, Addie, I sleep nude," he said, heading for the bathroom. "Bad habit I got into that I just can't break." He smiled teasingly and was clearly waiting to see if she'd take the bait.

"Good heavens," she said, "we'll have to work up a psychological profile on you, find if we can cure the nude disease."

"Gotcha." He closed the door to the bathroom.

He slept nude. Addie sat on the bed wondering just how she was going to handle that one. When she heard the sound of the shower start, she got off the bed, walked quietly to the closet and picked up the piece of paper.

There was an FBI imprint at the bottom and Jason's name printed on the top. The writer had used a ballpoint pen to inscribe travel plans and ferry schedules. A perusal of the handwriting was enough to make Addie sorry she had ever wanted to examine it. It was a script she recognized from the party. The writer wasn't Enigma, she held the proof of that between her fingers. But he wasn't the writer of Prospero's words, either.

This script matched the one used in the quotation from Alexander Pope. She hadn't been completely honest at the party. She couldn't just come out and tell someone he's cold, methodical, a sexual mechanic. She no longer remembered precisely what she had said about that one but Addie knew she had softened the blow considerably. No wonder Jason had thought her a fraud, although he wouldn't have appreciated the truth, either.

So the real Jason Farrell had presented himself in his handwriting after all. He was cold, an opportunist, methodical, and worse, his script had a certain sterility indicating sex was merely a matter of biology for him and that love had nothing to do with it. It reminded her of Rafe's, but this time she wouldn't make the same mistake. Saved in the nick of time. Once again she'd been attracted to a man by his outward appearance, by his smooth talk and his smile. She took the memo and tucked it into the pocket of one of his jackets.

He slept nude, did he? Well, good luck to him. The way her own luck had been running, he'd undoubtedly turn into Mr. Hyde halfway through the night. She thought of the hotel lobby and Tim Gruesin and Noah Roberts. Would they sleep out the night there or had the fog lifted sufficiently for them to return to West Wind?

She shivered lightly and rubbed her hands along her arms. Had Noah just come from Winehart when she met him out there in the fog? What if Jason hadn't appeared? Cold, methodical Jason. She was more confused than ever. Her knight in shining armor was a handsome, sexy-looking dud.

She went over to the window and peered out at the night. But of course the fog hadn't lifted and the mournful cry of the foghorn hadn't stopped; familiarity had just reduced it to unnoticed background noise. She turned around and surveyed the room. She'd have to make the best of things. She quickly stripped the top sheet from the bed. She'd show Jason Farrell a thing or two.

A quick search of the room revealed the one thing she needed: a long cord connecting a small radio on the night table with the one electrical outlet in the room, which was situated near the window. It unplugged at both ends, saving her the trouble of cutting it. She heard Jason singing some old blues tune in the shower. Then the shower stopped and so did the song. The foghorn sounded again.

Addie quickly ran the electrical cord from the light fixture to the clothes hook on the opposite wall. She slipped the sheet over the cord, arranging it so that her bed was totally hidden from the wicker sofa.

At the top of the closet she found a couple of extra blankets. She placed the blankets and a pillow, taken from the bed, on the wicker couch. Then she sat down behind the curtain and waited for Jason to appear. The trouble was the unusual rate her heart was hammering. She was certain he'd hear it. Addie didn't want a confrontation. She wanted Jason to head for the wicker couch. She wanted him to

crawl under the blankets, nude or not, and go to
sleep...without a word, without a single word.

The bathroom door opened. ''All yours, Addie. Plenty
of hot water on tap.''

She heard his padding footsteps and then his low
chuckle. ''Oh, Addie, you disappoint me.''

The moment Addie heard his warm, expressive voice she
wanted to cry. Cold, methodical, a man who used sex as if
it were controlled by an on-off switch. The facts didn't
square with what she felt about the man, or what she'd
seen, but then she had already learned a lesson about that
once before.

''I thought you'd decided to trust me,'' he said. She
heard him heading for the couch.

''But I do,'' she said from her side of the curtain.

''Ah, I get it. You don't trust yourself, hence Addie
Cordero's Iron Curtain.''

''Go ahead and laugh.'' She opened her suitcase and
pulled out her nightgown. ''I don't believe in giving off
mixed signals. I said what I mean and this should prove it.''

''Addie, you're not giving off mixed signals, you never
have. You're in control, I believe it. I may be sorry about
it, but I believe it.''

She took her nightgown and headed for the bathroom.
Jason was standing on the other side of the curtain, hands
on his hips, with only a towel draped around his waist. A
nest of dark hair on his chest glistened with droplets of
water. She liked his legs, too, muscular and strong. His hair
was damp and he had shaved.

Cold, methodical. He had shaved before bed.

Addie clutched her nightgown and dived past him into
the bathroom.

When she came out, he was sitting propped up on the
wicker sofa under the blankets she'd provided. He held a
glass of wine in one hand and a book in the other. He gazed
up at her, taking in the long flannel nightgown that was
buttoned to her neck. It had a little pink flower design
printed on it, delicate lace edging and didn't show one inch

of her body. As she walked quickly across the floor he started a low rumble that turned into a loud, belly-whomping laugh. His drink spilled and the book fell to the floor.

"Addie, I just don't know how I can resist you," he said. "You'd better get under those covers before I lose all control."

"Good night, Mr. Farrell." Addie spoke the words with as much dignity as she could muster, wishing she could share his teasing and much, much more. Instead she went behind the curtain and quietly got under the covers. A few moments later, Jason put out the light and in no time at all she heard his soft rhythmical breathing.

Cold, methodical, the off switch in place. And she still wanted to be with him, in his arms, in his bed, having him make love to her. She wanted desperately to believe her instincts and not the signals so apparent in his handwriting.

Graphology was a science, she'd stake her life on it, but for once, oh, how she wanted it to be wrong.

Chapter Twelve

As they came down the stairs into the hotel lobby early the next morning Addie glanced at her watch. "I could call Pam at home but she'll have her hands full with the twins," she told Jason. "I'll wait until nine and reach her at the office."

"What you're going to tell Pam is that Operation Enigma is a bust, you're catching the ferry out this afternoon and you'll be back in Boston tonight."

"Leaving everything to you and the FBI, I suppose."

"Just about sums it up, Addie."

"I never leave a job unfinished."

"That in your handwriting, too?"

"Jason, I'm not taking the ferry until I'm ready to take the ferry. And today I'm not ready to take the ferry."

They'd been snappish with each other that morning from the moment when Addie had come out from behind the curtain and found Jason, fully dressed, sitting by the window, staring out across the water, hands locked behind his head. He had told her rather smugly that he had been out, found the telephone had been repaired and placed a call to Washington. Afterward he had taken a bracing turn around the island. While she dressed in the bathroom, he pointedly took down the sheet and the electrical cord.

Now, as they entered the dining room, Addie tried to lighten the mood. "Let's have breakfast on the veranda," she suggested. He had, after all, rescued her from Noah

Roberts and proved a good sounding board for her ideas about Enigma. And for that she was grateful. She led the way onto the veranda, taking in her first breath of fresh morning air. The fog had dissipated overnight and the sky was a translucent blue, the color of certain morning glories. "Maybe I'll come back here someday," she said, "and just bask in the island's beauties. Although," she went on, "I think I've had enough of its people. Maybe Linus is the exception."

"Linus, whom you've irrevocably cleared of being Enigma."

"Graphology's a science," she said with a little too much emphasis on the word "science." "He's cleared."

Jason regarded her for a long moment. "But instinct cleared me."

"No. I mean yes."

He reached across the table and covered her hand with his. "Addie, once all this is over..." His gaze softened, but he didn't even try to finish the sentence.

"You'll return to Washington and I'll be deep into my practice in Boston." She slipped her hand out from under his, realizing she was still reacting strongly to the warmth of his touch and forcing herself to remember it was all mechanics.

"Don't even try to put up a mental curtain between us, Addie." Jason gave her a sudden, boyish grin and beckoned for the waitress. "Just remember the words," he continued in a low voice, " 'When this is all over...' "

"We'll meet in some neutral corner."

He laughed. "And not come out swinging. What's got your dander up, anyway? That sheet strung down the center of the room was your idea. I slept like a top."

"I know. I heard you."

"Well, now you know one more thing about me. I snore."

The waitress came over and handed them menus, although Jason waved his away. "Ham and eggs, coffee," he said. "Addie?"

"Coffee, juice, muffins." When the waitress departed, Addie said, "I don't know quite how to break the news to Pam about Enigma."

"The truth doesn't hurt and sometimes it even helps. Sending an amateur out on a job like this was a crazy idea in the first place, and doing it without providing a backup was certifiable."

"I was supposed to do one thing, use the expertise I possess. By hook or by crook, I was to get a sample of handwriting from the most logical candidates on the island. I was supposed to ID Enigma, then leave as soon as Pam contacted the local sheriff to pick him up. But I was snookered into a game of handwriting analysis with a bunch of jokers who wanted anonymity. And by then there was no way I could back off."

Jason looked over to the door leading out from the lobby. "Sheriff Clayborn is headed straight for us," he said to Addie in a low voice. "I think it's time we told the good man what's going on."

"No," Addie said sharply. "Not until I speak with Pam."

"You're in his jurisdiction, Addie."

"Believe me I know that. And I also know he could have a five-star fit and you and I would end up in a jail cell—"

"Together?" Jason gave her a crooked grin. "I might not object."

"Forget it. You snore."

The sheriff came over. "Glad I found you both here." He removed his hat, drew up a chair and beckoned to the waitress. "Could use a couple of eggs over easy," he told her, "bacon, hash fries, a quart of coffee. Ah, and some fresh squeezed juice." When she was gone, he sat back and perused them both with a self-satisfied smile. "Well, you two are some pair."

For a moment Addie thought he was talking about her spending the night in Jason's room. "Far as I know," the sheriff went on, turning specifically to Jason, "you're the first representative of the FBI to vacation on the island.

Sure that's all you're doing, vacationing? Besides coming up with the odd body, I mean.''

"Weather's been great," Jason said. "Been photographing the peregrine falcon, cormorants, terns, cliffs, rocks and, incidentally, one very interesting rare species known as the Addie Cordero."

"And tidal pools, I imagine."

Jason grinned. "And an odd, occasional tidal pool."

"I'd be interested in seeing some of those photographs."

Jason's reply was very careful. "I expect to have them on exhibit in Boston within the year. I'll send you an invitation."

"I may want to see the photographs a little sooner than that."

Jason, who had brought his camera with him, reached for it, then said, "This film's brand-new. I mailed the rest out already for developing."

"Too bad."

"I'll let you know how they turn out."

The sheriff stared at him for a moment longer, then turned to Addie, "Why didn't you tell me you worked with the justice department in Boston?"

"I thought it might complicate things. I'm on vacation." Perhaps he knew everything, knew she was lying. She felt Jason watching her closely but didn't dare catch his eye. She wanted desperately to speak to Pam, to throw the whole thing into her lap.

The sheriff shook his head slowly once again, clearly expressing his annoyance. "You might have saved us a lot of trouble speculating about you."

"I'm sorry," she said. "You asked me what I did for a living and I told you. Whom did you speak with in the justice department?" she asked after a moment.

"One of the assistant district attorneys, Pamela somebody. Vouched for you. Well," he went on after a brief look at Jason, "you might as well know it now as later. We have the victim's name and occupation." He waited a beat or two, then went on. "His name was Frank Masconi, a private detective working solo out of Boston."

"Private detective," Addie repeated, catching the calculating look in Jason's eyes.

"According to the coroner's report," the sheriff continued, "Masconi was dead before he hit the tidal pool. It was set up to look like an accident, but some wood fragments found imbedded in his scalp indicated a blow from behind."

"Poor sucker," Jason said. "Any idea what his business was on the island?"

The sheriff shook his head. "His secretary is a temporary employee, said he didn't want her doing anything but typing and answering the phone. She doesn't know beans about him and said all he told her was he'd be out of town for a couple of days. No wife, no kids, not even a landlady much interested in his whereabouts. I'm having the Boston police check his files with a fine-tooth comb."

"Temporary secretary," Addie remarked. "Sounds as if he was running his business on a shoestring. And something else," she added. "It occurs to me that the killer was new to Galbraith."

"How's that?" the sheriff asked.

"The tides. The victim was killed during the ebb tide. If he had been killed earlier, or much later in the day, his body would have been lifted by the tide and taken out to sea. Anyone familiar with the island would know that."

"Unless the killer wanted the body found," Jason said, "as a warning."

The sheriff picked up on Jason's remark quickly. "Got anyone in mind?"

Addie caught Jason's eye and almost imperceptibly shook her head. Not yet. Pam first. She hoped Jason could go along with her, though Addie knew they couldn't keep the sheriff in the dark much longer.

"And another thing," the sheriff went on without waiting for an answer, as though expecting they were innocent of everything but curiosity. "The telephone cable was deliberately cut and that took some doing. Telephone crew worked all last night to get it working again. Miss Cordero," he continued, "I want you to go back in your mind once again to your conversation with Masconi. Now that you know he was a private investigator, can you connect anything he said that would be of help? Anything unusual?"

"Everything he said was unusual," Addie said lamely. "But nothing was *unusual*, if you know what I mean. He said he'd come to see someone."

"And apparently he did," Jason threw in.

"I don't know," the sheriff said with a deep sigh. "We've questioned everybody on the island, and nobody knows nothin'."

"It's a tight little island. People here protect each other," Addie said.

The sheriff looked shrewdly at her. "You know that for a fact?"

Addie gave a small laugh. "Just what I surmise."

"As a psychologist."

"Oh, I've seen it with my own eyes. There's a lot of petty bickering, I imagine, but they do stick together."

The waitress arrived with their orders. The sheriff put a bright smile on his face and dug into his breakfast. Addie checked the time. Perhaps ten minutes had gone by. She had another half hour to wait before she could call Pam. Addie eyed the way the sheriff ate, reflecting that he might as well enjoy his breakfast now because eventually what she would have to tell him was likely to cause a massive bout of indigestion.

PAM'S VOICE at the other end of the telephone was the most welcome sound Addie had ever heard. "Addie, well, well, well. Am I glad to hear from you," she said as if she meant it. "Nice of you to call."

"The phone's been down. In fact I just found out why."

"I know why, and I ought to chew you out for not calling me the minute you landed on the island, but I won't."

"Look, before I go on, I want you to know this is a party line, meaning the telephone operator has a ball listening in."

"Okay, got the message. I've some information for you, which I'll give you anyway. I'm talking about our old friend, Eda," she said, referring to Enigma's last victim, Eda Barnstable. "Turns out her granddaughter, Ivy, is on the island. She's a musician married to a Russian violinist, Vladimir Tatlin. Seems Eda had a house on the island. Know the granddaughter?"

Addie let out an audible breath. "I do, but doesn't this put a new face on everything?"

"Possibly. Tell me about her."

"One of those well-adjusted people who wouldn't harm a fly. The husband as well. But still," Addie said as an afterthought, "she certainly doesn't act as if her grandmother had just gone over to the other side. In fact nobody on the island has said a word about it."

"Well, here's the kicker. It turns out that Eda's husband, the late Barney," Pam went on, "had a business arrangement with someone on the island. Steven West of Boston Bank. Know him?"

"Yes." The thought came to Addie at once, Jason and their conversation of the night before. The government was investigating Steven West. "Wonderful host," she said quickly. "Gave an absolutely smashing party the other night. As a matter of fact I performed my star turn and analyzed handwritings." Tilly would be taking it all in, but she had no choice. Pam had to be told everything.

"You were always pretty good at that sort of thing," Pam said. "Just let me add something else. An Atlantic City gambling casino may be involved. The Feds are interested. Need I say more?"

"No, I'm a fast learner. You'd be surprised how fast." Steve West and the late Barney Barnstable tied into a money laundering scheme, was it possible? She had to find Jason and let him know the connection between his case and Enigma. Yet it seemed equally clear to her that Ivy Tatlin was the reason Enigma had come to Galbraith. He must not have gotten what he was after from Eda.

"Speaking of your star turn, have you met our enigmatic friend yet?" Pam asked.

"Our friend is here, no question about it."

"Then it's time to come home, Addie. I heard about the accident on the island. The Port Clyde sheriff was on to us to follow up. Masconi's files came up empty concerning Galbraith."

"Sheriff Clayborn doesn't seem to know that yet."

"You're getting the news hot off the fire. We haven't learned any more than he already knows, but I don't like the smell of things. Pack it in and come back, Addie. All we wanted was the ID. I'll follow through from here. Who drew the lucky number?"

Addie hesitated a moment, then said, "You won't want to hear this but I don't have a name yet. I have, I mean *had*, a confirming sample of the handwriting but there's still no name attached."

"What? Have? Had? What's going on out there?" The question crackled along the wire.

"Don't ask for details, Pam, just take my word for it. The trouble is he may know I'm here."

"What?"

"Don't keep saying 'what.' You sent a beginner out to do the job, and it'll cost the entire program if I'm not careful."

There was silence from the other end of the line. Then Pam said in a worried voice, "Are you all right, Addie?"

"Fine, in one piece."

"Pack it in and get out of there. I'll call the Port Clyde sheriff and ask him to handle it. I want you out of there on the next boat."

"The sheriff is on the island now, Addie. Do you want me to—"

"I want you to pack it in."

"I've narrowed it down to one of maybe five, six people."

"I don't care. I want you out of there."

"And the six? You're just going to let them all go? I want to stop this guy."

"Addie."

"Pam, I'll call you back as soon as I can. I have to talk to someone."

"Addie," Pam shouted. "Don't hang up."

But Addie had already put the receiver down carefully and on her way out deliberately went past the reception desk. Tilly was at the switchboard, earphones on. Behind her stood the one person Addie didn't want to meet, Sheriff Clayborn.

Addie went quickly, quietly past, feeling a curious shiver race down her back. Then she heard the sheriff's voice.

"I'm waiting."

Addie stopped and swung around. Clayborn, however, was glaring at Tilly who just smiled at him and shrugged, then said into the phone piece. "Mom, I really have to hang up now, we've talked too long. I know, you've been worried. I'll call you later. The sheriff's been itching to get on the phone for ten minutes now."

Addie almost laughed out loud but she was distracted when the manager, sitting at the far end of the reception desk called out. "Oh, Miss Cordero, we may manage to have a room for you tonight. I'll let you know later."

"Thanks."

"And Mr. Farrell said he'd meet you back here at two and to stick around the hotel until then."

Damn, she had wanted to tell Jason about the tie-in between the Barnstables and Steve West, and about Ivy Tatlin. They had talked briefly earlier about his going up to West Wind to try to ferret out a few samples of handwriting for her. "Did he leave a note for me?" she asked.

"Sorry, just the message."

Of course he wouldn't leave a handwritten note. He still had no idea she'd already taken his measure.

It was nine-thirty, and four and a half hours was a long time for her to wait around for Jason. Agitated, she had to decide quickly what her priorities were. She could try to find Ivy Tatlin or she could wait for Jason at the hotel. Finding and warning Ivy about Enigma won easily. The stakes kept changing. The young musician, whom Addie had dismissed as a suspect early on, was now a player again, this time as Enigma's probable target. She'd see Ivy and then return to her cottage.

Whatever else Enigma might do, he wouldn't have any more reason to return to Winehart. He'd found what he was looking for and had undoubtedly discovered she was staying at the Inn. The logical thing for her to do, therefore, was to go back, pick up her clothes and assess the damage with a clear eye. She wouldn't touch anything except her clothes. The sheriff would want to take fingerprints, and then there'd be the insurance claim.

As she ran down the veranda steps, she noted that Steve West's launch was gone from its berth. The waters around the island were teeming with fish and Addie wondered if he hadn't taken his guests out. If so, Jason was out of luck.

Her map of the island didn't show the Barnstable house by that name so she asked at the general store.

"It's called Seal House," the owner of the store told her. "You'll find it on the north side of the island." He took the map and showed her where it stood on a lonely promontory.

"If you're lucky you'll see some seals sunning offshore," he said.

If she was lucky, Ivy would be safe and sound and ready to believe anything Addie had to tell her.

She found Seal House easily enough. It was a large, handsome dwelling with an open porch and a garden that had fallen into ruin. Apparently Ivy had made some attempt to get the garden going again, with plantings of begonias, impatiens and bright pink geraniums.

The house was closed up tight. Addie decided to stick around for a while. After checking offshore rocks for the sight of seals and finding none, she sat down on the top porch step and waited. After ten or fifteen minutes, a woman came up the front path eying Addie suspiciously.

"Can I help you?" she asked politely but with the faint mistrustful stare that most of the year-round residents seemed to reserve for visitors.

"I was hoping to see Mrs. Tatlin."

"She's off the island today, husband, too. Doing a concert in Portland. Can I leave your name?"

"When's she expected back?"

"Not until tomorrow morning, earliest."

"Thanks," Addie said. "I'll come back. Oh," she added just as the woman was about to unlock the front door, "how'd she get off the island? I saw her last night and the ferry hasn't even come in yet."

"They have the use of Mr. West's launch."

"Yes, of course. He's wonderfully generous that way," Addie said.

The woman shrugged as though she had no opinion of the matter.

"I was awfully sorry to hear about Mrs. Barnstable," Addie remarked, staying the woman once again. "It must have been a great shock to Ivy."

"Possibly," the woman said, opening up a bit as she realized Addie was not a total stranger to the family. "Although I can't say there was ever much love lost between those two. She hated the idea of her grandchild running all over the world." The woman clammed up suddenly, drawing her lips tight together as though realizing she had said too much. She went inside and closed the door quickly and firmly behind her.

"Well, thanks," Addie said, going back down the path. The fact that Ivy had been abroad when her grandmother was murdered had no doubt tempered her reaction. And anyway, Addie decided, not everyone made grief a public demonstration.

Winehart looked a lot less ominous during the day. But still, when Addie came close to the cottage, she realized she was dragging her feet. Nor was Fitzgibbon waiting for her. He was spooked, too.

When she approached her front door, however, she found a curious square of white affixed to it. A couple of seconds passed before she made up her mind. Then Addie reached for it gingerly.

Chapter Thirteen

"From women's eyes this doctrine I derive:
They sparkle still the right Promethean fire;
They are the books, the arts, the academes,
That show, contain, and nourish all the world."

"A quotation. And from Shakespeare. *Love's Labour Lost*." Addie read it aloud and laughed with relief. She brushed a hand along her brow. She was perspiring slightly. She hadn't known what the small square of paper would be, but Shakespeare written on a prescription pad belonging to Kevin Morgan was the last thing she'd expected.

She examined the script with interest. The neat upright hand had the cool self-consciousness she had seen before in British writing. Addie was astonished. The handwriting resembled the one she had decided belonged to Veronica West.

It all came together now. That handwriting could never have belonged to Veronica, who had to be the least self-conscious of women. As for Kevin, it was possible he had been educated in England and emigrated when young to the States. The neat, upright hand might be the last vestige of his earlier education.

Graphology wasn't meant to be a guessing game but a scientific tool in which one began with as many specifics as one could. She had indulged in guessing and had come up wrong. What she now learned was that Kevin might be aggressive when he'd had too much to drink but his nature was to be shy and even a little inhibited.

Abashed at his behavior at Linus Bishop's party, he had written her the poem and tacked it to her front door as an apology. And she now had absolute written proof the good doctor wasn't Enigma.

Apologies accepted. Addie tucked the note into her pocket. Kevin Morgan was decidedly not Enigma. That was all she cared about. And he clearly wanted her to be his poetical muse. Not likely, but the idea was a flattering one, anyway. She realized almost immediately that if Kevin was cleared of being Enigma, Veronica wasn't. Gruesin, Roberts, Evans, the Wests. Seven down, still five to go.

Addie unlocked the door to the cottage and pushed it open, wanting no more surprises. She went cautiously in, afraid to face the mess.

No fairy godmother had come by in the night and waved a magic wand to set everything back in place. Pillows and furniture were still overturned, picture frames smashed willfully, books turned out of bookshelves. She resisted the temptation to straighten up. Surveying the damage, Addie knew one thing. She wasn't going to flee the island. Her list of suspects had been reduced to five names. She would peel them away until the last one stood exposed. The noose was tightening around Enigma's neck. She wouldn't risk confronting him without Jason to back her up, but there was no way she was taking today's ferry off the island.

She checked her watch once again. Scarcely an hour had gone by since she had left the Island Inn. Time certainly flew when she was having fun. Hiding out from Enigma wouldn't necessarily be easy but a pleasant solution came to mind at once. She'd pack lunch and a thermos of coffee. The day was a beautiful one and she'd hide in plain sight in the Cathedral Woods where an artist sat on every tree stump.

At four-thirty, after the ferry had left, she'd return to the hotel and face Jason's undoubted ire.

"WHERE WERE YOU?"

Addie, coming into the lobby of the Island Inn, gazed at Jason with complete serenity. She carried the rest of her luggage and went over to the reception desk. "You promised me a room," she said to the manager.

"Ah, yes, of course, extremely happy to oblige. Room 203, facing the water. All ready for you."

"Forget the room," Jason said to Addie. "You're going back to the mainland if you have to walk there on water." He gripped her arm, pulled her over to a chair and forced her into it. "I said I didn't want you leaving the premises. I left a message telling you I'd be back at two."

"You didn't even bother to wait until after I talked to Pam. That really made a great deal of sense. Sort of gave me the feeling I could trust you all around."

A slight smile curled at the corner of his mouth. "I thought you learned all about trust last night."

It took but a moment for a soft flush to flood her cheeks. "And stop standing over me," she said with more anger in her voice than she felt, "I don't like being intimidated."

"Dammit, Addie, I've been worried sick about you, is that what you want to hear?"

"It'll do for the time being." She dug into her pocket, produced the note from Kevin and allowed herself a little smile. "One more down and five to go. Kevin Morgan is not Enigma. What do you have for me?"

He pulled up a chair and straddled it. "Should I ask how you arrived at that conclusion?"

"He's off the list, that's all you have to know. Come on, give, what did you come up with?"

"When you went in to telephone, I saw Steve West down at the dock with the Tatlins. He was taking them over to the mainland and I decided to go along."

"And if he was Enigma and wanted to dispose of Ivy...."

"You're completely on the wrong track," Jason told her, "but go on, spell out your scenario."

"She's the granddaughter of Eda Barnstable and is living in the Barnstable house."

"And?"

"And Mr. Barney Barnstable, Eda's late husband, was a lawyer with a firm that represented Boston Bank. Does that get the little hairs on your neck up? And according to Pam, there was some flak about money laundering and gambling in Atlantic City involving Barnstable."

"So you've decided Steve West is Enigma, who wants to do away with Ivy Tatlin for reasons unknown."

"Unknown?" Addie looked at him with disbelief. "Jason, she just inherited her grandmother's house and maybe she'd like to find her grandmother's killer."

"Did Pam say that?" he asked her shrewdly.

"No. I did. Did Ivy say when they're returning?"

"She told Steve they'd take the ferry back either tomorrow or in a couple of days."

"Well, at least Ivy's safe for the time being."

"Incidentally," Jason said, "you don't have to worry about getting Steven's handwriting. I remembered this morning that I have a note from him upstairs somewhere."

She smiled and got to her feet. "Great, let's go get it."

Jason reached for her luggage. "It'll wait, Sherlock. We'll have an early dinner and settle you in for the night. I'm going to keep you on a leash until tomorrow afternoon when the boat leaves for Port Clyde with you on it. Spending the whole day alone without a word to anyone was not a good move."

"Just a minute, Dr. Watson," Addie said, taking her luggage back. "Let's get a couple of things straight right now. One, I want to see the handwriting sample before dinner not after. If we've found Enigma, maybe we'll have better things to do than eat."

"All the more reason to eat first. We may be a tad busy once you see that note and Steve's not going anywhere."

"And," she went on, ignoring his remark, "if Steve is clean, you should know right now that I'm not leaving Galbraith until I'm clutching Enigma's ID in my hot little fist."

"Okay," he said, admiring her spirit if not her sense. However, it turned out one thing was certain, he was going to stick very close to Addie Cordero. He took her luggage again and headed for the stairs. "There's nothing I'd like better than to invite you to my room to discuss this."

"No," Addie said, following him. "You'll find me ensconced in room 203. I already tried to search your room once. This time you can look for the evidence I need yourself and when you have it, come by and show it to me."

"WERE YOU PLAYING games with the handwriting you claimed to be Steve's?" Addie asked the question later over dinner after Jason admitted his search for the note had been fruitless.

He shook his head. "Addie, there are any number of things I take seriously in this life, and whether or not Steven West is Enigma happens to be one of them."

"And you don't think it's strange that the note is missing. Maybe Steve is Enigma. Maybe he came here for the note just as he came to Winehart for the other samples."

"I've said it before and I'm going to say it once more, Addie, then we're going to drop the subject for just a little while. Steve West isn't a serial murderer. He's a banker. He may be committing a series of crimes with your money and mine, but he isn't taking the lives of innocent women while he's at it."

Addie opened her mouth to object but he reached across the table and deliberately put his fingers against her lips. "Don't even try to argue with me. I know Steve West."

Addie, instead, took his hand away and held it in a tight grasp. "One more question, and I promise we'll quit for the night. Even amateur detectives have to have a little time off. Do you remember anything particular about his handwriting?"

"It was handwriting."

"Thanks."

"Case closed for the night," Jason said. "Have another roll."

"SUNSETS on Galbraith can be pretty dangerous," Jason said to Addie as they wandered down to the water's edge after dinner. There were a good dozen other guests from the Inn gathered to watch the curtsy of the sun as it dipped plump and crimson into the horizon.

"Dangerous? I should think it would bring out the best in us."

"It does. That's what I mean. It's a little too heavy on inspiration, like fireworks. A man could lose his heart and have a hard time retrieving it in the cold light of reason."

Addie went over to a rowboat that had been pulled up to shore. She climbed into it, sat down and drew her shawl around her arms. The island, while hot during the day, always cooled off dramatically in the evenings. The sky was edged in red, which in a series of mutations turned gradually to a soft green overhead. When Jason joined her on the seat, she said, "I gather you don't mind losing your heart, as long as you can find it again the next day intact and all yours."

He took her hand, opened her palm and drew it to his lips. "Did I say all that?"

At the touch of his lips a trickle of exquisite pleasure eased along her spine. She couldn't bear it, knowing what she did about him and she abruptly drew her hand away.

The sun disappeared in a last explosion of light, leaving its trail of fading color behind. Overhead gulls wheeled and cormorants skimmed the water as though they now felt they had the sky and sea in their full possession. Slowly the other guests left and walked back up to the hotel, their voices faint murmurs against the cries of birds.

"I suppose this is too romantic a scene to photograph," she said, "this slow progression to night. I think you like everything stark and cold and full of irony."

"And I think you're being far too analytical, Miss Cordero. Come on," he said, reaching for her hand, "I want to show you something."

There was a series of stone steps, which led to the hotel's back garden; a carefully planted yet riotous array of flowers. "Not this," he said, urging her along. "I'm taking you back to my childhood." He drew her over to a small garden that was hidden by a carefully wound fence of grapevines. There were torches already lit, set among boxwood shrubs, and plantings of sandalwood and silvery herbs. The air was heavy with the lush fragrance of lavender and thyme, of tarragon and mint.

"An herb garden," Addie exclaimed with surprise. "How beautiful." She bent down and pinched a bit of leaf from a tall, healthy plant with abundant foliage. "Looks like celery, smells like celery, but is it celery?"

Jason took it out of her hand and tasted it. "If we're lucky, lovage. If we're not so lucky, hemlock."

"How come you know so much?"

"Grew up on a farm in Missouri." He drew her over to a small stone bench.

"That explains everything," Addie said. "I grew up in Boston in a small house with a garden that had two hydrangea bushes and plenty of ivy and very little else. Then, summers were spent at the beach; lots of sand, few plants. Mom was a great reader and not such a great gardener. I remember pots of geraniums and hanging baskets full of fuchsia. I called them ballerinas. How I loved them."

They sat side by side, not touching and Addie realized she had lost the remnant of fear that had been haunting her all day. She felt safe with Jason. She sensed he was looking at her and turned to catch his eye. She was very aware of Jason the man, of his intelligent, curious gaze, his unassuming talent, the blatant sensuality hidden behind a careful insouciance. He was not the man his handwriting proclaimed, not that man at all.

With their closing in on Enigma, she knew she'd be back in Boston soon enough. Everything would be over with and Jason, cold, methodical or blatantly sexual, would be merely a memory.

"Addie, what are you thinking?"

She turned to him and gave him a wistful smile. "Just vague, transitory thoughts."

He looked at her for a moment, then tipped her chin back with his finger. His lips came down on hers with a kiss that was strong and persuasive. "This," he said, "is for that electrical cord down the center of the room and the sheet separating us. You don't think I actually slept a wink, do you?"

His lips crushed hers. Addie closed her eyes and allowed the last of the resistance she was still harboring to drift away.

He nibbled her lower lip, coaxing her mouth open, tasting and teasing with provocative half kisses. And when she ached for more, his tongue explored her mouth with a thoroughness that had Addie gripping his shoulders, returning his kisses with complete abandon.

His cool fingers played along her back and she had no thought of stopping his hands as they took possession of her senses. She was falling under his spell.

And then of course it happened, the first faint tear in her eye, which she ignored, drawing her body close to his and hoping it would all go away. But once begun a whole array of symptoms presented themselves like soldiers on a battleground.

She pulled away from him, grabbed a tissue from her pocket and sneezed. Then sneezed again.

"What the devil." Jason looked at her nonplussed. "I'd hate to think you're allergic to me."

"Maybe." She tried to smile before sneezing overcame her once again. "But I think it's something else, more likely a cat." There was a faint rustle in the middle of the herb bed. A black tail stood high above the lavender. She watched as it moved along like an animated question mark. Then, with a lithe jump, the cat cleared the lavender and came stalking over to Addie.

"They always know I love 'em and I'm allergic to 'em. Let's go," she said in between sneezes.

"THAT YOU, Jason? Hold it, let me slip something on. I'm dying."

The odd nasal voice that greeted him through the door of Room 203 early the next morning didn't sound much like Addie, but as far as Jason knew, she was the room's only occupant.

The door was duly opened and a bleary-eyed, red-nosed Addie greeted him. "I feel awful," she said.

"You look lovely."

"Thanks. I had to take an antihistamine and if it works, I'll be falling asleep in about ten minutes."

"Good. You'll be safe if you stick to your bed. I'm going to Steven West now and the first thing I'll do is get a new sample of his handwriting for you."

"Great." She sniffled, grabbed a tissue and blew her nose. "But Jason, another day has passed and we've only removed one name from the list, Kevin's. You'll have to fill in for me. I want you back here by noon with five signatures." She beckoned him into her room and held out a slip of paper she'd retrieved from her wallet. "This is a photocopy of Enigma's handwriting. You may be lucky and spot it first thing."

He gazed at the dark, dense slant. "Lucky Enigma didn't find this along with the others."

"It wasn't any inspiration on my part to keep it separate," Addie told him. "I never needed to refer to this slip except when I double-checked it with the new sample the first night. It's all there in his handwriting. The muddied look, the overly forward slant, the sharpened m's and n's indicating we're up against a clever opponent. Think you'll be able to recognize Enigma from this?"

He nodded and took the slip from her and put it into his pocket. Then he leaned over and kissed her on the cheek, her ear and the back of her neck. "I'll get to the other zones later," he said.

"Mmm," she mumbled, her eyes half open. He waited until she had crawled back into bed and then left. He was supposed to meet Steven West out at Squeaker Cove where Steven would hand over the incriminating tapes. End of case. Jason was hoping the matter of Enigma could be resolved as easily. Then he and Addie could take the ferry together and he could try to sort out whatever was bothering her about their relationship. Something was obviously very wrong.

It was cloudy outside and the dark swollen clouds overhead were threatening to drop a torrent on the island. A distant drumroll and clap of thunder almost drowned out the sound of the turbulent ocean hurling itself against the cliffs. The first drops of rain had begun to fall as Jason entered the Cathedral Woods. He muttered a low curse as he hurried on toward his destination.

He burst out of the woods and headed for the path down to Squeaker Cove. Under any other circumstances he would have stopped to admire the scene. All color but black and white seemed to have been washed away by the successive waves of water rising and falling against great black boulders.

Sinister, he thought, drawing his collar up. Huge drops of rain pelted him as he made his way down the cove to the overhang where he was to meet Steven West.

He promised himself that the first thing he'd do when he returned to Washington was ask for a raise. This was above and beyond the call of duty.

As arranged, Steven West was already on the ledge when Jason ducked under the overhang. But the man wasn't moving. He lay sprawled on his back, his eyes open staring at nothing. Jason took in a great gulp of air and then quickly bent over West, feeling for a pulse. He found none. A spot on West's forehead was swollen and blue. A trickle of blood ran in a crooked line down his face. Not much damage, Jason thought. West wore a surprised expression, as though he still couldn't quite believe what was happening to him. Jason had no doubt he'd been murdered.

"Sorry old man," Jason said quietly. "I'll find out who did this to you." Then he slowly and methodically went through West's pockets, looking for the promised tape. Nothing. *Nada*. No tape, no notes, nothing. He was back at square one.

He got up and kicked his foot unmercifully at the rock. What could have gone wrong? West wasn't supposed to die. Jason moved out from under the protection of the ledge. The rain was now falling steadily and showed no signs of letting up. He studied the landscape above him and with the exception of some peregrine falcons he saw no movement at all, animal or human. He began the climb back up wondering just how he would handle this new development. Someone had messed up on his beat, wrote "finish" to something he'd worked on for six months, killed a man who had trusted him, and Jason had all he could do to repress his anger.

And what about Steve's widow? Veronica could hear the news from the sheriff or Jason could see her and try to break the news gently.

There was no real choice. It was his responsibility. He'd have to go to West Wind, tell Veronica about her husband's death and somehow search the house for the missing tape before the sheriff got there. He was banking on the possibility that Steven had guessed something was wrong and had hidden the tape back at West Wind. Jason had no qualms about spiriting evidence away.

Nevertheless, he felt a deep, worrisome pain in the pit of his stomach, the kind that had nothing to do with physical problems. He hadn't liked Steve West. He had no respect for the way the man chose to use his entitlements, but Jason didn't believe anyone should die in such a manner. That wasn't the price he'd expected Steve to pay for his crimes.

He wondered just how the widow would take his news and hoped somebody was with her to help her handle it. Veronica struck him as being an icy number, aware of every move she made. So self-involved, in fact, she had little love left to share with anyone else. But that didn't make having to break the news to her any easier.

Jason pulled up short within sight of West Wind when he saw a woman wearing a lightweight red raincoat heading for the house. At first he thought it was Veronica but upon closer examination he discovered it was Addie. He caught up with her on the porch.

"Always walk around in the rain?" His question was coolly stated, although he had no doubt Addie could see the concern in his eyes.

"I came after you," she said. "There are four suspects in this house and I want to scratch them off my list one by one."

"What happened to your allergy?"

"The humidity, I suppose, or the barometric pressure. Seems to have suppressed all that cat dander."

"Just like that?"

She shrugged. "Don't you trust me? The antihistamine did its job. I had a nap and now I feel great."

"Steve West is dead," he said without pulling any punches. "I just found his body at Squeaker Cove."

She gave a slight moan. "Murder?"

"Looks like it."

"Enigma." She said the word simply, neither as question nor answer.

He shook his head. "Addie, I don't know."

Veronica came to the door when they rang the bell. She was wearing a black caftan that was open at the throat and her hair was pulled back in a severe chignon. She wore no makeup and it struck Jason for the first time that she was considerably older than he had thought.

"Well, company, how charming. Come in. I'm just up and I was about to have some coffee."

She was in midsmile when she suddenly seemed to understand that they hadn't come by for a neighborly chat.

"I'd like to talk to you for a minute," Jason said.

"Is anything wrong?" She put her hand to her heart and her voice held a waver.

Jason took her arm and led her to a chair. "I found Steve at Squeaker Cove, Veronica." He exchanged a glance with Addie whose expression was one of barely concealed anguish. "I'm afraid he's dead."

"Dead." She murmured the word and then clutched at Jason letting out a long, low wail.

"Where's Kevin? Get Kevin," she said at last, looking at them through tear-stained eyes. "Oh, Lord, he said Steve was a bloody hypochondriac and not to worry about him."

Jason bent over the woman. "Are you telling me that Kevin was your husband's doctor?"

"Yes, I thought everyone knew. Kevin has been my husband's personal physician for the past three months. Of all the luxuries Steve could have had, he thought a personal physician the most impressive. Not paintings, not sculpture, not a museum or a Broadway theater named after him, a doctor." She threw out the last words with a surprising amount of contempt and then stopped short, and burst into tears again.

"Where is Kevin?" Jason asked.

She shook her head. "I imagine he's out walking. He does that. Stops somewhere after a while and shouts his poetry to the ocean."

"Is anyone here to stay with you? Tim Gruesin or Noah Roberts?"

"They went into town." She stood up painfully. "One of the local girls is in the kitchen. She does general cleaning. I think I ought to lie down."

"I'll go with you," Addie said.

Veronica gave her a wan, grateful smile. Addie wrapped her arm around the actress's waist to support her and exchanged a quick glance with Jason as she went out of the room. She'd keep Veronica in her room while he checked around for the tape.

Jason stood quietly in the living room for a moment. He could hear the sound of water running in the kitchen and someone muttering to herself. If the tape existed and was in the house, he had to find it. First he went into the library where the meeting between West, Gruesin and Roberts was to have taken place.

Jason swiftly rummaged through the desk drawers but came up empty. He dug behind curtains and beneath chair cushions. He checked the heavily laden bookshelves, fitting his hands behind the books to see if anything had been secreted there. Once again he came up empty. The leather bindings were burnished and shining but a bit worn as if they had been lovingly read through the generations.

With the expertise born of years of practice, Jason searched the other rooms in the house but his efforts proved fruitless. That left only the master bedroom where Veronica was ensconced. He could hear her soft murmur and Addie's reassuring answers. Since he didn't believe Steve would have put the tape where Veronica might find it, the only conclusion to draw was that the tape, if it still existed, was in the possession of Steve's murderer. And it took little imagination to pin the blame on the team of Gruesin and Roberts.

As he came back into the living room, Jason heard the front door open. Kevin Morgan came into the room dressed in hiking clothes, a sweatband wrapped around his forehead.

"Hey, Jason, how are you doing? Miserable sort of day out there," he said, pulling the band off and shaking his head.

"I'm afraid so. Got caught in the rain coming up here," Jason said, noting that Kevin wasn't soaked from the recent downpour.

"I sat out the rain on the porch at Winehart," Kevin told him. "Addie wasn't home, but I figured she wouldn't mind."

Jason nodded then said in a steady, quiet voice, "There's been an accident. Steve. I just found his body out at Squeaker Cove."

Kevin blanched and grabbed the edge of the chair to steady himself. "Steve? Wait a minute, are you telling me—"

"He's dead. I've just talked to Veronica. Addie's with her."

Kevin closed his eyes for a long moment, then said, "His heart. I can't believe it. As far as I was concerned the man

was obsessed about his health but there was nothing actually wrong. To die just like that—''

"I'm afraid there's no knowing how he died, Kevin.''

"Are you talking about murder?''

"I'm not saying anything. Look, do me a favor, check in
on Veronica.''

"Right,'' Kevin said springing to life. "She'll need a
sedative.''

Jason went with him into Veronica's bedroom and found
her dramatically propped up against half a dozen small,
lace-trimmed pillows. When she saw Kevin she exploded
into a fresh paroxysm of tears. Jason explained that he and
Addie would go into town to call the sheriff and then
grabbed Addie before she could protest.

Outside, the clouds were still low and heavy, but the rain
had stopped. When they were clear of the house, Jason
turned and took both Addie's hands in his.

"I want to make one thing clear,'' he told her. "I have a
lot at stake here. No, amend that. The government has a lot
at stake. Besides murder, we're dealing with about a
hundred million dollars in gambling proceeds being ille-
gally transferred to an offshore bank. Gruesin and Roberts are on the top of my list of suspects. I don't want you
prying into their affairs looking for scraps of handwriting
until I settle this. It's too dangerous. I want you to stay put
at the Island Inn.''

"I've been tracking a serial murderer, Jason. I'm afraid
I don't care about your hundred million dollars.''

"Listen, you little fool, if Enigma is the link, as you seem
to believe, messing with him is big trouble.''

"Wait a minute,'' Addie said. "I've been in big trouble
all along, remember? What are we quarreling about? I'm
scared. I admit it. If you don't want me chasing after little
scraps of paper until after you settle your business, believe
me, I won't. Come on. Let's dump it all into the sheriff's
hands. I won't interfere.'' She began to jog ahead of him.

Jason caught up to her. "Mind telling me why you came
to your senses so easily?''

"Jason, the sheriff isn't going to be too happy about your finding Steve West's body. He's going to ask a lot of tougher questions this time around."

He gave a short laugh. "I doubt if our friendly sheriff is going to take on the FBI."

"Oh, I'll bet he'd take on a lot more than that if he thought it was his job." Addie paused, then said, "Is it possible Veronica murdered her husband?"

"Veronica? I personally think her grieving widow act was pretty good. But whether she loved her husband or not, when the government gets through with the case, she's not going to be a very merry widow. By the way, did you find a sample of her handwriting?"

Addie shook her head. "No, on the contrary. Veronica obliged me in another way by showing me a note Steven left her this morning. Just a few words stating he was going fishing and wouldn't be back until noon."

"Enigma?"

"No, not Enigma but someone cold, mechanical, who can turn sex on and off like a very, very cold faucet."

"And that's why you wonder if the lady could have killed him?"

"It's as good a reason as any. Oh, and something else, it matches a note I found in your room. I had thought it was yours, but I realize now that though it was written on your memo paper the handwriting was Steve's."

He gave her a look of surprise. "You little sneak. Where'd you find the note? That's the one I was looking for."

"You couldn't have looked very carefully. It floated to the floor of the closet when you moved your clothes over to make space for mine. Naturally I picked it up and read it."

"And naturally you thought it was my handwriting." He laughed. "I had Steve write down the ferry schedules and travel instructions for me and you're ready to convict me."

"I guess I'd have to see your handwriting to make a judgment. Which poem was yours, anyway?"

He looked at her and for a moment the forbidding expression on his face was replaced by one of incredulity. "Last night, you never had an allergic attack, did you? You figured you were beginning to like being with me a little too much and that wouldn't do at all. I was cold, mechanical. I could turn sex on and off by the flick of a switch. My supposed handwriting told you all that so you faked an allergy attack. Amazing. Addie, I wouldn't show you my handwriting if it guaranteed you'd hop into my bed in a minute."

"Is that what you believe? That I faked an allergy attack? I wasn't lying."

"About what? About wanting to get away from me, or about that fine act of sneezing?"

"It wasn't an act. Oh, forget it," she said, plunging on ahead of him. "Let's go call the sheriff. The whole case has been *blown* to bits, anyway and I don't mean with a handkerchief."

Jason nodded his agreement of her solution, but the expression on his face clearly told her that they would have to talk more about this later.

THE HELICOPTER landed on the cliffs at White Head just yards from the West house. Jason and Addie were waiting for the sheriff when he stepped down. As before, a couple of men from the Galbraith Volunteer Fire Department were ready with a stretcher carried up in the island's only vehicle, the Jeep owned by the proprietor of the general store.

The sheriff's cool appraising expression took in them both. "You two have a penchant for discovering bodies," he remarked.

"Not I," Addie said. "This one's all his." Addie turned and whispered to Jason. "I thought I could hack it, but the antihistamine I took is catching up with me again. You're on your own, but don't worry, I'm heading back to the Inn as we agreed."

Jason nodded. "I'll take Clayborn out to Squeaker Cove and try to get away as soon as I can. It's imperative that I locate that tape."

"If it exists, Jason."

"If it exists, and I certainly mean to find it before the sheriff does."

Addie struggled with a yawn. "We've got to get those other handwritings," she began.

"Ready, Farrell?" The sheriff glared at him.

"Get some sleep," Jason advised Addie. "We'll handle it all later in the day."

"All," she confirmed before walking away.

Jason turned to the sheriff. "I found the body down at Squeaker Cove."

The sheriff squinted up at the gray sky. "What were you doing at Squeaker in this weather?"

"The worse the weather, the more beautiful it is to be a man with a camera," Jason told him, evading the question easily.

After a moment's thought, the sheriff nodded. "I guess I can agree with you there."

When they arrived just above the cove they found the rocks still slippery from the recent rain. Jason pointed down to the overhang. "I discovered him just beneath that. You can't see the ledge from here."

"A little too private, if you ask me." The sheriff gave Jason a keen, curious look, then gazed back down the cove.

"It's a bit of a scramble to get there from here."

"I think I've managed my way around a few tougher spots in my day."

"I imagine you have," Jason replied. The sheriff, however, moved more agilely down the incline than Jason had expected. The sheriff came up behind him, a little out of breath, but his words, full of disbelief, were clear enough.

"This is where you said you found him?"

Jason looked at the long drop that led from the ledge straight to the turbulent sea. "This is where I discovered Steven West, dead, flat out, face up." He bent down and examined the rock. It was wet, but because of the rain, there was no sign that it had been the site of recent violence.

"Any other witnesses?"

Jason stood and accepted the sheriff's hard gaze without flinching. "If there had been, I wouldn't have left the body alone." He remembered looking around for signs of life and finding movement only in the flight of some peregrine falcons. What had happened to the body was perfectly clear. Gruesin and Roberts, separately or together, had been there all along, waiting out of view. When Jason had left, they came back and finished what they had started, consigning Steve's body to the sea.

The sheriff dug his hands into his pockets. "If this is a crime scene, then we're going to have to treat it as one," he said. "If on the other hand, you're lying, Mr. Farrell, I think I can safely say the FBI might just have to put up bail bond to get one of its own out of jail."

Chapter Fourteen

The sound of the fire siren later that afternoon awakened Addie from a deep sleep. Her first thoughts were instinctively for Jason, although there was no reason to suspect he was in any kind of trouble.

She dressed quickly and went outside where she found George Evans and what seemed to be the entire population of Galbraith heading for the town hall. She swallowed her dislike of George Evans and called out to him. "What's going on?"

"Organizing a search party. Steve West's disappeared."

Addie, still rubbing sleep from her eyes, was nonplussed. "Wait a minute, I thought he was—"

"Dead? So did Jason Farrell. Body's disappeared if there was a body to begin with," George said in a single breath, "and the best way to get at the truth is to organize a sweep of the island. Maybe Jason was mistaken, maybe not. He says he wasn't so he's out there with the deputy sheriff combing the rocks around Squeaker. Figured if Steven wasn't dead, he'd be wandering around out there dazed."

"Wandering around? More likely he'd have fallen into the water," Addie said. "There's a terrific undertow at Squeaker."

"That's what happened if you ask me. The fishermen are out trolling the waters now. Come along," he said, waving at her to join the crowd, "we need all the hands we can get."

"Right," Addie said. "I'll catch up. There's something I have to do first."

He waved again and went on his way while Addie took off in the opposite direction. George Evans was headed for the town hall to help organize a search party. That would require teams of people sweeping the island from one end to the other. George Evans's house, like the Winehart cottage, would eventually be reached in the sweep. Eventually. The words for what she was about to do, were breaking and entering. She picked up her pace, feeling a little awkward as she went against the flow of people heading for the town hall, but there was nothing more important than discovering whether George Evans was Enigma.

His two-story shingled house was set back from the road. Unlike the Winehart cottage, however, the land around it was cleared of trees and undergrowth. There was no one around except for Fitzgibbon, who sat on the porch railing. When she approached the house, the cat jumped down and sauntered off. Addie felt a sneeze coming on. "I believe you started the whole thing," she told him.

He disappeared around the side of the house.

Addie approached the front door and rapped briskly on it a couple of times.

"Hi, anybody home?" She waited a reasonable time, knocked again and called out a greeting again. The silence remained profound and a little awesome. Addie then circled the house to confirm there was no one lurking about. Back on the front porch she tentatively reached for the doorknob, then drew her hand back as if scorched. She wasn't used to entering other people's homes uninvited. She closed her eyes, counted to ten and reached out once again, this time taking the knob firmly in her grasp. The door was unlocked. She pushed it open and stepped inside, her heart hammering wildly.

She stepped directly into the living room, which was painted a stark white. It was a striking contrast to the others she had seen on the island. George Evans was a minimalist painter; his works were great attractive swathes of white space with thin lines of color. His paintings dominated the room, which held spare, modern furniture strictly, yet stunningly arranged.

She shook her head in astonishment. She had to find his handwriting if only to explain the dichotomy of George Evans, man and artist. Beyond the living room she found his studio. It was filled with paintings, drawings and sculpture but was also almost compulsively neat.

There was no need to search desk drawers or bookshelves for samples of his writing. On his drawing table lay a journal. A quick glance at the interior cover established that the journal belonged to George Evans. The information it contained was mostly technical. A record of his daily working habits. His handwriting matched the signature on one of his drawings.

No, she thought with a satisfaction that surprised her, George Evans wasn't Enigma. He wasn't Enigma but he also wasn't the overbearing buffoon he wanted everybody to believe. His small, neat, angular script showed a certain amount of caution; an obsession with details and also with himself. Trapped in the large bear of a body George Evans tried very hard to be comfortable with, was a pussycat the size of Fitzgibbon.

Addie quickly realized the portent of her discovery. If George wasn't Enigma, then there were only three people left on her list: Veronica, whose husband's dead body had just mysteriously disappeared, Tim Gruesin and Noah Roberts.

She left the house quickly and quietly and joined up with the first group of searchers she came across.

It was nearly seven by the time Addie returned to the village. No sign had been found of Steven West, neither by the fishermen who had scoured the waters around the island nor during the careful sweep made of Galbraith itself by its inhabitants. There were few people milling around at that time of day and even the dock was empty. It was as if Galbraith were turning in on itself to contemplate this latest shock to its collective system.

Only the sea gulls performed as usual, diving after fish or sitting like carefully rendered sculptures on the pilings. The sky was covered with clouds and mist was rising from the sea. A hundred yards from shore one lone rowboat had a towhead sitting in it with a fishing pole in hand.

Addie saw that the West launch was still at dock, and noted its name for the first time: *Verry*, for Veronica, she supposed. The boat might have to be renamed *Enigma*.

Back at the Inn, she checked through the public rooms for Jason, but he was nowhere to be found. The receptionist handed her two folded notes and said, "This is from Pam Hellman, who asked you to call her. The other's from Jason Farrell."

Addie held her breath for a moment, then said without looking at the notes, "Mr. Farrell wrote this note, I suppose."

The receptionist raised an eyebrow, held up her pen and showed it to her. "In front of me, with this very pen. Something wrong?"

"No, nothing." She was afraid to open the note, afraid that somehow Jason might be Enigma after all. But he couldn't be. She had already shown him Enigma's handwriting and he had been curious, but that was all. No, she was afraid of what she might find out about him and it had nothing at all to do with Enigma.

She ignored Pam's message and saved Jason's until she reached her room, but once there Addie still didn't look at the note. Instead she went over to her window, which overlooked the dock, and tried hard to concentrate on the world outside her window. Sea, boats, lobster traps and sea gulls. She didn't want to know one more thing about Jason. She couldn't afford to.

She watched as Tom Gruesin and Noah Roberts appeared. She watched them board the *Verry* and contemplated the possibility of going after them and asking for samples of their handwritings. It wouldn't wash. Even at this late stage, subtlety was called for.

Subtlety. She had waited long enough. She looked down at the note, guaranteed by the receptionist to be in Jason Farrell's own hand.

The handwritten words were simple enough: "I suppose you heard about Steve. Back soon. Down at the dock and verry busy." Her heart bumped and she gave a sharp little cry. His was the writing she had admired first at West Wind: intelligent, creative and sensual. She caught the word *verry*. Intelligent, creative and sensual Jason Farrell couldn't spell worth a damn.

THE SHERIFF'S DEPUTY had carefully searched the sleek handsome launch owned by Steven West, but then he wasn't looking for an innocent appearing tape, he was looking for the whereabouts of the man himself, dead or alive.

Jason, however, reasoned that if Steven had wished to hide the tape, the *Verry* was as safe a place as any from prying eyes. When the deputy emerged empty-handed, Jason, who had waited for him out on the veranda of the Island Inn, got casually to his feet. The gun he carried fit into a shoulder holster hidden under his denim jacket.

Jason had left a note for Addie at the reception desk and walked down to the dock. It was early evening and he had the place to himself. He looked up at the hotel, checking windows to see if he had an audience. One of the windows belonged to room 203. He thought with a surprising little pang that he wanted it all to be over, wanted to be with Addie, enjoying her, enjoying all the ordinary diurnal events the beautiful island had to offer. No curtain moved, no shadows were seen. But then, he knew she wasn't in. He was beginning to be worried about her. Still maintaining his slow pace he went down the narrow private dock where the *Verry* was berthed, then slipped up the ramp onto the deck and ducked down low into the helmsman's cabin.

He examined the instrument panel, looked through the map case, felt for loose boards and hidden cabinets. He found no tapes and nothing incriminating. Next he went below deck where he found a couple of cabins, a galley and a small, comfortably furnished salon. It was an admirable layout and Jason wondered whether the boat had been purchased with mop-pail money or laundered money. Either way, it was no soap: the government almost certainly would lay claim to the property.

He searched the salon first, admiring the thoroughness of the deputy, who had left no unbolted piece of furniture unturned. There was also a tape deck and a couple of dozen tapes. He was going through them slowly but thoroughly when he heard a footstep behind him. He whipped around but wasn't fast enough. Noah Roberts was grinning at him, a .32 in his hand. Tim Gruesin stood one step behind Noah, hands dug into his pockets, a nasty smile on his face.

Jason thought about the possibility of reaching for his gun but Noah merely shook his head. "Take the gun out nice and easy and pass it on to our friend here."

Jason had no choice but to obey. His only route out of the place was past Gruesin.

"Checkmate," Tim said, picking up the gun and examining it for bullets. "Where we first saw you, Farrell, was in Boston but not at a baseball game. You were coming out of Steve's office and we were on our way in. Now why would you bother to deny that? we asked ourselves. Oh, and when we asked Steve the same question, he told us you were one of Veronica's pickups. We almost believed him, knowing Veronica."

"Tim's a chess player," Noah said. "You make a move, he thinks a dozen moves ahead. Steve blamed your presence on Veronica, but he didn't act like a jealous man. That made Tim decide to try out several possible plays."

"And the one that fit best," Tim went on, "was Steve selling us out to the feds."

"I'm a professor of medieval history."

Tim smiled crookedly and hefted Jason's gun. "Pretty well-armed for a professor of medieval history. Tilly over at the hotel's reception desk isn't above taking a twenty for a little information. The number you dialed in Washington was no university.''

"And that's why you killed Steve?"

"Killed him? A pity we didn't." Noah screwed up his face. "Don't make the mistake of thinking we're stupid. You said he's dead but there's no body. Which makes us think you're in it together. Nothing like a renegade officer of the law. As far as we're concerned, Steve is safe in the Bahamas milking an offshore account. Maybe you're his new partner, and maybe not."

"Steve is dead, you'd better believe it, and you both head the list of suspects," Jason said. "Don't make things any tougher on yourself than they already are. We know all about you. I'll offer you the same deal I gave West. Cooperate and the government will go easy on you."

Noah gave him a level stare. He raised the gun a little higher. "By getting rid of you we've got nothing to lose and everything to gain."

"Everything?" Jason asked.

"This launch is quite capable of taking us to safety."

"And somewhere along the way," Tim added, "you'll go deep-sea diving. It's a shame you didn't bring your equipment along. It could be a pretty long swim back to the mainland."

ADDIE STOOD on the beach just beyond dockside staring at the *Verry* dead ahead. While she watched, Tim Gruesin came up on deck and after looking around for a moment, went into the helmsman's cabin. Even in the half dark she could see Tim quite easily. He gazed at the paneling with a perplexed look on his face, then came back out to the stairs leading below deck.

She heard him quite clearly in the quiet early evening air. "Where's the key to the ignition?"

Addie glanced at the note in her hand. "Down at the docks and verry busy." It had taken a while for the word to connect. Jason was on board the *Verry* and so were Tim Gruesin and Noah Roberts. It was possible he had connected them to Steve's murder. Or had proof one of them was Enigma. She didn't like the feel of it.

No, the note simply meant he was searching the *Verry* for the missing tape. It was possible Jason had been surprised by the two bankers and that he was still on board the boat. Possibly in trouble. Maybe she should go for help.

Gruesin's voice floated up. "Look behind the control panel."

Tim went back into the cabin. Addie didn't even stop to think of her alternatives. There was no time to go for help; Gruesin and Roberts were about to leave. While Tim was distracted searching for the ignition key, Addie made her first move. She searched quickly around the rough gravel beach for a piece of driftwood and found one with a suitable knob head that had a good heft to it. Clutching it tightly she made her way onto the dock, keeping close to the boat. She looked up at the safety of the inn. She could see the window to her room and thought of the sanctuary it offered. Perhaps Jason wasn't on board the *Verry*, after all. Perhaps he had already found what he was looking for and left before Gruesin and Roberts arrived. Perhaps all Tim Gruesin and Noah Roberts wanted to do was a little deep-sea fishing.

The truth became evident pretty quickly. She heard Noah's voice again from below deck. "Tim, need help?"

"I'm still looking for the stupid key."

"Behind the control panel, I said."

"Okay, okay, keep your shirt on. You just entertain Farrell. I don't want him to get lonely. Right," he said after another moment, "I've found it. We'll be on our way in another minute. All I have to do is pull up the ramp and cast off."

Addie couldn't wait any longer. She had to act now or watch the *Verry* go to sea with Jason aboard it. She crouched low and took the ramp in a couple of steps. She hit the deck and, still crouching, moved swiftly to the front of the cabin where Tim couldn't see her.

"That you, Noah?"

"What?"

"I thought I heard... Wait."

Addie went silently around the cabin and positioned herself behind the door. She took in a deep gulp of air in an attempt to calm the pounding of her heart. It didn't help. She found herself gripping the wood so tightly, it seemed embedded in her skin. Tim came out of the cabin muttering to himself. She raised the piece of driftwood but he caught sight of the movement and turned around, his mouth open, his eyes wide with surprise. She saw him reach for the gun tucked into his belt and brought the driftwood down on his skull. He dropped to the deck. Addie was just about to retrieve the gun when she heard Noah's voice.

"Hey, what's going on up there?"

She heard someone move heavily up the stairs. "Sit tight, Farrell. You're not going anywhere."

Roberts poked his head out and Addie raised the driftwood high again, as though it were a baseball bat. She waited while he took another step. Then she brought the driftwood down hard. She heard his sigh and a loud thud as he fell back down the stairs. The gun clattered down separately and bounced below step by step. Addie waited, stunned, still gripping her club with both hands. When she heard no further sound at all, she went quickly over to Tim's prostrate body. She gingerly retrieved his gun and only then did she put the club down. Holding the gun before her, Addie went below deck, easing herself down quietly. Her heart was still hammering.

"Well, I'll be—" Jason, sitting on a chair, his hands tied behind him, grinned up at her.

Relief washed over her. She could scarcely speak over the lump that lodged in her throat. "Are you all right?"

"Never better," he said. He nodded at Noah Roberts who lay very still at the foot of the stairs. "You did all that?"

She nodded. "How'd you get yourself into such a fix?"

"Just lucky, I guess. How about untying me, or do you think I'm Enigma?"

She laughed and ran over to him. She took his face between her hands and kissed his lips. "No, Jason, you're not Enigma. You're not even a puzzlement."

IT WAS only later, when they were back in Addie's room, that she noted the gash over his eye. "How'd that happen?"

"You didn't get there fast enough. If I'd known you were coming, I wouldn't have tried to arm wrestle Noah for his gun."

"You lost."

"Don't tell my boss."

"I might tell him anyway just so you can be kicked out of the FBI. That's no job if you plan to keep breathing."

"Odd words coming from a graphologist with a penchant for tracking down murderers."

"Have we tracked the murderer down?" Addie asked. "We don't have a sample of Veronica's handwriting, even if Tim and Noah are off the hook as far as being Enigma is concerned."

Jason laughed. "I really have to hand it to you, Addie. There was the sheriff hauling them away in handcuffs and you stopped the action for autographs."

"Well, the district attorney might hassle them for threatening to kill you, but they aren't Enigma and you haven't found the tape that proves they're involved in the money laundering scheme. They'll walk away, believe me."

"Addie, it's not over until it's over. Steve West is dead and so is an obscure detective named Masconi."

"Better let me apply some first aid to your battle wound. That kit I bought at the general store the other day is coming in entirely too handy."

He followed her into the bathroom, sat dutifully down on the edge of the tub and let Addie tend to the gash.

She removed a Band-Aid from its wrapping, saying, "Jason, I'm worried about Veronica running around loose."

He reached up and stayed her hand for a moment. "Pam said to pack it in and go home. The Boston d.a.'s office is going to contact Sheriff Clayborn and you're out of it entirely."

"I still think we should have told Clayborn ourselves. He could have posted a deputy right outside of West Wind."

"The lady is acting the wife in confusion," Jason said. "She feels safest in her bedroom, surrounded by white lace pillows, catered to by Dr. Kevin and her servants. As for telling the sheriff, telling him what? That you have a scrap of paper in a handwriting you think belongs to Veronica West? He wouldn't buy it. You're not judge nor jury on her guilt or innocence. Step back, Addie. Let the professionals finish the job."

"This is a fine reversal of events. The last time we talked about Enigma, you wanted to spill everything to the sheriff."

"It's a different game now, Addie. It's no longer a guess who Enigma is."

Addie pulled her hand out of his grasp and then carefully applied the Band-Aid to the wound. "No, it isn't. Veronica is Enigma by default. There were a dozen people in the room...."

"Plus you."

"Plus me. I know the handwriting I saw belonged to Enigma. Everyone else has been scratched. I don't have to see her handwriting. But Jason, she's free to leave the island anytime. She could fly to England, or disappear anywhere in the world. She doesn't even have to wait for the ferry. The launch is still at the dock."

"Somehow Veronica doesn't strike me as a sailor. I wouldn't worry about her plying the high seas alone."

"Now that you know that tape wasn't on the *Verry*, are you closing up shop, too, Jason, leaving the island tomorrow with me?"

He shook his head. "I'm not writing it off quite yet. If I don't find the tape, my whole case goes down the tubes."

Addie put away her first-aid kit. She went over to the window to gaze out over the water. "Funny but the signs were there, you know. About Veronica, I mean. The killer was trusted by her victims. All signs pointed to someone who killed but didn't like the act of killing. And Enigma had to be in a position to meet wealthy women of a certain age. Veronica fits all those criteria, especially since her husband was an officer of the bank."

Jason came up behind her and put his hands on her shoulders. "Let's forget Enigma and all its variations. What made you come after me?"

"Forget Enigma, just like that."

"Just like that. I asked you a question. What made you come after me?"

He drew her into his arms. Addie knew he was waiting for her to say something and it had to do with his handwriting. She had insisted upon knowing who he was by the signs he made on a piece of paper and now she knew and in a way she was a little sorry. It wasn't psychology or graphology or even instinct that had made her fall for him, but her heart, her corny old waiting heart reacting in a brandnew way. And nothing and no one else had ever mattered so much before.

She studied his face and his deep-set intelligent eyes that still held just a hint of mockery. "I caught your pun," she said. "You were *verry* busy." She rolled the r on her tongue. "I thought you wanted me to come to the launch after you and that it had to do with a missing body and a missing tape."

"And no other reason?"

She hesitated. No, she wouldn't tell him. She might let him guess forever about his handwriting. "Can't think of one."

He eyed her skeptically, with a little grin on his face. "I like making puns," he said, "and I'm glad you came after me, but it wasn't what I had in mind."

"Really?" She drew her arms around his neck. "What did you have in mind?"

It happened so naturally that neither of them knew who'd made the first move. The kiss started out tentatively and then almost at once encompassed another dimension. Time on the tiny island took on a fresh meaning; familiar sounds produced a music that was full of heady excitement—birds calling, water lapping, a distant horn searching.

Lips crushed together, breaths mingled, tongues dueled as Addie and Jason moved slowly toward the bed, entwined. Addie had never been so overwhelmed by her feelings for anyone before. She wanted to be held so tightly there would be no space between them, no particle that could separate them.

Her heart beat wildly at the thought that she had almost lost him. Now, when she was aware of everything about him, she realized how much he had come to mean to her. His breath was warm against her cheek. He was murmuring her name in a way no one had ever done before. He gave a low primal growl and he sought her mouth again. The urgent rhythms of his mouth matched the pulses that throbbed through her body.

All thoughts of the danger they faced were gone in the quiet of their kiss. For this moment the world stopped and every threat disappeared in the heated whisper of their small, isolated space. She entrusted herself, without reservations, to his love.

With exquisite tenderness Jason removed her clothes and then his own, his eyes never leaving her. Addie held her breath. He was muscular and tanned and virile and she raised her arms toward him. He held himself over her, then lowered his body to hers until they touched everywhere from head to toe, warm flesh meeting warm flesh.

She needed to know him, to feel the warmth of his flesh and the strength of his body. She explored the outline of his rib cage, skimmed over hard and narrow hips and firm thighs. He lifted his head and gazed at her with a hot, sweet and unbearably gentle look and then his mouth moved slowly over her face and throat, lightly gliding down until he had one tingling nipple between his lips. He traced heated kisses down the length of her body. A cloud of pleasure enfolded her and she called out his name through a sharp rush of desire.

She shivered as she thought how close they had come to never having known each other. Nothing would get in their way now.

His touch confirmed all she already knew about him. His lovemaking was gentle and yet it had a primitive edge, a raw heat that radiated from his body to hers. He was a treasure she had found by the sea and he was taking possession of her.

"I could never bear to lose you now, you know that, don't you?" His voice was ragged and Addie knew she was on the brink of incredible joy. The heat of his body seemed to course directly through her. His fervent kisses deepened as the hard demands of his body hinted at the irresistible forces gathering within him. Then there was no more thinking as he entered her, murmuring her name and claiming her soul.

Chapter Fifteen

Jason watched her sleep. The soft rise and fall of her breasts sent a shiver through him of such intense possessiveness that, without thinking, he caught his breath and held it. Her hair lay spread out on the pillow, dappled with the fresh light of the morning sun. Her face was radiant even in sleep.

Addie's passion had moved him more than he'd anticipated. She was more giving, more intense than he had dreamed. She was, in fact, a wonderful contradiction; a professional able to separate herself from her emotions, then when it meant the most, revealing a surprisingly deep and pure instinct for love.

She was a rare woman with rare courage. She had taken on both Tim Gruesin and Noah Roberts to rescue him without stopping to consider that she might not be able to win. He smiled at the memory. Even unflappable Sheriff Clayborn had raised an eyebrow when Jason told him that story.

Jason bent over her and realized he had never kissed a woman awake before. Addie stirred at his touch and opened her eyes. Her smile promised him that he had just become whole, that he would never be alone again.

"What time is it?" she asked.

"I haven't any idea."

"Check, crazy, my watch is on the table."

"Ten o'clock. Time for me to get going."

"Where on this tiny island do you intend to go?"

"West Wind."

Addie pushed herself up on her elbows, eyes wide. "What? You're not going to take on Veronica."

"I'm not talking about Veronica. I'm talking about turning West Wind inside out again to find that tape."

"For which Veronica will give you unconditional permission with a wan smile developed through years of practice on the best stages of London and New York. Jason, leave it. The tape may not even exist. There's no guarantee it was ever made. We don't know why Steve was killed but he's gone and the case is history."

"I hate a smart Alec," Jason said, bending over and kissing her. "I'm going to give Veronica my true credentials and tell her to get out of the way. She'll cooperate just to make herself look good."

"What if you need rescuing again?"

"I think there's only one way to shut you up." He took her lips greedily, not really wanting to leave her again so soon. Addie moved under him and Jason knew that the tape would have to stay in hiding, wherever it was, a while longer.

"Ah, Jason, Addie." Kevin Morgan answered the door at West Wind and gave them a surprised smile. "What are you...? Hey, come on in but Veronica isn't here." He stood aside and beckoned them in, then preceded them into the living room. "Listen, that business about Noah and Tim has her all upset. Her life is crashing down around her shoulders, poor kid." He dug his hands into his pockets and surveyed them as though their dour expressions made him expect a fresh infusion of bad news.

But when Addie and Jason said nothing, he gave them a perplexed smile. "They've found Steve, then? He's okay?" He made the statements in the form of a question.

"Is that a question or something you know for a fact," Jason remarked.

"Asking, but the truth is I don't really want to hear the answer."

There was a long moment of silence, then Kevin said, "Veronica took the launch into Port Clyde."

Jason caught Addie's eye, a tacit admission of a mistake of colossal proportions. They'd have to race back to the hotel and alert the sheriff.

"She has some idea that Steven is playing fast and loose with her. That he's back in Boston. I tried to talk her out of it. How could he have left? The launch is still here and no one saw him take the ferry. I told her to stay put."

Addie frowned. It was obvious Veronica had lied to Kevin, too. She didn't care about her husband, dead or alive. She had just wanted to get off the island.

There was a sudden movement and Addie jumped, but it was only Veronica's long-haired black cat brushing lightly against her. Addie made an automatic movement toward it, drawing her fingers through the silky fur. Jason thought he knew the reason. With Addie's soft heart, she was probably wondering what would happen to the cat with Veronica gone.

"Listen, how about a drink?" Kevin waved his hand around the living room as if offering them a seat.

Addie, however, seemed to be having a sudden allergic reaction to the cat. She sniffled and reached into her pocket for a tissue. Her eyes had begun to tear.

"Are you all right?" Jason asked worried.

"I'm a little clogged up. Damn, each attack gets worse. This one's going to be a honey."

Kevin solicitously took her arm and led her over to the couch. "The cat, right? I remember now, you said you suffered from allergies."

"That's right, Fitzgibbon and now this cat." But when Addie sat down on the couch the attack increased. "I keep away from cats at home," she explained in a hoarse voice, "and I'm not used to carrying antiallergy medicine around with me."

Kevin bent over her solicitously. "Do you have any medication with you?"

"No. Truth is I ran out. When I feel good I don't even think about..." She was clearly unable to finish the sentence, ending it in a cough.

"Maybe she could lie down for a while," Jason suggested. He'd make better time anyway if Addie stayed behind.

"Come to think of it, there's probably cat hair on the pillows and that's why she's reacting so strongly," Kevin said to Jason. He reached for Addie's hand. "What you want is the chaise, which is about as far away as you can get. And you need a prescription for something strong."

"It's the worst I've had in ages," she told him gratefully. "I feel I've just been hit on the head with a hammer. I'd really like to get back to my room at the Inn." She tried to smile up at him through watery eyes. It was also a convenient excuse for returning to the Inn quickly so they could warn the sheriff.

"Listen," Kevin said to Jason, "let her stay here. I'm going to write out a prescription for something strong. The general store should be able to fill it. Meanwhile I'll remove the cat and the pillows and see that she stays comfortable."

"Thanks, Doc." Jason looked over at Addie. "He's right, you know."

"I'm convinced," she said, reaching for her bag and more tissues. She didn't feel much like walking anyway, and Jason could talk to the sheriff perfectly well without her.

Kevin handed Jason the hastily scrawled prescription, saying, "Addie, it'll take him a half hour at the most. And to keep you comfortable, I'll make a pot of tea since we're fresh out of chicken soup."

"Kevin," she said, smiling between coughs while she dabbed at her nose, "you're an angel."

All the way back to the village, Jason rehearsed how he'd handle the next crucial half hour. First he'd drop the prescription off and then he'd race over to the Island Inn and place a call to the sheriff. If Pam hadn't already apprised Clayborn of the facts about Enigma, the sheriff might decide to sit tight and not act. Steven's body still hadn't been found and the sheriff was bound to take the news with a grain of salt about Veronica being a serial killer. Jason thought with a bitter smile that if he were in Clayborn's place, he certainly would question the probability. Well, if Veronica was off the island at least that meant Addie was safe. Once he'd called the sheriff he figured he'd pick up the prescription, retrace his steps to West Wind and tell Kevin to stand back, that he was going to go over the place with a fine-tooth comb.

Kevin, you're an angel. Addie's words to the doctor rankled. Jason didn't want Addie grateful to anyone but him. He thought of how her body looked and felt and how much he wanted her, tears, headache, cough and all.

The owner of the general store was in an expansive mood when Jason came in.

"A bit too much excitement around here," he remarked. "Been here almost my whole life and I don't remember a summer like this. You'd think someone had put a curse on the island."

"How long before I can pick up this prescription?" Jason asked handing over the slip of paper.

The manager shook his head as he examined the prescription. "Chicken scrawl, can't figure out what he wants." He squinted and held the paper up to the light. Then he showed the prescription to Jason who glanced at it and shook his head.

"Beats me. Do what you can with it, I'll be back in about ten minutes. I'm going to make a phone call." He left without waiting for an answer.

If he couldn't get the prescription filled, Addie would just have to make do with an ordinary antihistamine. He was putting her on the Port Clyde boat that afternoon and she could always find what she needed on the mainland.

The one and only public telephone on the island was in use and Jason paced the floor for three minutes before asking Tilly to ring the sheriff for him on the switchboard.

"Find another body?" she asked, barely containing her sarcasm.

Sheriff Clayborn wasn't at his desk and had to be beeped in his car. When Jason finally got through to him, he told his story quickly and succinctly.

The sheriff had already spoken to Pam and said someone was on the way down from Boston. He also said that he wasn't about to arrest the wife or widow of Steve West on the basis of an unsigned scrap of paper.

Jason knew he was right.

"That launch is capable of landing down at Booth Bay or any other port along the coast," the sheriff added. "If Veronica West wants to run away, she won't have any trouble at all doing so."

"Put out a bulletin."

A long, drawn-out sigh rumbled along the wire. "Farrell, I'm going to be real sorry when you leave that island. I'll put out a bulletin to track the lady, but there's no way I'm going to issue a warrant for her arrest, not without proof."

Jason hung up, smiled his thanks to the switchboard operator and made his way outside. He was half way to the General Store when he heard someone call out to him.

"Hey, Jason, you look like a man who'd go for a spot of fishing."

Jason looked around to see Linus Bishop headed toward him.

"Come on," Linus went on, "I could use the company. I just met poor Veronica. It's awful for her to be held in suspense like this. Is Steve dead, or isn't he?"

"What do you mean you just saw Veronica?"

Linus gave him a quizzical look. "I just saw Veronica. What's the problem? I saw her heading up the road and we stopped and talked. She's pretty low. Incidentally, she gave me carte blanche to use the *Verry*—"

But Jason didn't even wait for him to finish the sentence. He sprinted down to the dock and saw the *Verry* in her berth. His mouth went dry and he could feel his heart pounding unnaturally. He turned and raced up the road, passing an astonished Linus. "Which way was she headed?"

"Back to West Wind."

He passed the general store but didn't even give a thought to the prescription. If that woman harmed Addie, he'd kill her.

Chapter Sixteen

"How are you doing, Addie?" Kevin came over to the chaise carrying a mug of hot tea which he put down on the table beside her.

"Lousy." She eyed the tea but had no desire to try some.

"Lucky for you," he said with a small smile, "allergies aren't usually fatal."

"No, that's true. Never thought I'd have something good to say about allergies."

His smile didn't go away and it struck Addie that something strange was going on. He was staring at her in a new way, as if he were a cat that had just cornered a mouse. Oh, damn, she thought, he's going to make another pass and I can't even breathe.

"You're a nosy little thing, aren't you?" He sat down beside her and began stroking her hair.

He was sitting too close and his touch made her squeamish. She drew back. "I'm sorry, what did you say?"

"You heard me quite clearly. You may be a little fuzzy around the tear ducts right now, but there's nothing wrong with your hearing."

Something had happened to his eyes. His pupils had contracted and he was gazing at her through laser points that were black as tar. His mouth curled up at the corners but she would no longer describe his expression as a smile. His breath on her cheek was sharp and hot.

Enigma. The word came to her unbidden. Her flesh crawled with the chilling knowledge of it. Enigma. He was far cleverer than she had ever imagined and she had to put her hand to her lips to keep from speaking the word aloud. It seemed to her that he must know everything, even the code name given him by the District Attorney's Office.

Enigma. He was no more than inches away. He'd murdered at least four women already and she was alone with him in the huge, empty, quiet house.

All she could think of was the prescription Jason had tucked so carelessly into his jacket pocket. He hadn't even looked at it, hadn't connected the handwriting to Enigma's. There had been no reason to suspect. She had told Jason that Veronica was Enigma, and he had believed her.

"Catching on?" Kevin asked quietly.

Reason told her to take everything slowly, to divert him, to ease herself out from under his gaze, his touch, to run straight for town. She was afraid he could even hear the wild hammering of her heart and all she could do was lie there with Kevin cutting off all possibility of escape.

"Where's Veronica?" she asked. Was it possible Veronica was in the house after all, drugged or worse?

He smiled. "Conveniently out of the way for the moment."

"You mean she's gone to the mainland?"

"Veronica always had exquisite timing. Imagine leaving me here at West Wind and not even knowing you'd come by for a little visit. But we're not here to discuss Veronica," he told her, an edge of hardness creeping into his voice. "Those handwriting samples. Did you think I wouldn't see you sneaking them into your bag?"

"Kevin, you don't make sense. What are you talking about?"

But she already knew. The note stuck on the door of Winehart must have been in Veronica's handwriting, not Kevin's and Jason was trying to chase Veronica down as though she were Enigma.

Kevin had succeeded only too well in playing an elaborate game on Addie and had won. She didn't know how he'd gotten Veronica to write the poem he'd used at the cottage but somehow he'd managed it. And Addie had walked right into his lair and allowed him to send away Jason, the one person who could save her.

If Jason would only look at the prescription, recognize the handwriting, *believe* it was the same one as on the photocopy she had given him.

"Ah," Kevin said in a tone of satisfaction, "you see the error of your ways. Incidentally, that one little gesture, that furtive look around the room just before you spirited the samples away, that's what made a believer in graphology out of me."

Keep him talking, Addie told herself. She had known men like him before. She had seen them behind bars coolly boasting of crimes as if they were accomplishments to be proud of, men who'd gone through life on the slant, leaving human debris all along their trails, men without the slightest bit of empathy for their fellow human beings. Madmen.

It was an effort to speak in a normal tone but she had to. "It was purely an automatic gesture," she protested. "I didn't even know I'd taken them until I got home."

"That's why you took the trouble to select a frame, pull it apart, hide the samples between the picture and mat and carefully put a backing on, cut neatly from a grocery bag. Tsk, tsk, how unimaginative." Kevin shook his head slowly, a smile playing around his lips. "Oh, Addie, give me a better excuse for your behavior than that. You didn't even know you'd taken them." His tone of voice mimicked hers.

He traced a line along her cheek with his fingertip. She felt the touch as though it were given with a razor blade and only reason told her not to draw back, not to present a sign that she was frightened.

"I knew you weren't the amateur you pretended to be," he went on. "You tripped over your tongue reading Blake's poem and then to make matters worse, you perpetrated the most outrageous lies about me. I'm really rather a nice man with nothing in the way of a temper. You said I was determined. Correct. I can't fault you there. You said I was creative. Decidedly.'' He pouted, then said, ''You never even asked to see one of my poems, Addie. Bad move. Usually they want to see a poem. Veronica, in fact, keeps a notebook full of them. I'd have written one for you, by the way, but decided on Shakespeare, a quotation beloved of Veronica. It was easy enough to ask her to copy it down for me on my prescription pad. She actually believed I wanted something written in her own little hand.''

''But you see I knew all along that it was Veronica's hand,'' Addie said.

He shook his head. ''Somehow I don't buy that, Addie. Extremely intelligent, that's what you called me. In fact, I've a very soft, sensitive side. You didn't catch that, did you? Well, it's not a perfect science, is it, graphology? Still, I now know handwriting reveals facts about oneself best kept hidden.''

Addie eyed the mug of tea he had brought her. It was still steaming. If she could only ease herself to a sitting position, she might grab it and throw it in his face. But at her slight movement, he smiled and forced her back against the chaise. ''By the way, you can scream if you like. No one will hear you. You know how isolated West Wind is and there are no servants around at the moment. I told Veronica we'd leave today, the two of us, together. Lovely Veronica, she has a strong romantic streak and I'm the current object of her affections.''

''But Veronica's already gone,'' Addie said. ''You told me.''

Kevin smiled. ''I'd like to take a look at your handwriting someday. Do you always believe everything you hear?''

So Jason was chasing after a will-o'-the-wisp. Veronica was still on the island. Did she know about Kevin or was she completely innocent?

"You're thinking about Jason," Kevin said. "Don't bother, Addie. Even if he runs all the way to town and all the way back he'll be too late."

"He knows who you are, Kevin, and so does Sheriff Clayborn, and the district attorney's office in Boston."

"Addie," he said in an admonishing tone, "Addie, Addie, Addie, they have no proof, none of them. Uh, uh, by the time they put two and two together, I'll be long gone." He reached out once again and entwined her hair between his fingers. "Quick temper, you said. Mix everything together, you said, and I'm a volatile companion." He shook his head slowly. "No, wrong there. I'm deliberate, Addie. I plan. Temper tantrum? I'd never call it a temper tantrum. Someone gets in my way, I'm reasonable. See?" He drew his hand away, held both his hands up and turned them back to front. "No temper, no anger. I'm calm."

Addie couldn't let herself think about how scared she was. She wanted to remain detached, pretend he was a patient. She banked upon his need to show off his superior reasoning. "Why all those—"

"Deaths?" He finished the sentence for her. "All necessary. I already told you. And my handwriting should have told you, too. I'm not a violent man by nature."

"No," she said quietly. "I saw that. You're a doctor, you're supposed to save lives."

He laughed, a long dry sound that ended abruptly. "I'm trying to figure you out. Psychologist, graphologist. From Boston, right?"

"Why did you kill Eda Barnstable?"

His eyes narrowed. "Ah, so that's it, poor, silly Eda. A little too grasping and clingy but generous to a fault. And in the end, a lot more trouble than she was worth, believe me."

She saw him move and it seemed to Addie as if all the action had been speeded up. His lips parted in a grin and then his hands loomed large and menacingly over her. "This whole conversation is for your benefit, not mine. Don't take me for a dolt, Addie. Not in my handwriting, remember? Definitely not in my handwriting. I can watch a clock, too. Your boyfriend should be on his way back with the medicine that won't do you a bit of good." He reached over and pulled a pillow from the couch. "Goose down, incidentally. Not at all nice for people with allergies. But it hardly matters one way or another. It'll do nicely. Without a doubt your death will be taken as the result of a severe allergy attack."

Addie took in as deep a breath as she could. Fear gave her the surge of adrenaline she needed to push against him with both hands. Kevin was taken by surprise, as if all his previous victims had gone willingly to their deaths just to please him. He fell backward and Addie had just the moment she needed to break free and run for the door.

"Come on, Addie, you're being stupid."

Her hand felt icy and the doorknob slipped under her grasp. She gripped it with both hands and jerked it open. She ran through, slamming it behind her.

"Addie!"

She heard the door open again as she raced for the road, then she realized he was making his way through the shrubbery and would cut her off before she could reach the road. She had no choice but to turn back, head around the house and take the route along the cliff. Her only hope now was to outrun him.

"Hey, Addie," he called as she angled back, "dumb move."

But it wasn't dumb at all. She sprinted around the house heading north along the cliff, disturbing a conference of gulls as she ran. They flew shrieking into the sky.

"Addie."

She glanced back and saw that Kevin was less than a hundred yards away and catching up fast. Addie thought she could see him grin. She picked up speed. The one thing he hadn't counted on was her endurance and she blessed the time she'd spent running around the park in Boston.

The trouble was, she was headed into territory she didn't really know. The verge of the cliffs was a virtual patchwork of rock, tufts of green grass, narrow fissures, small twisted pine trees and thick bushes. She twisted in and out, breathing evenly, hoarding her energy. When she checked back again, Kevin hadn't gained any more ground.

Then suddenly his words came to her with frightening clarity as though pushed toward her by the wind. "Hey, Addie, you're finished. There's nowhere to go now but down."

She pulled up short, realizing she had indeed reached the tip of White Head, which ended abruptly in a steep hundred-foot drop into the churning sea.

She was boxed in with Kevin cutting off her route back and nothing but rocks and death below. There was only one chance and that was to round the tip, hoping the other side would reveal a different face.

Kevin angled toward her, gaining several yards in the space of seconds. "Addie! Give it up. You're just wasting your time."

She found what she was looking for, a crevice wide enough to take a human body. There were even hand- and footholds she might negotiate with care. The crevice narrowed a couple of yards below to a small boulder-cluttered ledge. If she could reach it, she might be able to edge her way along the cliff wall until it began its gentle slope toward town.

"Addie." Kevin's voice was closer.

She had no choice. As she hesitated a moment longer, she felt a sharp object glance off the back of her head; her knees buckled and she slid down into the crevice. Even as she fell she heard the stone Kevin had thrown at her shatter against the cliff before scattering in fragments into the sea.

Addie reached out, her fingers splayed, grasping for a handhold. She landed on the clutter of stones and boulders, which graced the ledge she had seen from above. It wasn't a soft landing and she lay very still for a moment, wondering which parts of her were smashed and which remained whole.

"Hey, Addie."

She looked up to see Kevin on the crest of the cliff above her, hands on his hips. The most extraordinary thought occurred to her; that he *was* extremely attractive and charming. Even now she could understand his appeal to his victims and why they would have agreed to give up everything for him.

"I wouldn't move if I were you," he said. "One little shift and you'll slide all the way down to oblivion."

"Isn't that what you want?" She tried to raise herself but her ankle was wedged tightly between two rocks. When she tried to move, several stones came loose and bounded away.

"This isn't how I planned for things to end," Kevin said. "It could all have been so different. I'm the type to forgive and forget. You know, you shouldn't have rejected my advances the other night. That hurt my feelings. I'm a poet, sensitive to rejection. You saw that in my handwriting, it's there."

"Oh, yes, of course I did," she said in as cajoling a manner as she could. She had to ease her foot out from between the rocks without his noticing it. She winced with pain but realized almost at once that nothing was broken.

She looked up at him. He was watching her efforts with a small smile on his face. "Kevin," she began in an attempt to divert his attention, "when you tacked that note in Veronica's handwriting to my front door, I knew it didn't quite match the psychological profile I had of you so I called the sheriff and told him of my suspicions."

Kevin merely laughed. "Good try, Addie, but it won't wash. Trouble is, I detest violence. I wanted it all to be neat and quick. Don't you want to know the whole story before you . . . go?"

Another moment and her foot would come free. "You mean you're willing to talk to me . . . about Eda Barnstable and the others?"

"Fools, all of them," he said. "Devoted patients and loving contributors to my famous clinic in Switzerland. Poor darlings, they thought sheep glands and monkey glands would give them a new lease on life. Never had a chance to find out, did they? Yes, indeed, they never had a chance to find out. It was so much easier to put them out of their misery once I had their money and before they discovered the folly of their ways. For you see, there was no clinic, never had been.''

He shaded his eyes from the sun and appeared to be looking around for something. ''Ah, there we have it,'' he said. ''You'll wait a minute, won't you?''

The moment he was out of sight, Addie carefully and painfully managed to pull her foot free. Her ankle was bruised, but she could move her foot even though she wasn't quite certain yet how much weight she would be able to put on it.

''Here we are,'' Kevin said, appearing above her again. He was kicking at a large stone, nudging it toward the edge of the cliff until it sat directly above her. He left again and returned carrying several others, which he piled up nearby in a small cairn.

Addie stared at him, mesmerized.

''No,'' Kevin went on, ''I had to come to Galbraith because of Eda, you see. Her husband had tied up her inheritance offshore. 'Terrible of him,' she used to say. 'Didn't trust me at all, did he?' She knew about his ties with the mob and Steven and his laundered money coming out of the Atlantic City casinos. I sometimes wondered if Eda hadn't done old Barney in. Didn't do her any good at all, even if she did.

''She had a devil of a time getting at her funds. Steven West's bank controlled every cent she had. Wouldn't let her withdraw a penny without his express approval. No, Eda wasn't quite like the others. But you see I still came away with her power of attorney. All I had to do was learn from Steven West where the money was banked and how I might get to it.''

''Then you knew Steve all along.''

Kevin shook his head, smiling at what he clearly thought was her stupidity. "Knew Steve? Hardly. I had to do a lot of fancy footwork just to arrange to meet Veronica."

"But you managed it nicely."

"I always finish what I set out to do, Addie."

"Except that Steve is dead and you're no closer to Eda's fortune than you ever were."

"Wrong, Addie. Wrong. I learned everything straight from the man's mouth. Via a very useful tape, which I took from Steven West and left for safekeeping at West Wind, in the music library, mixed in with all those other tapes. Clever hiding place.

"West's tape of his conversation with Gruesin and Roberts spelled out just how they laundered the mob money and where it was kept. It was Eda's husband Barney who worked it all out for them, you know. Cash was skimmed from slot machines and games, turned over to the three bankers who nicely legitimized it for the mob and, of course, for their cut of the profits. Now all I have to do is go to the Bahamas, present my power of attorney at the proper bank and collect Eda's fortune. If anyone tries to stop me I'll just threaten to blow up the whole works."

He crouched down and ran his hands along the cairn. "And I'll take Veronica with me so she can pick up Steven's share."

Then Veronica *was* alive although for how long Addie didn't even dare guess.

Kevin stood, picked up a stone and, after hefting it, looked down at her. Addie cringed. She might be able to make her escape if she could just get to her feet and edge her way along the north cliff wall.

"'Cruelty has a Human Heart,'" he said, raising the stone above his head.

Then, all at once Addie heard voices and laughter from a little way off.

Jason. Relief washed over her. Kevin threw the stone so that it cleared the cliff and fell into the ocean. He shook his head. "Don't even try screaming, Addie. We'll just let these nice folks go on their merry way." He smiled and shouted at them. "Hi. Nice day."

"Great weather," a man called back. His voice seemed to come to Addie from some distance away.

So it wasn't Jason after all. Addie pulled herself to her feet while Kevin was turned away, praying the hikers would come to the edge of the cliff and peer down, but they didn't. There was a slight twinge in her ankle, the kind that she knew would disappear with a little exercise and use if she ever got the chance. She looked up to find Kevin with his foot braced against the huge stone, which was now teetering on the edge.

"Couldn't ask for better," Kevin called to the man. "Where you headed?"

"Back to town. Time for a tall glass of beer. Well, *ciao*."

It was her last chance. Addie took a deep breath and cried out, using all her lung power. "Help! Help!"

There was a fluttering of wings. Several gulls rose into the sky screeching.

"Noisy little beggars, aren't they?" Kevin called out with a charming smile. The stone moved slightly again under his foot.

"You can say that again." The voices faded off with more laughing. A lone gull let out a long, mournful cry.

"There's a good girl," Kevin said after a moment. "You see? Miracles don't happen." He regarded her with the same charming smile, then wiped it off in an instant. He bent on his haunches and looked earnestly down at her.

"Listen, I didn't mean for Steven West to die any more than I wanted you to have to die, Addie. I was his doctor, I was responsible for him, but he found that detective's briefcase and he had to look inside. Poor Steven, I suspect his body will wash up one of these days."

Addie closed her eyes briefly. It was all tying together and it looked like as if the knowledge she'd gained would die with her. "Masconi's briefcase?"

"Foolish of me to keep it, but I intend to burn the papers in the fireplace and I haven't had time yet. Shame on you, Addie, you've kept me entirely too busy."

He reached for another stone from his pile, hefted it and threw it down, deliberately missing her. " 'And Jealousy a Human Face.' Steve hired the detective," he went on, "to find out who his wife was playing around with. And Masconi was the type to leave no stone unturned. He checked into my background and found out. Came up here with the papers to show me. He tried to blackmail me. I didn't have much choice in the matter, did I?"

"And so you killed him."

"Took him for a long walk out to Gull Rock. Told him it was a condition for getting his money—I didn't want Steve to see us together. One thing I can say about Masconi, he didn't trust the clements. The trouble was, he shouldn't have trusted me, either."

"And you killed him because he tried to blackmail you about your affair with Veronica?"

Kevin gave an impatient shake of his head. "I'm a doctor no matter what anyone would have you believe. You don't need a degree, you don't need all those years in medical school. You need brains. You need interest in the field and the ability to retain information."

Addie felt a cold chill come over her at his words. "Are you trying to tell me you never went to medical school? That you're a fake?"

His expression darkened. "A fake? No, not a fake, never a fake. Just a man trying to make people happy. You don't need a diploma for that. No, it's all so easy. Even you wanted to believe me, wanted to think I could cure you of your allergy. And Steve? He didn't even bother checking my credentials, just believed his wife when she suggested he have a doctor all his own. He liked the idea of shelling out a fortune for someone who'd give him all the pretty little pills he could swallow. Hypochondriacs, every one of them. Women who were tired of being alone and not having anyone pay attention to them, men who woke up every morning listening to their hearts tick. But you know what, Addie? This whole thing is beginning to bore me. It's time.''

She felt her heart freeze. To die now when she had just found love. It would be too cruel.

"Hey, come on, it'll all be over in a second. You know what they say, Addie, 'Terror, the Human Form Divine.'''

'And Secrecy, the Human Dress,' Addie thought when she saw the figure looming up behind Kevin.

Jason with a gun in one hand reached out his other hand and grabbed Kevin around the neck. He poked the gun in his ribs. "Don't make a move or you're dead.''

Kevin, his eyes bulging in surprise, kicked at the stone beneath his foot. Addie watched in horror, a scream stuck in her throat as it rocked in place for a moment. Jason pushed Kevin back and dived for the stone. Kevin gave a maniacal scream of laughter as the stone plunged straight down toward Addie before Jason could reach it.

Addie flattened herself against the cliff face and the hurtling object missed her by inches.

She heard Jason shout her name. "I'm okay," she called back. She saw Kevin standing stock-still on the crest of the cliff.

Jason, still holding the gun on Kevin, called out to her. "Can you make it, Addie, or do you need help?''

"You just take care of Kevin," she answered. "I'll manage on my own.''

Kevin lunged at Jason with a curse, Addie watching in horror. He misstepped and began to slide down the crevice, groping frantically for a foothold. He went plummeting past her. She heard his long terrible wail as he fell the hundred feet to the churning sea below. Her own scream was stuck deep in her throat, and it was several moments before she found the energy to climb back up.

Jason was waiting for her. He held his arms out and took her in, cradling her and crooning her name.

"Did you hear everything?" she asked.

"Enough.''

"How—how'd you find us?"

"You weren't in the house. When I came back outside, I heard a commotion that turned out to be the cries of sea gulls rising into the air. I figured something had disturbed them and came running. I saw Kevin standing alone by the edge of the cliff. But when I got closer I could hear both of your voices."

"And then you just waited for Kevin to confess everything." She straightened and pulled out of his arms. "You let me lie there, scared to death, facing a madman, just so you could hear what he had to say?"

He grinned. "I planned to move before he did anything, but I had to close my case. And besides, I figured you were all right. After all, you were the one who decked both Gruesin and Roberts. And you sounded just fine, calm and collected."

"Correct, but you owed me one for that rescue. I may never forgive you."

"Want to bet?" He pulled her into his arms, silencing her with a kiss.

After he released her, she remembered something else. "Even if we weren't in the house, why did you come out after us? Are you telling me you were jealous?"

"When I was in town, I learned that Veronica had never left Galbraith and that she was on her way back to West Wind. I went tearing after her, intent on keeping her away from you—protecting you from Enigma. I came across her when I was halfway to West Wind. From the look on her face, I could tell she'd been crying. Perhaps she misses Steven, after all.

"At any rate it seemed a pretty odd emotion for Enigma. Then all at once I realized that Kevin, not she, must be Enigma. I told her to go down to the Island Inn and wait for me there. The rest is history."

"And just how did you figure out that Kevin was Enigma?"

"Graphology, my dear Watson. I had seen Kevin's handwriting on the prescription. Enigma's handwriting. It took a little while to sink in, that's all."

"Ah, so this case has made a believer out of you. Good. Then maybe you'll agree with me now as far as one Jason Farrell is concerned—you're creative, you're smart, and you're sexy. I saw it in all those little squiggles you make. You can't deny it, Jason, try as hard as you might. You *are* going to quit your government job and take up photography full-time, aren't you?"

He shook his head and after a moment said, "We'll see. I have that exhibition ahead of me." He tapped her nose gently. "By the way, I left your prescription behind, Addie. How's the allergy?"

She sniffed, realizing that fresh air, the absence of cat hair, and facing death had done the trick. She wriggled her nose, thinking that narrow escapes were not a cure she'd care to try on a regular basis. "What allergy?" she replied, raising her lips again to be kissed.

"GIVE YOUR HEART TO HARLEQUIN" SWEEPSTAKES

OFFICIAL RULES

NO PURCHASE NECESSARY TO ENTER OR RECEIVE A PRIZE

1. To enter and join the Harlequin Reader Service, rub off the concealment device on all game tickets. This will reveal the values for each Sweepstakes entry number and the number of free books you will receive. Accepting the free books will automatically entitle you to also receive a free bonus gift. If you do not wish to take advantage of our introduction to the Harlequin Reader Service but wish to enter the Sweepstakes only, rub off the concealment device on tickets #1-3 only. To enter, return your entire sheet of tickets. Incomplete and/or inaccurate entries are not eligible for that section or sections of prizes. Not responsible for mutilated or unreadable entries or inadvertent printing errors. Mechanically reproduced entries are null and void.

2. Either way, your Sweepstakes numbers will be compared against the list of winning numbers generated at random by computer. In the event that all prizes are not claimed, random drawings will be held from all entries received from all presentations to award all unclaimed prizes. All cash prizes are payable in U.S. funds. This is in addition to any free, surprise or mystery gifts that might be offered. The following prizes are awarded in this sweepstakes:

(1)	*Grand Prize	$1,000,000	Annuity
(1)	First Prize	$35,000	
(1)	Second Prize	$10,000	
(3)	Third Prize	$5,000	
(10)	Fourth Prize	$1,000	
(25)	Fifth Prize	$500	
(5000)	Sixth Prize	$5	

   *The Grand Prize is payable through a $1,000,000 annuity. Winner may elect to receive $25,000 a year for 40 years, totaling up to $1,000,000 without interest, or $350,000 in one cash payment. Winners selected will receive the prizes offered in the Sweepstakes promotion they receive.
   Entrants may cancel the Reader Service at any time without cost or obligation to buy (see details in center insert card).

3. Versions of this Sweepstakes with different graphics may appear in other mailings or at retail outlets by Torstar Corp. and its affiliates. This promotion is being conducted under the supervision of Marden-Kane, Inc., an independent judging organization. By entering the Sweepstakes, each entrant accepts and agrees to be bound by these rules and the decisions of the judges, which shall be final and binding. Odds of winning are dependent upon the total number of entries received. Taxes, if any, are the sole responsibility of the winners. Prizes are nontransferable. All entries must be received by March 31, 1990. The drawing will take place on April 30, 1990, at the offices of Marden-Kane, Inc., Lake Success, N.Y.

4. This offer is open to residents of the U.S., Great Britain and Canada, 18 years or older, except employees of Torstar Corp., its affiliates, and subsidiaries, Marden-Kane, Inc. and all other agencies and persons connected with conducting this Sweepstakes. All federal, state and local laws apply. Void wherever prohibited or restricted by law.

5. Winners will be notified by mail and may be required to execute an affidavit of eligibility and release that must be returned within 14 days after notification. Canadian winners will be required to answer a skill-testing question. Winners consent to the use of their name, photograph and/or likeness for advertising and publicity in conjunction with this and similar promotions without additional compensation. One prize per family or household.

6. For a list of our most current major prizewinners, send a stamped, self-addressed envelope to: WINNERS LIST, c/o MARDEN-KANE, INC., P.O. BOX 701, SAYREVILLE, N.J. 08872

LTY-H49

Harlequin Regency Romance™

Romance the way it was *always* meant to be!

The time is 1811, when a Regent Prince rules the empire. The place is London, the glittering capital where rakish dukes and dazzling debutantes scheme and flirt in a dangerously exciting game. Where marriage is the passport to wealth and power, yet every girl hopes secretly for love....

Welcome to Harlequin Regency Romance where reading is an adventure and romance is *not* just a thing of the past! Two delightful books a month, beginning May '89.

Available wherever Harlequin Books are sold.

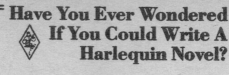

Have You Ever Wondered If You Could Write A Harlequin Novel?

Here's great news—Harlequin is offering a series of cassette tapes to help you do just that. Written by Harlequin editors, these tapes give practical advice on how to make your characters—and your story—come alive. There's a tape for each contemporary romance series Harlequin publishes.

Mail order only

All sales final